Wicked Promises

Fallen Royals
Book 3

S. Massery

*Special thanks to Kristy, Alaina, Beth, Lindsey, Kandis,
Shari, Alex, Denisse, and Whitney for your support!*

patreon.com/smassery

Introduction

Hello dear reader!

First and most importantly: this is **not** a standalone. Wicked Dreams and Wicked Games must be read prior to this, as Wicked Promises is the final book of the trilogy.

If you've read me before, you know my stories run quite dark. This book contains themes common to dark romance, including bullying, blackmail, stalking, and dubious consent. This story also includes mentions of childhood trauma.

Stay safe out there, friends, and happy reading!

xoxo,
Sara

P.S. This series was previously published (under the same title) in 2020, but has since been revised.

Unknown

My accomplice is chagrin.

My prey is unconscious.

I run my fingers through her hair, contemplating what to do. I wanted her captive, yes, but the way my accomplice went about it...

When I received the text to meet here, I was curious.

Her hair is silky. There's a bit of blood matted at her temple that I avoid. I don't want her blood on my hands. Physically anyway.

The car crash was a bit extreme. My accomplice, properly scolded, knows their place. We're not trying to *kill* her. All I want is for her to suffer a little... And, perhaps, to leave Rose Hill once and for all.

The cold breeze rushes through the wide cracks in the wooden slats. The old hay barn we stand in has been abandoned for some time. It's a hazardous structure, pitched to one side. Weeds and grass climb up the weathered boards, and it smells like dust on the inside.

I didn't choose it, but it's as good as anything.

"What now?"

I think of the chessboard in my room. I rather like the game now that I understand it. There's the opening, the middle game, and the endgame.

Both players start with a clean slate, and the opening is all about development.

Then the middle game: maneuver your pieces into attack or defensive positions.

And finally, the endgame. Where the attack becomes more targeted. Pieces are exchanged.

This is what we're entering.

"How did you leave Robert Bryan?" I turn to my accomplice, eyebrows rising.

They dip their head, still so embarrassed by what they did. "Unconscious. The car was upside down."

A death on our hands... Well. Perhaps not mine, per se.

"Caleb Asher?" I question.

A pause. Then, "None the wiser."

I nod. Not planned—but perfectly acceptable.

Our strategy is set. My pieces ready to triumph. Caleb will crumble.

And Margo is in prime position to fall.

Chapter 1
Caleb

A balled-up sock hits me in the face.

I jerk and glare at Eli. "What was that for?"

"You were zoning out," he says.

One thing we can't get away with in the Black household is laundry duty. Everything else is taken care of except this one task. It's soothing, the warm fabric sliding through my hands. It also reminds me that things have changed since my childhood.

My mom left, my father is dead.

The house I spent the first ten years of my life in is now no better than a mausoleum.

Eli and I stand on opposite sides of his dining table with piles of clean clothes. The faster we fold, the sooner we'll be done. That's what I keep telling myself anyway. And the sooner we finish, the faster we can escape to the garage and practice our shooting.

I can't afford to get rusty because Coach suspended me from a few games.

Right now, Margo is with her dad. I woke up this morning filled with a sense of dread, and even though I tried to hide it... She'll find out the real truth. The ugliness we've been hiding.

Her dad killed mine. Snuffed his life out—

"*Dude.*"

I grimace.

The last thing I want, in this exact moment, is for Margo to be hurt. It's kind of annoying, actually. I was hell-bent on her destruction just a few months ago. I turned the whole school against her. And now I can't picture anyone else harming her. It can only be me.

Just as surely as only she can hold my heart.

My heart. How fucking sappy.

The doorbell rings. Eli moves off to answer it. My phone goes off, stopping me from following him, and I grab it. My brows furrow at the blocked number. *Private* scrolls across the top of my screen.

A blocked number probably isn't Unknown, Margo's harasser. *Stalker.* In all reality, it's a telemarketer or a scam. And if Margo didn't have a stalker who liked to text her creepy things from a blocked number, I would probably dismiss the call entirely.

Instead, I answer it.

"Hello, Caleb," a robotic voice says. It sounds like an automated voice reading a line of text. "I've been eager to speak with you."

A chill sweeps down my spine. "Who is this?"

The voice laughs. It sounds fucking weird as shit. It doesn't translate well—which probably bodes well for the future of humanity. Can robots take over the world if they can't imitate a human laugh?

"They're going to ask you about Margo," it finally says.

"What?"

"When they ask, just remember: anything you say will

be held against you. Like you're already under arrest." The hydraulic laughter picks up again.

"What happened to Margo?" My heart beats faster. Worry takes over.

"Don't worry, Caleb. You got your wish."

I fight back the growl. "What the fuck did I wish for?"

Pause. "For the foster parents to be... removed from the situation."

"That is the opposite of what I want," I snap. "You've been stalking us—haven't you been paying any attention?"

Eli's mom walks into the kitchen. "Caleb, hang up the phone."

I want to keep arguing with the sicko on the other end of the line, but there's something in her expression... something bad. I lower the phone, my body stilling. Pressing the red *end* button is easy. Automatic. I'm glad, as soon as the call is cut off, to be free of it.

But what has Norah Black spooked?

"The police are here," she says to me in a low voice. "They wanted to talk to you."

Anything you say will be held against you.

Somehow, this—this *person* knew the police were on their way to the Blacks' house. Taunted me with it before I realized. Are they outside right now? Watching the house?

"Who was on the phone?" Eli's mom questions. "Your uncle?"

I shake my head, suppressing the bad feeling rising in my throat. "No one important."

"I've called Josh. Eli is holding him off in the front room." She tips her head. "Don't admit to anything."

Josh is Eli's father and a very skilled defense attorney. It would make sense to have him around for a conversation with the police. He often told us that innocent people think they don't need an attorney—and that lands them in hot water more often than not.

"Did they say why they need to speak with me?"

If something happened with my uncle...

My chest tightens.

Worry flits across her face, but it's gone before I can latch on to it.

"They didn't say." She smooths my shirt and straightens the collar. She's been more my parent than my family ever was. Taking a deep breath, she turns and leads me into the sitting room.

Eli leans against the doorframe that separates the front room from the foyer. The only other person in the room is an older man. He's big and wide, a black leather jacket stretched across his shoulders. Bald. He faces the window, but his body is angled toward Eli.

At our entrance, he twists to face us. His eyes are light blue and piercing. His eyebrows are dark, set on a heavy brow bone. He doesn't smile or react in any other way.

This isn't a pleasant visit, then.

And he's certainly no patrol cop. No uniform in sight, just a badge at his hip.

"Caleb, this is Detective Masters." Norah gestures for us to sit. "Since Caleb is still a minor, I'm going to stay. Although I would prefer if we waited until my husband was home."

"I just have a few questions for Mr. Asher, and then I'll be out of your hair." His voice rasps. "We can wait if you'd like."

I lift one shoulder. "It doesn't matter to me."

Norah lets out a breath, then nods.

I take a seat. Eli stays where he is, visible out of the corner of my eye.

The detective takes the seat across from me. "Have you been home all day?"

My eyebrow jumps. He's wasting no time. And it isn't every day the police come asking for an alibi.

"I dropped my girlfriend off at home this morning and came back here."

"Been here all day," Eli confirms.

Masters glances at him. He consults a notepad, then refocuses on me. "Girlfriend is Margo Wolfe?"

My stomach twists. Why is he asking about Margo?

"Did something happen to her?" I lean forward.

He waits.

"The last time I saw her was in front of her house this morning," I reiterate.

"And as far as you know, what were her plans today?"

I frown. "She had plans to see her father."

"Her father, who happened to be in jail on murder charges—"

"He pled out to voluntary manslaughter, Detective," Norah interrupts in a low voice. "And this line of questioning seems rather extreme. Are you insinuating something happened to Margo?"

Detective Masters leans back, his eyebrow twitching.

Smug asshole.

"I'm not insinuating anything, Norah. Margo is missing."

I bolt to my feet. "Missing?"

He stands as well. "Her foster mother has reported her as such."

"Why?"

He stares at me, then checks his notes again. "At approximately two p.m. this afternoon, Robert Bryan's vehicle was struck. Reports from the prison showed that

Margo Wolfe was listed on the visitor's log. She, unlike her foster father, was not found in the vehicle."

And they haven't been able to find her.

"And you're here? Questioning me when you should be —I don't know, out there searching for—"

"Caleb." Norah puts her hand on my arm.

I jerk away from her. Margo is *missing*—and has been since two o'clock? It's nearly five now. That's three hours. I suddenly can't breathe around my fear. Images of someone dragging her out of a wrecked car fill my mind.

"This is bullshit," I spit. "She wouldn't just wander away. What you really mean is someone took her. Since you seem to be implying it was me, I'll save you the trouble—it wasn't." I narrow my eyes at the detective. "Get the fuck out of here."

Masters' expression sharpens. "Has anyone been paying too much attention to Margo? Her foster mother was unable to confirm anything, but I suspect Margo would've been more open to talking with friends."

Fucking Unknown. I'm no closer to figuring out who they are. And we're not *friends*—she's something else entirely.

"You have quite the obsession with her, don't you, Caleb?"

Norah makes a noise of protest. "They're dating, Detective. Young love is intense."

All my *training* to keep calm is slowly going out the window. Lessons with my uncle have gone to shit. My temper is snapping—*fast*.

"I think it's time for you to go," Norah continues. "If you'd like to talk to Caleb further, you can go through my husband."

The detective narrows his eyes—not at her, but at me.

"You can't hide from this," he tells me.

A chill sweeps down my spine.

I don't have anything to hide. Not when it comes to Margo.

While Eli's mom shows him to the door, I go downstairs. I shove my sneakers on, lacing them tightly, and grab my sweatshirt.

Eli intercepts me at the top of the stairs. "Where are you going?"

"Get out of my way," I snarl.

"He's still *out* there, you jackass. What do you think, he's just going to tell you Margo's missing and then drive away? You burst out the door now, he's just going to follow you."

"I know—" I grimace. "I don't *know* who has her. But I kind of know."

He rears back. "What?"

All I know is that Margo's stalker played a part in this. And for this detective to believe me, I need proof.

"It's complicated." I shoulder past him, forcing him to follow me. "We don't have time for this. I lost her once. I will *not* let someone else take her from me."

Eli stares at me for a moment, then he shakes his head. "Fine. I'm in."

I pause. "What?"

"I'm *in*. Fuck off with that look of surprise. Do you think I'd just let you handle this on your own?"

Well...

"Asshole." He elbows me. "I'll lead the detective away. As soon as I lose him, I'll meet you at the school." He snatches my keys out of my hand. "You're not even supposed to be driving anyway."

He pulls the hood of his sweatshirt up over his head and

hurries toward the garage. A second later, the familiar purr of my car engine reaches my ears.

He's going to lead the detective away.

With Eli... a little bit of hope comes back. I'm not ten years old, pushed along by my family's current. I can make my own choices.

I will bring her home.

Past

Where did she go?

Mom grabbed me, and my eyes flew open. I knew it was her before I was even aware, because she always smelled like roses and baby powder.

"Caleb," she said. "Wake up."

I was already staring at her. Her order came a few seconds too late.

She moved to the foot of my bed, her arms wrapping around herself. Her glare cut through my misery. Through *me*.

"Why did they take her away?" I sat up slowly, the desperate need for answers clogging my throat.

"Her father—" Mom pressed her lips together. "After what *that man* did to our family, you still want to see her?"

I frowned. "*She* didn't do anything."

Mom laughed. I flinched at the sudden loudness of it in my room. It was dark, practically the middle of the night. No moonlight came in through my windows. There wasn't even a breeze to cool my skin.

I was hot. Burning impossibly bright.

"She didn't *do* anything?" Mom turned on my overhead light.

I cringed. She was being mean. Grief made people do crazy things, right?

"Do you even care that your father is dead?" She glowered at me.

Long live the king.

I'd been repeating that since the day he'd died. Why? Because he was still here, haunting the house. Lurking. His memory was pungent enough to suffocate a bear, and Mom just wouldn't let it go.

Her grief was loud. Hard. But my aunt whispered in my ear at the funeral: we're supposed to bear witness. That's the only way she'd get better.

The loss I was dealing with was twofold. My father, yes, but also my best friend. Dad being gone was kind of incomprehensible. It was too abstract to imagine. But my best friend being torn away for good... that, unfortunately, I could picture. Mom had already painted it in such fine detail, the way my friend was never returning to Rose Hill.

And when I think of my father, I think of his yelling. I think of his cold expression.

So, I did care that my father was dead—just not like I cared about *her*.

I wanted Margo. Plain and simple.

Mom huffed at my silence. "Get up."

The digital clock on my nightstand proclaimed the time: 2:06 a.m. A thrill of nerves went through me. Why were we getting up in the middle of the night?

"Get *up* Caleb Asher, or so help me—"

"Okay, okay." I threw back the blankets and stood, keeping my attention half on her while I found my jeans and a clean shirt.

"Pack a bag."

"What?"

"Pack a bag, Caleb. Why do I have to ask you to do something twice?"

I shuddered but did as she'd asked. I threw clothes in a backpack. She disappeared into the hall, then returned with my toothbrush and a few other toiletries. She checked what I had already tossed into my bag and added underwear and socks. With a firm hand, she zipped it shut and slung it over my shoulder. She steered me down the stairs with a tight grip on my arm.

Her bag was packed, too. A suitcase sat by the door.

"Where are we going?"

"Away from this house." She gave me a brittle smile.

I cast a look around at the familiar space. "For how long?"

"Forever, as far as I'm concerned. The will reading is tomorrow, and I doubt your father left the house to me. Everything was locked up tightly in a trust. Irony at its best."

Those words were foreign. I thought Dad trusted her? How could trust lock something up?

Outside was just as warm and still as it was in my bedroom. The night wasn't silent—not like the house. Quiet, yes, but there was life out there. Crickets. The wind rustling through the trees.

Not like in there.

"I don't understand." I trailed her to the back of the car, where she tucked both our bags in the trunk.

"You don't understand what?"

How is Margo going to find me if I leave?

"You're going to stay with family," she said in an even tone. "Get in the car."

She opened the door behind the driver's seat and waited for me to climb in. I secured my seat belt, and she closed the door softly. She climbed behind the wheel.

"What family? Uncle David and Aunt Iris?"

She jerked her head in a nod.

My stomach pitched. I swallowed hard. If I threw up, it would only make things worse—but Uncle David had a mean streak worse than Dad's.

She wanted to leave me there with him?

"You're coming, too, right?" I leaned forward. "Mom?"

She met my eyes in the rearview mirror. "There are some things I need to take care of, Caleb. I need to find someone to get the blood out of the carpet, for one. The sooner we can sell that godforsaken house, the better off we'll be."

White-hot fear flashed through me.

"You can't sell it! Margo—"

"Do *not* speak her name." Mom slammed on the brakes, jerking the car to the side of the road. She twisted around and pinched my chin. Her long nails dug into my skin. "She's dead to us. Okay, honey? I need you to understand. That vile girl will not be a problem anymore. After what she's done to this family..."

"Just like Dad?"

Mom stared at me for a moment. There was a softness in her expression, but now it was gone. "Didn't you ever love him? Do you not get it? He isn't coming back. This isn't a dream you can wake up from, Caleb. Things won't go back to how they were. And I sure as hell will *not* trap myself in Rose Hill while the rest of the world keeps turning."

I did love him, but he screamed. Threw things. Instilled terror into us.

Us. Like Margo was sitting beside me.

Mom released her grip on me and turned back around. She breathed deeply, while I shook in my seat. I understood what Mom was saying. In Rose Hill, bad things happened. She wanted a new chance at life.

But I didn't. I wanted things back to normal.

She started the car again, pulled back out onto the quiet road.

I rubbed the bracelet on my wrist absently. I should've removed it and thrown it away, but the hate Mom kept insisting on wasn't there. It wasn't Margo's fault. It was her *dad's* fault.

"Silly boy," Mom said, more to herself than me. "You think she didn't have a hand in this?"

Had I spoken out loud?

"You'll learn. You can't trust a Wolfe."

Chapter 2
Margo

Some people come back from unconsciousness slowly, one sense at a time. Hearing, smell, taste. Drifting out of a slumber-like state peacefully.

Not me.

I rush into awareness like I'm bursting from underwater, gasping for air.

And the next thing to hit me?

Memories.

They burn through my mind, one after another, a flipbook of information.

It hurts. I cry out as I relive it.

Someone grabs my arm, threading their fingers through mine. They squeeze my hand, but I'm inconsolable. The truth is blinding, but I finally have answers.

I remember.

<h1 style="text-align:center">Chapter 3
Caleb</h1>

I curl my fingers into the hat on my lap. It's hard not to critique Eli's driving. For one, he's driving *my* car. And we've been going in circles for hours. Literally and figuratively.

After he picked me up at the school, the detective sufficiently ditched, he pried the entire story out of me. At some points, I let information go willingly. But others... He slowed the truck, and out my secrets came. It was impulsive, like vomiting. I couldn't have stopped the words if I tried.

They now float between us, although I'm suffocating.

We have made *no* progress searching for her. We started near the prison. I stood on the corner of an intersection three blocks away, bits of shattered glass under my shoes. The car had already been towed. Robert...

I don't know. Hospital, I imagine. The detective didn't mention anything else.

"Just so I'm reading this right... your folks hate Margo because of something her dad did?"

"Basically." I run my hand over my face.

"And your mom just... left. She dropped you off with Uncle Evil and said, bye honey, see you...?"

"She went upstate. To some sort of... I don't know. She called it treatment, but I'm pretty sure it was a resort." I laugh at the memory of her selling it to me that way. That she needed this place to recalibrate and deal with her *grief*. "She'd call every once in a while, drop in when she needed more money from my uncle. She's been around more recently, although I'm not sure if that's a good thing."

"Oh, Lydia." Eli scowls. "And meanwhile, you were a punching bag for your uncle."

"He's a twisted fucker," I mutter.

"Karma will get him."

He's confident in that assessment, but he's wrong. Rich men don't often bow to fate. They're the exception to the rule. Always have been... always will be. I'd love nothing more than for my uncle to pay for what he's done, but it just won't happen.

I feel as helpless as ten-year-old Caleb.

My phone buzzes. I freeze at the text from Unknown, but it's just a string of numbers.

Followed by...

UNKNOWN

Time's ticking, Asher.

"What the hell is this?"

Eli pulls over to get a better look. He copies the numbers over into his phone's web browser, and a location pops up as the first result.

In Rose Hill.

I sit up straighter. "Is this—did they—?"

"I mean, it looks like it."

He zooms in on the area. It's an old, abandoned farm.

The owner was a bit crazy, totally believed in the end of the world, and built a bunch of bunkers in one of the pastures. An old hay barn is still standing, and I think the place is littered with rusted equipment.

It would be the perfect place to hide Margo.

"Fuck." Eli squints at it. "What if we actually find her here?"

Time's ticking, Unknown said. Which makes me think they did something to Margo. I withhold my fear, my throat closing, while Eli taps on his phone again.

He puts the location into the maps, and it routes us there.

Ten minutes away.

I glance at him. "What did you mean, what if we actually find her?"

Eli chews his lower lip. "The detective seems to think you're involved. Suddenly finding her..."

"It's better than *not* finding her," I argue. Consequences be damned. "Go."

He nods and hits the gas. We fly toward the swath of no-man's-land between Rose Hill and Stone Ridge. Rumor has it this area is haunted, but every story is different. Some say the owner of the bunkers was convinced the apocalypse was coming and locked people in. Others say we had a cult on our hands and it was mass suicide. Ghosts, buried bodies...

None of it is true, but the temperature seems to noticeably drop when Eli turns onto the gravel driveway.

Coincidence. The bunkers are in the distance, the roof of the barn just visible over the hill. There's swampy, dark water on either side of the road. Feeble stalks of grass poke out, waving in the wind.

He stops the car just shy of the top of the hill. "What if they're there?"

I laugh. "You're asking me this now?"

"I mean, they could be armed."

"That's not stopping me." I raise my eyebrow. "And your headlights give us away."

"Shit." He lets off the brake. "If we get shot, you owe me."

We crest the hill.

Nothing.

Nothing visible in the darkness anyway. My car's headlights only illuminate so much. The barn is the first thing, and beyond that, remnants of a fence and the first bunker beyond.

I shove all my emotions down. I can't afford to be hopeful or nervous or... terrified. We're going to be smart about this. Logic over emotions. I want to burst into the buildings, scream her name, get her back.

What are the chances this is a trap?

I find the folded knife he keeps in his glove box and flip it open. With the tip, I point to the white-walled bunker just behind the barn. "You check that bunker. I'll take the barn."

"You want to split up?"

I glare at him and hop out without answering. With a groan, he follows.

We split up. The barn is old. It creaks and rattles in the wind, like it's protesting even still standing. There's a chain on the huge sliding doors, a thick, rusty padlock hanging from the center.

I keep moving. If someone got her in here, there would be a sign. Knife in one hand, my phone in the other, I use its flashlight to search for any disturbance on the ground.

All the while keeping my ears open for Eli. His shout of success could come at any moment.

My heart races. It might burst before I find her.

I come to a smaller door. Without hesitation, I kick it in. The frame splinters with a *crack*, and the door bangs against the wall.

I step into what was once an office. There's a desk in the corner, heavily tilted to one side. Thick dust covers everything. I creep through the door, into the main part of the barn. There are some stalls, but the rest is open. My attention goes to the hay stacked along one wall. The debris on the dirt floor.

And then... *her*.

My hopes soar. I rush to where she lies on the floor, curled on her side.

Her dark hair covers her face, and her hands are bound in front of her with duct tape. Her ankles are bound, too.

I fall to my knees in front of her and brush her hair back. Her eyes are closed, but she's breathing. There's a gash on her head. It's not bleeding anymore, the trail of it down her temple and jaw tacky to the touch. It's down her face and neck, soaked in her shirt collar.

No jacket.

No shoes.

"Margo," I whisper, rolling her onto her back. "You're okay. I've got you. You're safe."

She groans. My heart jumps at the sound.

Her lips are nearly blue, her skin too pale.

I swing my light around, making sure we're alone in the barn. I need to get her out of here. She was in a car accident, and then who knows what happened to her between now and then. I pick her up, wincing at how cold she is.

She's been out here for hours. I didn't notice the bite of the wind, but for her to be alone, with no coat or shoes...

She could've almost died.

I cradle her head to my chest and hurry back the way I came.

I almost crash into Eli. His flashlight sweeps across my face, then Margo's. His eyes widen, and without a word he leads the way back to my car.

He opens the back door for me. I slide in without releasing her, holding her close, and he makes sure her feet are fully in before he shuts the door. His eyebrows hike when he makes contact with her skin.

Without asking, he blasts the heat. He cranes around. "Hospital?"

"No shit."

He lifts a shoulder. "Just making sure you don't want to do this the private way."

I scoff.

The *private* way would probably land me in more hot water with the Rose Hill Police Department, and it would involve asking my uncle to call his physician. That old man has patched me up a few times in the last seven years...

But since Uncle has a grudge against the Wolfe family, I think he'd rather enjoy denying her care.

I stroke Margo's hair and will her to wake up. Her face is peaceful—minus the blood—and she could almost pass for sleeping. Still, it doesn't negate that some asshole abducted her and left her for dead. Without a coat *or* shoes.

I'm going to kill them.

I shift and slide my phone out, thumbing a message to Unknown.

ME

I'm going to find you.

"You don't think your family was behind this, do you?" Eli glance back.

The ride is smoother now that we're back on the main road.

I tug at the tape on Margo's wrists. "We've been operating under the assumption that Unknown is our age. I think that is still accurate. My uncle wouldn't be so..."

Sloppy comes to mind.

As harsh as it sounds, I don't think he'd leave Margo alive, let alone somewhere I could find her. Even more unlikely that he'd point me in her direction.

He grunts. "Does she have her phone on her?"

I shift her, feeling her pockets. "Nope."

"How's she doing?"

"It'd be great if you could drive faster," I grit out.

I'm not a doctor, but Margo being unconscious isn't a good sign.

It's probably a really fucking bad one.

Eli's already driving fast, but he stomps down on the accelerator and learns what kind of engine is under the hood of my car. It whines as we climb faster and faster, and he barely makes the turn into the hospital's emergency entrance.

"We're here, we're here." We coast to a halt.

As soon as the car stops moving, I fling the door open and maneuver out. I keep Margo tight against my chest so she doesn't bounce.

Eli follows me inside, the car forgotten.

I should've taken the tape off her arms and legs.

A nurse rushes toward me. "What happened?"

"I—she was abducted. We found her."

Chaos.

We're swarmed with nurses or doctors—maybe both. One instructs me to set her on a gurney. Another leans over her with a penlight, cracking open one eye, then the other. They shuffle me backward, but the first one's gaze stays on me.

"This is the missing girl?"

I nod woodenly. "Margo Wolfe."

"Sit down, son," someone orders. "We'll take good care of her."

The original nurse leads me to a chair in the waiting room. "Is that your car?"

I open my mouth to say it is, but Eli puts his hand on my arm.

"I'll go move it," he says.

"It's in the way of the ambulance bay," she explains. "There's a parking—"

"I know. I've got it."

He leaves, his back straight. He was just in Chicago with his parents... we didn't talk about his trauma—or family drama. Seems like it was better left in Illinois. But I imagine he won't be eager to rush back here, after spending so much time in a hospital only weeks ago. He'll be gone for a while.

It doesn't matter. He helped me by getting Margo here, and that's all I needed.

I hunch lower in my chair and eye the people going in and out of the emergency department. Margo is behind a locked door. Just when I had her in my arms again...

Eli's dad bursts into the waiting room, gaze swinging around before he finds me. He's usually a composed man, but right now... he hurries in my direction, motioning for me to stand up.

"Where's the fire?" I ask.

He grimaces.

The next person through the sliding glass doors is Detective Masters.

"His goal is to make a scene," Mr. Black says to me. "He wants to trip you up because he has no evidence."

"Evidence of what?"

"He wants to bring you down to the station for questioning. He thinks you—it doesn't matter. It's best if we go along with it, let him talk to you with me there. He's threatening to get an arrest warrant if you don't go amicably. It's a bunch of bullshit, if you ask me, but it's harder to scrub that from your record."

"I can't leave Margo." I grab Josh Black's wrist. "I just found her."

"Mr. Asher," Detective Masters calls.

He's got a gleam in his eye like he's about to enjoy this next part. I wish I knew what I did in our ten-minute interview to make such an impression. I've never met the man before—and *Masters* as a family name doesn't sound remotely familiar.

"You need to come down to the station with me," he says.

What will be the first thing Margo sees when she wakes up? Someone who doesn't give a fuck about her? Her social worker, or worse, the detective himself? *No.* She needs to know it was me who found her—

"I need to be here for Margo," I say.

"Now, Caleb, I doubt Margo would want to hear that you refused to help on her case." He sighs. "Just imagine how hurt she might be by that information."

"Come on, son," Josh Black whispers.

I feel the detective's sharp eyes on me, waiting for some hint of my guilt. It's no different to how my uncle looks at me—although I'm not so sure Masters would take a swing at me just for the sake of it.

Maybe only if no one was watching.

It's clear I'm not going to win this fight. The sooner I answer his questions, the faster I can return to Margo's side.

"Fine," I grit out.

The detective grips my upper arm. His hold is strong, his fingers digging into my muscles, and he forcibly guides me out of the hospital. At the curb beyond the ambulance bay, his unmarked police car flashes blue-and-red lights.

Lenora, Margo's foster mom, nearly crashes into us on our way out. She grabs my shoulders, stopping my forward movement.

"Caleb! D-Detective Masters!" Her attention bounces back and forth, and her brows furrow when she realizes he's still holding my arm. "What on earth are you doing?"

"Just have a few questions for Mr. Asher here," the detective says.

I would very much like to punch him in the face.

Break his nose maybe.

"But—"

"We've got to get going." He sounds apologetic. "I'll be back to the hospital once Margo is awake."

She nods, scanning my face, then steps to the side. Mr. Black pauses beside her, and I crane around when she says something to him. I can't make out their words.

Masters hauls me along faster, and his grip gets tighter. "Like that little show, did you, boy? You have a grim look on your pretty face. Heh. Not used to getting caught, more like."

I say nothing, even if he couldn't be farther from the truth.

He puts me in his car, his hand heavy on the back of my head.

He hasn't arrested me, but it sure feels like he's about to cart me off and lock me away. My mind jumps ahead to the implications, and what my uncle would do when he finds out, then circles back to Margo.

Uncle David will get me out if Josh Black fails to negotiate with the detective. Even if he has to pave my exit in gold.

It wouldn't be the first thing the Asher family has covered up.

Chapter 4
Margo

Past

The room was cold. The surface of the table in front of me was sticky. Spilled milk maybe, or coffee that hadn't been wiped away.

I avoided putting my arms on the table, keeping them crossed over my chest instead. The entire house smelled like spoiled food. It was rotten, and the scent seemed to have climbed into my nostrils and dug in.

Even when I went outside, I still smelled it.

"Some lady is here for you." The foster mom swept into the kitchen like she was the queen of the castle and she didn't notice it was rotting. "Not sure why anyone would want to visit with you. Did you even brush your hair this morning?"

My hair was often a wild tangle, even after brushing. I was fourteen, not four. Basic hygiene had been part of my routine for a while, without any oversight from previous foster parents.

I left my cereal—*maybe that was the spoiled smell?*—and

went to the front door. If it was my social worker, Ms. McCaw, the foster mom would've said. She probably would've seemed more anxious, too, seeing as how the state of the place was not great.

But because she didn't, I was left with a mild curiosity about who awaited me.

I yanked the door open.

Houses like this always had porches. Big wraparound ones that made everyone else in the neighborhood jealous, but it was the inside that was bleak. Pretty outside, sick inside.

My mother stood on this one, within reaching distance. Only a screen separated us.

Shock filtered through me. Her brown eyes, much like mine, bore into me. She fidgeted. There were spots on her neck, bruises. A scrape across her cheek.

My heart kicked against my ribs.

She hated me, but she checked up on me.

It was our little secret.

I pushed past the screen door and took a few steps out onto the porch. I wrapped my arms around my stomach, fighting an immediate shiver. Winter was sliding into spring, and more often than not the days were warm. But at this time of the morning, before school, the air still had a bite to it.

Her attention went from my face to the thrift store clothes, then down to my boots. They were falling apart. The laces broke the other day, and I had to duct tape them back together so I could keep wearing them.

Boots were more practical in everyday life than soft-topped sneakers. You could run in boots. Kick shit in them. Stomp on your enemies in them. Never mind that my class-mates laughed at me for them. They always pointed and whispered about my clothing, my hair, my boots. The worn, hand-me-down backpack, the short pencil I meticulously sharpened to make sure it lasted.

I cleared my throat and waited for her to speak.

Her gaze snapped up. "I heard you moved."

"Shithole house." I slipped past her. Down the stairs, all the way to the sidewalk. It wasn't often I got to take a deep breath of clean air, but sure enough, that rotten stench was still there. Ruining it once again. "The foster mom's a bitch. Her husband is even worse."

He leered.

They had sex in the middle of the night when they thought we were asleep. The box spring squealed loudly, never failing to jar us awake. She never made a noise, but he did. Grunts that filled our ears. The smallest girl would climb into bed with me, burying her head in my chest under the covers.

At my age, I knew about sex—but I didn't want to think about it. And I definitely didn't want to hear it almost every night.

Mom followed. "Karma's a bitch, too."

I snorted. "Gee, thanks."

"They giving you an allowance?"

Part of me still wanted to be loved by my mother, and I would do anything to get her to stay. If I gave her money—like I had in the past—she would come back.

It wasn't guesswork.

She would run out of money again, and then she'd show up wherever I was. Even if it was only for a few minutes.

But right now, I had nothing.

"Can you tell me about your adventures?" I stall. "Where you've been, or..."

"I've been dealing with a loss," she told me. She kept

tapping her finger against her arm. Crossed and uncrossed them. Shifted her weight. "And coping the only way I know how."

I sighed. "What is it now?"

I knew it was drugs. Ms. McCaw and Lydia Asher had both told me, in very different ways, that my mother was giving up her parental rights. She'd been checked into a rehabilitation center only a few months after Dad was locked up, but that didn't seem to solve anything.

They let her go when the state funding dried up, and as soon as she had something to barter, she was getting high.

I blamed Dad for her addiction. But while I hated him for what she'd become, I couldn't give her the same level of loathing. Some little voice in the back of my head whispered that it wasn't her fault.

I wondered who she'd lost. Dad, maybe?

"You could go see Dad," I suggested. "If you're feeling like he's gone."

She scowled.

It'd been four years. Maybe she saw him and didn't want to tell me. She tended to be petty like that. Everything was my fault in her eyes, just like her addiction was Dad's.

Simple... but sometimes I wondered how we got here.

"Margo, I need to go." She inched closer. "You were right. I've been traveling a lot. I had a job in the city, but I was late because my car broke down, and they fired me..."

"What do you need?"

She turned away from me. I hated the sharp angles of her body. She used to be soft—someone worth hugging. Now, her bones threatened to slice through her skin every time she moved. There were pockmarks not only on her neck and face, but track marks in the crooks of her elbows. I saw them even when she tried to hide.

"If you can't help me, I'll leave." She took three quick steps back, her shoes scraping on the concrete.

"I can find something." I reached for her, but she was already out of range. "Please. I don't have anything right now, but—"

If I couldn't make her stay, she wouldn't come back.

"It can't wait." Mom shifted again, pulling at the hem of her shirt. Strands of dark hair slid from the clip on top of her head and caught in the wind. She finally turned around and walked away. She went down the sidewalk like she wasn't fleeing from her daughter.

The pain started slow, but it grew the farther away she got. There wasn't a kind word she could've said to staunch the flow. Not that she would've said it.

"Take care of yourself," I whispered. She was out of earshot, so it didn't even really matter. I'd only said it to make myself feel better.

A tear slipped down my cheek.

I hastily wiped it away and glanced back at the house. The new coat of paint, the manicured lawn. Nothing but the ivy burrowed in the stucco walls, gripping like its life depended on it, betrayed what was on the inside. Rotten hearts.

They wouldn't notice if I went for a walk.

All my belongings were on my back anyway. Shirt, pants, shoes. I reached into my pocket and ran my finger across the threads of the blue-and-gold bracelet. I stopped wearing it some time ago, afraid it would fray and break. But I didn't trust this house. It stayed in my pocket, safe and comforting.

Mom didn't want me. The foster system certainly didn't want me.

Caleb...

I exhaled, and my stomach cramped. I missed him, but he was so far away. There was no chance of his family taking me in. The angry look on his mom's face, the way she told me, with no small amount of gleeful malice, that my mother wouldn't be taking custody of me...

No one would take me.

Maybe I'd just keep walking until I found someone who did.

Present

Pain crashes through me. It goes straight to my head, and so do my hands.

Someone rushes in. Their warm fingers wrap around my wrists, pulling my arms down.

"Margo, Margo. Can you hear me? You're safe. You're in the hospital."

Stars burst behind my eyelids, but I recognize Lenora's voice. She eases me back, muttering about the lights. A second later, everything in my peripherals goes dim. I lower my fingers away from my eyes and blink.

It still hurts, but not nearly as bad.

Lenora hovers at the side of the bed. She strokes my hair, leaning in. "I was so worried, honey. Oh my God. You gave us a scare."

A nurse comes in, followed quickly by a doctor. My foster mother's expression is worried... and afraid. Why is she afraid?

"You have a concussion," the doctor says. "Expect headaches, maybe memory fragments. And... there's a detective outside who wants to speak with you."

I just woke up.

I glance at Lenora, whose lips flatten into a straight line. "Do you think she's in any state—"

"No," the doctor agrees. "We can put him off for a little while, but he knows you're awake. Now, ma'am, let us check out your daughter."

The nurse takes Lenora's place. She checks my eyes, blood pressure, heart rate.

"You're not going to tell me how I got here?" I ask her.

"The detective wanted to speak with you." He gives Lenora a look. "You should be present, as her guardian."

"Of course."

I think back. It's hard with the headache pulsing behind my eyes. I was at the prison visiting my father. He said some upsetting things... like how he was there because he murdered Caleb's dad.

He said he didn't do it.

There was the plea deal. I told him I went to see his lawyer, and that upset him.

When I got outside, I fell into Robert's arms...

The collision of cars is suddenly all around me. Like I'm reliving it. I jerk. The weightless feeling of rolling, the crush of my seat belt across my chest...

"Where is Robert?" I grab for Lenora.

She slides her palm against mine, gripping tightly. "He's in intensive care. His lung collapsed, and he has a few broken ribs, but he's going to be okay."

I bite my lip. The metallic taste of blood blooms across my tongue.

Someone pulled me out of the upside-down car. Away from the wreck. But instead of helping me, they were taking me away.

They knocked me out, and when I woke up...

Shit.

"Where's Caleb?"

A man walks into the room as I'm asking. "He really fooled you, huh?"

Who the hell is this?

The doctor groans. "Really, Masters? You're supposed to wait for Angela—"

"I'm here," Ms. McCaw comes in behind the detective. "Traffic. I was across town. Margo, how are you feeling?"

Overwhelmed, scared. Confused.

None of those seem satisfactory, though. Growing up in the system—and also being literally torn away from my father when he was arrested—I do not trust the police.

So this guy, who seems like he could easily strip out of the leather jacket and enter a caged MMA fight, who has a badge on his belt and a scowl painted on his rather scary face, flies to the top of my Do Not Trust list.

I school my features into some sort of stoicism. "I'm alive, so..."

"Detective Masters wants to chat with you about what happened," Ms. McCaw explains. "I'm here to be your advocate."

I haven't seen her in a while.

The nurse and doctor file out with a warning to take it easy on me.

The detective drags a chair over to the side of my bed and makes himself comfortable.

He has piercing blue eyes and a smooth head. His leather jacket doesn't scream *detective*, but it definitely fits his personality. Besides the badge at his hip, there's a holstered gun on the other side of his body.

I don't like guns.

He leans forward, staring like he could see straight

through me. "As your social worker explained, I'm Detective Jim Masters. I'm just going to ask you some questions about yesterday."

I shoot up. "*Yesterday?* It's been—"

"About twelve hours since the accident," he says. "Your abductor brought you in around eight-thirty last night."

Making it eight-thirty in the morning. I glance toward the window, at the pale sunlight streaming in. But then the first part of his sentence registers. My abductor brought me in?

I frown. "Why would they do that?"

There were two of them. Talking. I cross my arms and pinch my skin where he can't see. The localized pain centers me, although what they were talking about, even their voices, slips out of my mind.

He leans forward. "They? How many? Did you see anything that could identify them?"

"I..." I hesitate. "No. I didn't see anything."

My head freaking *kills*. At my request, they turn off the overhead lights, letting the picture window illuminate the room.

The detective stares at me in a way that tells me he thinks I'm lying. "A friend of Caleb's?"

I freeze. "What?"

The detective waves his hand impatiently. "Come on, Margo. I know Caleb had something to do with it. So who was he working with?"

"Are you saying *Caleb* brought me to the hospital?" My mouth dries. I risk a glance at Lenora, who nods carefully.

Yes. Okay. Caleb brought me in—but he wasn't the one who took me.

"He would never hurt me, Detective," I say in a low voice.

Not quite the truth. He's hurt me plenty the last few months.

But to this degree? *Never.*

Masters watches me. "Caleb Asher orchestrated the whole thing. He has motive and the arrogance to pull it off. You said you heard another voice. Was it one of his friends?"

No, no, no.

No matter what dark hole you go down, I will find you and bring you back. Isn't that what he promised me?

He kept that promise. He found me.

I have to keep mine.

I glare at the arrogance of this man who thinks he has everything figured out. "It wasn't him, Detective. I know him. I know his *voice.* The person who dragged me out of the car talked to me before he pressed a cloth to my face. I'd know Caleb's voice anywhere—and it wasn't him."

He narrows his eyes.

I focus on Ms. McCaw. "Can you get a nurse? I have to use the restroom."

She nods and ducks out. The detective and I lock into a staring contest until she and a nurse return.

The latter takes one look at me and faces Detective Masters. "I think she's had enough for today."

After a long moment, the detective nods and exits the room.

The nurse flips the blankets off my legs. She quickly disconnects the wires that monitor my heart, and the long cord attached to my IV port taped to the back of my hand. I swing my legs over and touch my socked feet to the cool tile, and she helps me stand.

"Slowly now."

I'm as wobbly as a newborn deer. The room slants and spins. We pause, allowing me to close my eyes for a second.

"Head injuries do nasty things to our balance," the nurse murmurs.

I heave a sigh. I really do need to pee—but I could also use a moment alone. Thankfully, the nurse agrees to my request for privacy. She tells me to ring the bell when I'm done and closes the door.

I hover by it, listening as hard as I can.

It's quiet, and then, "He really carried her in here?" That from Ms. McCaw.

My heart picks up speed.

"Her arms and legs were still duct taped," the nurse says. "Although the detective didn't see how distraught he was."

Caleb. My heart gives an extra kick.

I focus on my wrists. The skin is red and angry. There are little abrasions around where the tape must've pulled as they removed it.

I scratch at my wrist and groan at the slice of pain.

"You okay, Margo?" The nurse's voice is jarringly loud through the door.

I sit on the toilet and reply, "Yep, almost done."

When I'm finished, I scrub my hands under hot water until they match my wrists. Stinging and pink. I rip open the package on the sink counter—a toothbrush and little squeeze tube of toothpaste.

My mouth feels a thousand times better with a minty freshness.

Then, slowly, I cast a glance at myself in the mirror. I've avoided it until now, afraid of what I was going to find.

There's a wound on my head that's been bandaged— and presumably stitched underneath. Various scrapes across my face. A bruise on my temple, coming down onto my cheek, and the skin around my eyes is puffy. If I had more time, I'd do a more thorough examination. I imagine my ankles, hidden under the thick socks, are in the same sort of shape as my wrists. Unless they went over my pants...

I take a breath. My ribs don't hurt as much as they did when Ian kicked me, but there's still a deep ache. My hair is a wild mess. I finger-comb it as best as possible, but it really needs washing to tame it.

Enough stalling. I open the door and smile at the nurse.

"You're supposed to ring the bell," she admonishes.

"I'm already feeling better."

She doesn't have to help much on the way back, and soon enough, I'm tucked into bed, hooked up to the monitors and IV of fluids.

Detective Masters returns not long after. "Can you walk us through the day? Everything you remember."

I heave a sigh. What I really want is to go back to sleep. But since Lenora hasn't moved from her spot on the wall, and Ms. McCaw seems impatient for this to be over... I should just answer his questions.

As long as they're not incriminating.

"I got home—"

"Who dropped you off?"

"Caleb."

"So he knew where you were going?"

I narrow my eyes. "Objection—leading the witness."

He jerks, then laughs. "Okay, okay. Proceed, Ms. Wolfe."

"Caleb dropped me off at my foster parents' house, then left. Robert and I went to the prison soon after that. I visited with my dad for the first time in..." I shrug. Not relevant. "I visited with him. Once it was over, I left and got in the car with Robert. On our way home, we were hit by another vehicle."

I try not to think about the crunch of metal. The car flipping. Or the way he hung upside down. He's in the ICU while I'm being interrogated.

And what about Caleb? Did they arrest him? Masters already seems to think he did it, and since Caleb isn't here...

Is he sitting in a jail cell?

"We went off the road," I continue. "I hit my head, so everything is kind of blurry..."

"Just do the best you can," Masters urges.

"Someone helped me out of the car."

"Did they unbuckle you?"

I frown. "No... I think I did that. I released my seat belt so I could get to Robert. I was right-side-up, trying to reach him, when I was yanked out."

I was dragged over glass. I flip my hands over. There are scratches and cuts from the glass on my palms. Probably elsewhere, too. Little pieces everywhere. I can smell the snow and smoke.

"The guy who had ahold of me kept apologizing. Saying it was going to be okay." My fingernails are on my wrist again, scratching. "I believed them up until they put something over my face. It hurt to breathe."

"The nurses took a blood sample," Ms. McCaw tells me. "The hospital is running a full lab to figure out what happened."

Searing pain flashes through my head. I cover my face with my hands and groan. My heart monitor shrieks.

A nurse rushes in, followed by the doctor who helped me.

"Out," he orders the detective. "Thought we already told you she was done for the day, Masters."

He puts the bed flat, his hand on my shoulder. "Margo, it's okay. We're going to give you oxygen to help you breathe. Okay?"

He lowers a clear mask over my nose and mouth.

I'm so sorry—

It's too similar to what just happened to me. My head pounds. A ringing noise fills my ears. It takes a second to realize I'm the one screaming, pushing at the mask.

A sob breaks through me like a crashing wave.

Is it too much to ask for a little peace?

"I'm giving you something to help you sleep," the doctor says.

Ice rushes into my vein through the IV. It spreads through my body, weighing it down.

Panic still crushes my chest, though. Just because I'm about to be dragged under doesn't mean all my fear goes away. No, it's being pulled down with me... right into my own personal nightmare.

My memories.

Chapter 5
Caleb

Mr. Black meets me outside the county jail, and I can't say I've ever felt like more of a miscreant. But at least Uncle isn't the one waiting for me.

After our 'interview', the detective said he had enough cause to hold me without pressing charges. So there I sat, while Margo was in the hospital without me.

"I found her," I say once we're in the car. "And they just—"

"He already suspected you. When you showed up with her at the hospital, her arms still fucking bound..."

Eli's dad isn't a swearer. He drinks expensive whiskey when the occasion calls for it—after a big day at work, maybe—but otherwise, he doesn't like alcohol. For years, I've been trying to find his vice. Smoking, gambling, women.

There had to be something.

Instead, I found a good man. He went to church with his wife on Sundays and tried not to disappear into his office on the weekends. He was present. At the games, cheering us on. When we were younger, he'd pick us up from school and we'd grab ice cream.

Eli's family was more like mine for a long time. And if I had to pick a man to emulate when I got older, it was him.

He hands me my phone. "Your uncle called."

I grimace. "I was hoping to avoid telling him I'm out."

"Did the time in jail make you delusional?" He shakes his head. "I can sometimes pull a rabbit out of a hat, but I'm no miracle worker."

"Maybe." I fiddle with it. "How is she?"

It's been just under seventy-two hours. Almost three days exactly since I saw her. And every moment of it has been hell. My skin has been crawling since they put me in the holding cell. There was an odor in there, but now that I'm out, I think it's me.

I should be ashamed, but I'm just mad. At the detective, at Unknown and whatever fucking game they're playing.

Finding their identity is my new priority.

Eli's dad glances over. "She told the detective it wasn't you."

I didn't expect anything different. It *wasn't* me. But the sudden relief at knowing she knows... indescribable. My shoulders lower a fraction, and I take a deeper breath.

"Is she still in the hospital?"

His grip flexes on the steering wheel. "They discharged her this afternoon."

It's a little past seven. Winter has well and truly arrived, because it's already dark. And there's a fresh layer of snow on the ground.

"She could be home already," I muse.

I scroll through my missed calls and texts. Falling off the radar doesn't go unnoticed in Rose Hill. But I'm only scanning for one name in particular. Instead, another catches my eye.

RILEY

It's Margo. I'm home.

Not sure where my phone ended up.

That's an invitation if I've ever heard one.

"Robert is still in the hospital," Eli's dad offers unexpectedly. "They moved him out of ICU. But with Margo home, Lenora is trying to be in two places at once."

I scowl at him. "Margo shouldn't be alone. Not with a kidnapper on the loose."

And Unknown still harassing us.

They knew I was going to get arrested. Knew I'd find the barn... but how?

He nods. "I figured you would say that. I checked with her case worker and made some calls. Riley and her dad are going to stay with Margo while Lenora stays at the hospital."

Not good enough, I almost say.

I swallow. "Is the detective going to come after me again?"

"I'll make sure he doesn't." He sighs. "She wasn't able to name anyone. Says she didn't see, although she swears it wasn't you."

Something funny happens in my body. Every muscle gets tight. Alarmed. A lump forms in my throat, and it's hard to breathe. She was held—they pulled her from the wreckage and did who-knows-what, and she never saw them?

"Even more reason to stay with her," I bite out. "Who—"

"Caleb. I'll drop you off at Margo's house, but do not, under any circumstances, talk to Masters or anyone else about what happened."

Mr. Black is a badass defense lawyer. He has sway in the prosecutor's office and all over the county. Hell, half of New York City knows of Josh Black. I don't think the district attorney has ever had a worse record in court against one lawyer.

And right now, I'm grateful for it.

I barely slept while in holding. There was an officer keeping watch, but it was county jail. All sorts of crazies were brought in.

My phone vibrates again.

UNCLE

Tomorrow morning. My house.

I can hear his anger from here. He thinks I did it, but he's more concerned that I got caught.

I don't respond to Margo, or my uncle, or any of the other messages. I need to see her with my own eyes.

"I should've taken off the duct tape." I don't realize I've said it out loud until Mr. Black has slowed the car and twisted toward me.

"Caleb." His voice is stern. "You cannot say things like that, especially around the detective. You understand?"

"I found her on the floor of the barn." I meet his gaze. He already heard this story when I told the detective, but it bears repeating. "She was unconscious. I was more worried about getting her to the hospital."

"All they'll see is someone who wanted to keep her in check. Under their thumb."

I bristle. "That's not it."

"I *know* that's not it. I know you. But that's what they'll say, and that argument is what they'll build a case on, if Masters decides to charge you."

"She said it wasn't me."

Eli's dad tsks. "She was drugged. She could've been confused."

"I *found* her!"

"How? How did you know exactly where to go? Why didn't you call the police?"

"Fuck!" I'm tempted to jump out of the car. Of all the things, I kept the detail of Margo's stalker leading me right to her a secret.

"Son, I'm just trying to get you to see how the prosecutor would—"

"Yeah, I get it. Can we just..." I wave toward the road. We're close to Margo's house, and I'm eager to see her. And be done with this line of questioning.

He chuckles to himself. "I suppose it's a good thing we're going to see her now. Saves you a midnight trip."

Ah, shit. "You know?"

"Just because you *think* you're quiet doesn't mean I don't know everything that happens in that house. But your *runs* don't usually end with you coming home in a reasonable time. And sometimes they involve your car."

I chuckle. "Yeah, that may be true."

We pull into Margo's driveway, and he stops me from getting out with a hand on my shoulder.

"Seriously. We had the sex talk when you were fourteen. I don't need to tell you to be safe, right? You're smart enough to already—"

"Yeah, we're good."

He drops his hand, and I get out. Lenora's car is in the driveway. Robert's is probably at the junkyard... or in police custody. I didn't see it, but I have enough mental imagery to last a lifetime.

Lenora yanks the door open before I have a chance to knock.

"Caleb." She's decidedly unfriendly.

I narrow my eyes. "Mrs. Bryan."

"Angela told me..." Her attention slides past me, to where Josh Black comes up behind me. "The charges were dropped?"

"I didn't do it." I stare at her, willing her eyes to come back to me. "I would never."

She scoffs. "You seem to be the cause of a lot of heartache."

"I can't really do much about that unless you let me in to fix it," I say quietly.

She only steps aside once Mr. Black is behind me.

The living room is empty. I glance into the kitchen, find that empty, and head up the stairs. The longest walk of my life. It's been the longest few days of my life, actually.

My imagination runs wild. I walk down the hall to her room, and it stretches out in front of me. Her door is cracked open, and it doesn't make a noise when I nudge it open farther.

She's... *cleaning.*

Shoving papers into drawers, straightening her books. Her small trashcan is in her hand, and she periodically shoves random things—a bauble, a paper, something that appears to be a seasonal decoration—into it. Her sheets are off the mattress, balled up in the center of the room. Comforter thrown on the floor. All her clothes are stacked in a pile on top of her nightstand.

Maybe cleaning was the wrong word. She's doing more harm than good.

And she's sniffling.

The whole room feels different. Like I left it—and her—one way, and now I'm coming back to someone new.

"Margo."

I startle her. She nearly jumps out of her skin, and my heart gives a nasty thump.

Her face is bruised. A few butterfly bandages are taped over stitches across her forehead—that gash was the source of a lot of blood. She probably has more injuries, but those are the only visible ones.

That, and her expression.

I step toward her, and she steps back.

That's not how this normally goes.

"You don't think I had anything to do with this, do you?"

Her eyes widen, then skip to the window. I can't help but notice it's locked. A message if I ever saw one. I want to howl. Instead, I keep approaching. Her back bumps against the bookshelf—the very same one I found the spying figure on—and she freezes.

I relish the heat of her body, but I don't touch her. I stop just a hair's breadth away and meet her dark eyes. There are hours unaccounted for after the accident, and I would kill to give them back to her.

I force myself not to trace her jaw. To inhale the scent of her shampoo—because even that is off, tainted by the antiseptic smell of the hospital.

She's breathing heavy, like me being in her room has stolen her oxygen.

This isn't you, I almost say. This girl is scared—but she doesn't need to be scared of *me*.

"Are you angry?" she blurts out.

"Furious," I whisper. "But not at you."

I give in to temptation and drag my finger across her lower lip. It's split, a little swollen, but she doesn't move when I press, parting her pretty mouth.

Her tongue darts out, touching my thumb, and I grin. I'm getting harder by the second, but I think Margo knows what she does to me.

It's so fucking good to see her.

"I thought you might be happy to see me." I stroke her hair. I want to kiss her, but she seems scared. I don't know why she'd be scared of me. "You okay, baby?"

A ridiculous question to ask, given the circumstances.

"Caleb..." She trembles, but she reaches out and steadies herself on me. "I'm so far from okay, I don't know what to do."

I can't read her expression, but she seems terrified.

"Tell me," I demand. "Let me make it better."

She sucks in a breath, then blurts out, "My memories came back."

And all the things I was trying to keep from her are suddenly... not so hidden.

Fuck.

Chapter 6
Margo

Past

Caleb and I were playing hide and seek, which required me to be extra quiet. I tiptoed through the house, planning on balling up under the sink in the kitchen. It would take him *forever* to find me, and I'd be victorious.

We weren't supposed to be here, though. Lydia—*Mrs. Asher*—had taken us to the park, but she dropped us off about an hour ago and told us to play in Caleb's room until she got back. There were only so many things we could do in his room, and he was sick of me touching his Legos. The puzzles were built. I wasn't allowed to play his violent video games, so that was out.

We were used to being let loose, and eventually, Caleb caved.

My dad was working, his mom was out. We could hear his dad downstairs, which should've been reason enough to stay locked up.

Caleb and I had experienced an odd thrill of imminent

capture when his dad got home. He wouldn't just yell at us —he'd probably scream his voice hoarse at Caleb's mom, too. Leaving two ten-year-olds unattended? Not wise. But hide and seek was an excellent game. It got us out of the room, and there was a bonus of sneaking around Caleb's dad. It was *meant* for devious kids like us.

And yeah, it may have been my idea.

There was an odd thumping noise coming from the kitchen.

I pressed myself to the wall and tiptoed closer, more driven by curiosity than anything.

Upstairs, Caleb was probably counting as quietly as possible. I counted in my head, keeping track of my time. That's how you were supposed to do it when being stealthy.

"Fuck, Amber," a voice growled.

My whole body got icy.

I stopped just before the doorway and poked my head around the corner.

My mother and Caleb's dad were in the kitchen. She sat on the counter, her bare legs wrapped around Caleb's dad's hips. It was the same counter she cooked on. But she was moaning like she was in pain. Her mouth was open. Eyes closed.

His hand was tangled in her hair, keeping her head back.

His ass flexed as he moved, and horror filtered through me.

I knew about sex. We'd learned about it in health class just a few weeks ago. All the kids had laughed and shrieked their way through the birds and bees discussion.

But I didn't think it would be like *this*. Caleb's dad was still wearing his pants. Barely. They clung to his upper thighs. That wasn't the disturbing part—besides seeing his hairy ass, *ew*. No—it was that the words coming out of his mouth were vicious.

He called her dirty, even as he kissed her neck.

Mom was cheating on Dad?

I knew what that was, too. We had learned about it from Savannah. Her dad had a shiny new girlfriend who sometimes picked her up from school. Sav said her dad called the girlfriend the newer model—whatever that meant.

That's not this.

This is something worse.

They're doing something *bad*. Worse than picking up someone else's kid from school.

Dad would be heartbroken if he saw them. But before I could let out a shout, a hand wrapped around my mouth and dragged me backward. I kicked, then realized it was Caleb. He pushed me into the pantry, closing the door behind him with a soft *snick*.

"What are you doing?" I needed to scrub my eyes out with soap. I was shaking.

"You can't tell," Caleb said.

That wasn't what I expected.

"Please, Margo, you can't tell them." He was desperate. Reeked of it. He came at me and grabbed my wrists. His thumb caressed my bracelet, as if to remind me that it was there. "That won't be us. Okay? But it's them, and doing whatever you're about to do will just make everything worse."

"Caleb, Mom is cheating on my dad—" I took a step back, shaking him loose. "You knew?"

Slowly, he nodded.

"Cheating is wrong," I said. Decisive.

Dad always talked about morals. Morality. It was such a

hard thing to wrap my brain around, but he made it easy. Right and wrong. Stick up for the truth.

This... this was a lie. Plain and simple.

I shoved past Caleb and into the hall, where Mom was standing. She was dressed, luckily. Her hands were on her hair, pulling it up, but they slowly dropped when she saw me.

I swallowed.

Her pants were still unbuttoned.

"Margo!"

I turned and fled. Up the stairs, down the hall to Caleb's room. Caleb chased after me, and once we were inside he slammed the door, flipping the lock.

The doorknob rattled, then Mom pounded on the door. "Margo Wolfe, open up right now."

Caleb stared at me. "You're not going to tell, right?"

The door flew open. Caleb's dad straightened, triumphant, but my mom shoved past him.

She grabbed my shoulders, shaking me slightly. "You don't know what you saw, Margo. It was nothing."

Her voice was angrier than I'd ever heard it.

I shook my head. "But, Mom—"

"No buts. Please, Margo." She put her face right in mine. "If he found out, it would ruin everything. And nothing even happened. It just looked bad. Do you want to be responsible for ruining it all?"

It looked like sex, but what did I know? I'd never seen it before.

Her fingers dug into my shoulders. Caleb's dad stared at me. Caleb was breathing heavily behind me, the entire room waiting on my answer.

"I won't tell," I promised.

I promised.

Present

"All of your memories?"

I shift. "I remember catching my mom and your dad. Running to your room. We were playing hide and seek."

All I want to do is throw myself into his arms. He found me. Took me to the hospital. Detective Masters *arrested* him.

And yet, I'm grappling with this truth he kept from me.

Two, actually. He never mentioned that my dad allegedly killed his. I can see why he thinks that, now knowing what I do.

"Your mom said it was nothing," he says.

"She was trying to minimize it. I know that now. And you—" I break off. My head hurts. I'm under concussion protocol, which should mean limiting my physical activity. And this conversation feels like a physical altercation.

What did Caleb say the first time we went into his house?

One day I'm going to fuck you on this counter. And then he did. Mirroring our parents' fuck-up. Making me role-play some sick and twisted game when he knew I didn't remember.

He did, and he didn't have any regrets. He took my virginity like that.

"I never claimed to be the nice guy." He comes closer and reaches for me. "If you're remembering that day in the kitchen..."

"I hate you for putting me in that position. For doing that to me... *there*."

The image is burned behind my eyelids. My mom and

his dad. Even if I convinced myself at the time that maybe it wasn't what I thought, I now know I was right. They were *fucking*. Cheating. He was degrading her, but I think she liked it.

"Margo, there are dark memories all over that house. How are we ever going to move on if we don't erase them?"

I push at his chest. That's a cop-out. The worst excuse I've heard.

I've been so *stupid*. I thought the truth was going to release me. But it turns out, it's just another shackle. The truth is that he asked me not to tell, but I did. And everything fell apart because of me.

Caleb was right to be angry with me.

He tugs on my wrists. I fall into him, unable to stop myself.

"I wasn't the one to block away my memories, baby. I've had to live with this for years all alone." His lips touch the top of my head. "I'm not sorry for our beginning. But I *am* sorry for not keeping you safe."

My emotions are on a pendulum swing.

I slip away from him and go to the window. My room is a wreck—the first thing I did when I got home was yank it apart, and now I feel like I'm bleeding from every seam. All the while, his gaze follows me. His eyes see too much.

"You found me," I say softly. "How?"

He's suddenly behind me. His hand lands on mine, stopping it. I had been scratching at my wrist again.

"I need you to touch me," he says softly.

I turn slowly. Touch him?

Do either of us deserve that?

"It feels like you're not really here," he whispers. "I'm going to wake up in bed and you'll still be missing."

My chest aches.

I raise my hand. One touch won't kill us.

"Caleb!" someone calls from downstairs.

I'm about to drop my hand when Caleb snags it, holding it to his cheek. We both exhale.

"Margo? Come down, please."

I tilt my head. "Ms. McCaw is here?"

Caleb shrugs. "No idea. She wasn't when we got here."

The story of how Caleb found me will have to wait. I pull away and grab a sweatshirt, carefully zipping it up and heading downstairs.

Before we left the hospital this afternoon, I got to see Robert. He was intubated and sedated in ICU, and I couldn't get close, but seeing him through a window was enough. He looked beat up and scary, but the nurses assured me he was in good hands.

Me, on the other hand? Lenora kept worrying the entire way back. She asked me how I was feeling, if I needed anything special at the house.

If you know who took you and you're scared to tell the police... you can tell me.

I didn't. I promised her I didn't know.

Three days in the hospital. The detective visited me twice, asking much the same questions. But apparently, they can't just take witness testimony as fact. There has to be *evidence*. And so far... nothing.

No fingerprints on the tape, no CCTV footage on that intersection. No idea about whose car hit ours.

The detective is eager for me to admit Caleb took me. It's odd that the detective has such disdain for him... and such bias. But who am I to know? All I can keep repeating is Caleb's innocence.

Lenora, Ms. McCaw, and Eli's dad—who I've only met

once—are seated at the kitchen table when Caleb and I come down.

Ms. McCaw meets us halfway and puts her finger under my chin, lifting my head and inspecting the bandage. "How do you feel?"

I shrug. "I don't know. As good as can be expected, I guess."

"Let's sit," she suggests.

I wonder if this is the part where they tell me the accident was too much—that I can't stay. I'll get a few minutes to pack my bag. At least Caleb will be here to say goodbye. *Again.*

"Originally, Riley and her dad were going to stay here." Lenora's eyes are puffy from crying. She stretches her arm across the table, taking my hand. "But they're not approved by the county for any sort of fostering. Including respite. We all thought it wasn't going to be a problem, but..."

But it is. Respite is temporary housing. Also known as a foster kid's nightmare. It's a house you don't know, with rules you're unaware of or unfamiliar with, and strangers trying to boss you around. For a day, a week. However long your long-term place is unable to have you. Be that vacation or sickness...

Ms. McCaw takes over. "That wasn't a possibility, unfortunately. However, the Blacks have been approved to take in fosters."

My gaze shoots over to Eli's dad.

"You can stay with us until Robert is out of the hospital," he says.

Lenora squeezes my hand. "Does that make me a bad mother? Wanting to stay with him?"

I shake my head. "No, of course not."

"Is that allowed?" Caleb asks. "The detective—"

"That's why we wanted to sit down and discuss it," Ms. McCaw says. "Yes, you're a person of interest in the case, but everyone here believes that you didn't have a hand in it."

My eyes fill with tears. "Lenora? You believe me?"

She hadn't... "If you say he didn't do it, then yes. I believe you."

Caleb scoffs.

Mr. Black rises. "Gather some things, Margo, if you would. I've got an early start tomorrow."

What a whirlwind. Like so many other things in my life, this is happening almost too fast to comprehend.

Accident. Kidnapped. Hospital. Home. And now— Caleb's home.

I shove clothes into a bag. I don't know how long I'll be, so I take only a few items. My school uniform. Toiletries from the bathroom.

Caleb is in my room when I return, sitting on my bed again.

He frowns. "You're crying."

I swipe at my cheeks. They're wet. "I don't know why."

And yet, it keeps building. The sadness.

"Mom told me not to tell." I stare down at my boots. "I promised."

"I know."

"I have a history of not keeping my promises, Caleb. How can you believe anything that comes out of my mouth?"

He may be a liar, but so am I.

I was the original.

"I know you," he says. "Okay? I know *you*. And some promises you won't break." He reaches out and snags my wrist, pulling me closer. Between his legs.

"Why can't we go back to normal?" I ask.

He laughs. His thumb brushes my cheek. "Normal? What's that?"

I giggle—and then abruptly stop. I *laughed*. Robert is in the hospital and I laughed. And—

"Stop."

His gaze is dark. I could run from it, but what's the use? He'd just find me again.

I back away from him and grab my bag. It's an improvement from the garbage bags I've had to use in the past. This one is thicker canvas. It won't break on me.

An omen if I've ever heard one.

And then... I leave him there. Sitting in my room, staring at me like I'm still his salvation.

I'm not. I'm so not.

I'm *dirty*. Just as dark as him. Maybe worse. Because I remember the start of my awful betrayal, and I know what came next: I told someone.

I betrayed my mother.

No wonder she hates me so much.

It's in my blood. It's in my history. What if I do that to Caleb? What if the next time the detective asks, I lie and say he did take me?

Would I do that to him?

Chapter 7
Caleb

I watch her when she thinks I'm not.

Or maybe she feels my gaze and is an expert in ignoring me. Fuck if I know.

We loaded up into the car and drove in silence. I sprawled across the backseat, my eyes on the back of her neck, and turn over the revelations.

She knows what she witnessed.

Mother insisted Margo made it up, but I figured it was a little too far-fetched for a ten-year-old to create. So I held on to the belief that Margo saw Dad fucking her mom, and let my own mother live in the fantasy world she created.

Without that truth—that Dad *had* cheated—her whole world stayed intact.

I long to reach forward and touch her, to move the hair off her neck and kiss down her shoulder. To chase away the shadows in her eyes.

Margo Wolfe has her own demons now.

I know all about them.

At the house, I take the bag out of the trunk. She follows Eli's dad slowly, like the porch will suddenly realize she's intruding and catapult her onto the lawn. Needless to say, her worries are for nothing. I trail them upstairs. The room closest to the steps, right across from the bathroom, is all hers.

Norah has an eye for design. Normally the room is a bit sterile—used most often as a guest room for visiting extended family—but in the short time she had, she's transformed it.

There's a fuzzy, hot-pink pillow in the center of the bed. The comforter and throw pillows, which used to be all white, have been replaced with a floral print. Muted colors, but color nonetheless.

A desk in the corner has a vase of flowers. There's a standing lamp beside it, and a shorter matching one on the nightstand. The ambiance has a warmer feel instead of the overhead light.

The curtains are closed for now, warding against the chill and darkness. It also probably helps lessen that watched feeling. I don't know if she's been getting that vibe, but the hair on the back of my neck is permanently up.

I can't shake that Unknown was here the other night, waiting for the detective to arrive and interrogate me. But the more important thing is that Margo feels safe.

No—the most important thing is that she *is* safe.

I put the bag down on the desk chair.

"Make yourself comfortable," Mr. Black tells her. "Norah is heating dinner, it should be ready soon."

He leaves, and then it's just us.

My phone has been steadily blowing up in the last hour, but I've ignored it. Now, I pull it out and scroll through the messages. Half of them are from Riley, which would be weird if...

Well, Margo texted me from hers. Which means—

"Did you find your phone?"

Margo flops on the bed. Her dark hair fans across the pink pillow, and she bites her lip. "They took it, I think. Or I lost it in the accident."

I frown.

"Lenora texted Riley, who met us at the house. She stayed until Ms. McCaw called and said they weren't approved…" Her cheeks pinken. "I don't really have anyone else to talk to except her or you."

I hand her my phone.

She sits up and scrolls through. A small smile creeps across her face at the messages from Riley. They start off formal, with Margo's name at the top. As if I'd get confused about who she wants to reach.

She taps out a reply, then goes to hand the phone back.

"There are others. People who are either nosy or think they care." I stay standing. What I really want is to climb on top of her and kiss her until we're both breathless and she's trembling on the edge of an orgasm…

But I can't risk the Blacks kicking us out.

"I notice Amelie and Savannah don't give a shit," she says on a laugh. "Amelie's nowhere to be found, and Sav's latest ones all seem a bit desperate."

I chuckle. "Yeah, well. She *is* desperate."

She sobers. "What if I'm misremembering stuff? Like my brain just put in a person who didn't really make sense—"

"You don't trust yourself?"

"How could I?" She stares at the ceiling. "I forgot that my own mother cheated on Dad with yours."

My stomach knots. While I'm glad her memories finally opened up, I hate her forlorn expression. "It was traumatic, but I'm glad you were able to live without it for a little while."

She cocks her head. "What do you mean?"

I could give her this. A taste of my side.

"After Dad died, Mom couldn't stand to be in the house. She was self-destructing."

"Not as bad as mine," she whispers.

"No, Mother didn't turn to drugs. But she did think she couldn't parent me anymore, so she carted me off to my aunt and uncle's house only a few days after the funeral."

Margo knows exactly what that means. She's seen my uncle's handiwork firsthand.

"All I wanted was to get you back." I cave and sit beside her. My hand lands on her thigh. "Uncle David employed a very specific type of behavior modification. He was relentless in blaming not only your father, but *you* for everything."

Her eyes fill with tears. "Why?"

Everything is so fucking fragile right now.

"Because if I didn't hate you, I would've done anything I could to get back to you. And he couldn't have that lingering over him. It would've hurt our family reputation. His reputation means more to him than anything else."

I can't resist anymore—I lean over and steal a kiss from her lips. Cup her bruised jaw. Slide my tongue into her mouth and taste her mint toothpaste. I thread my fingers in her hair and tip her backward. Her hands fist my shirt, pulling me closer.

I get a knee between her legs and pin her with some of my weight. Her kiss goes straight to my groin. My dick wakes up, pressing against my zipper.

"Hey, I heard—*Argh!*" Eli makes a retching noise. "Dinner is ready, you sex beasts."

Margo freezes under me.

I groan against her lips and slowly extract myself. "Sorry, baby."

The barest smile creeps across her lips. I help her to her feet. My dick throbs. Her hair is ruffled, her lips redder than they were. She's so fucking perfect, I can't stand it.

"It's okay," she whispers. "You know where to find me later."

Chapter 8
Unknown

They're going to clip your wings, Margo. Caleb Asher isn't interested in your flight. He only wants your song, and you can do that perfectly well behind bars.

He'll keep you locked away forever.

Except you think your cage is a house, and your keeper is your lover.

Foolish. It's foolish to believe in love when it's nothing more than noise, thunder rumbling over our heads.

And luck is just a flash of lightning, brief and bright.

I only need one strike.

Chapter 9
Margo

Family dinners still seem foreign. Robert, Lenora, and I developed our own routine. It didn't always involve the kitchen table—and very, *very* rarely involved the dining room table or the fancy place settings—but we were usually together.

At the foster home I shared with Claire and Hanna, they got everyone together on Sunday nights. It set the week up right, they said. Although those dinners were awkward more often than not. I liked the family, don't get me wrong. We just didn't really know how to talk to each other.

This is different.

I sit with Caleb on one of the long sides of the table. Eli faces us. Mr. and Mrs. Black have the heads... or head and foot? I'm not sure of proper etiquette. What to call it.

All the food is in the middle of the table, and we pass stuff around to fill our plates. But there's never a lull in the chatter. Eli mainly fills it with hockey talk. Or school. Or gossip.

"No one wants to hear about Savannah's dad's new girlfriend," Caleb finally says. "He's a sugar daddy. I'm pretty sure he pays them to date him, but that's not news."

My eyes widen.

Mrs. Black—who told me to call her Norah, but that still feels weird—coughs. "Perhaps we should discuss something else."

Caleb glances from her to her husband. "Maybe we should discuss Detective Masters."

Mr. Black grimaces. "I hadn't wanted to say anything earlier."

"But?" Caleb presses.

"Jim Masters went to school with your dad," Mr. Black explains to Caleb. "There's some bad blood there."

"Did you know him back then?" I ask.

Mrs. Black shifts. "We all did. And we knew your parents, too, Margo."

"*What?*"

They look guilty. Under the table, Caleb catches my fingers and squeezes.

Eli's mom explains, "Josh, Ben Asher, and your dad, Keith, were friends in high school. Josh and Ben played football together, and Keith..."

My dad.

It's surreal to hear his name on her lips after so many years of nothing.

"He was the smart one of the group." She smiles.

"But you said you knew my mom, too?"

Her smile fades fast. "We didn't meet her until after college. Your parents came back to Rose Hill engaged. They were partially proud, but he was also returning with his tail between his legs. His family disowned him in the process of their engagement."

"Disowned?" By family? We didn't have any family.

Mr. Black sets down his silverware. "You have a grand-mother. Had? I'm not sure if she's still around. She had a home in England, but she may have relocated or passed away... I wish I could tell you for certain."

"That's..." *The first I'm hearing of this.* I have a grand-mother? Bizarre. "I always figured any grandparents I had died before I was born. Dad never mentioned having anyone, and neither did Mom."

It's the reason I went into the foster system. The state couldn't find anyone who would take me. No relatives they could contact. Not on my dad's side, and not on my mom's either.

Another thing occurs to me. I face Caleb. "I thought we moved into your guest house because Mom got a job?"

Norah clucks her tongue. "Keith called us asking if we knew of any opportunities. From my understanding, the three of you were living in the city at the time and strug-gling. Josh and I didn't have any leads for him, but we suggested he reach out to Ben."

"But Eli and Caleb didn't meet until later," I say slowly. "Right?"

Mr. Black nods. "Ben and I had a falling-out when you all were young—probably in diapers. For the sake of our family, we put some distance between us and the Ashers. And then, of course, the terrible tragedy that happened to Ben..."

The true tragedy is that no one is innocent. The Blacks played a hand in getting my parents back to Rose Hill. Ben Asher and my father knew each other. *Well*, apparently. Even though, from my perspective, they seemed more like enemies.

If Dad was disowned, it probably meant his family had money. And the quick fall from grace with his new wife might cause some rifts between him and his friends, right?

Ben Asher most of all.

Would that have led Ben to cheat on his wife with my mom? How could he have done that to one of his oldest friends?

"Enlightening," Eli says, breaking the silence. "But can we talk about the rumor of Amelie being engaged?"

I tune him out.

After dinner, I excuse myself and grab fresh clothes, then lock myself in the bathroom. Once I'm alone, I strip off my shirt and grip the edge of the counter. I blow out a slow breath, trying to keep control of myself.

My dad was best friends with Ben Asher in high school?

I focus on my eyes. They're brown, which is usually nothing to write home about. Heroines in romance novels don't often have brown eyes, or they're described as honey, amber, or chocolate. Nothing wrong with any of those things. Mine just seem a bit more plain.

My attention drifts from my eyes to the bandage on my forehead. The nurse gave me instructions on washing—basically, try not to get it too wet. If I take a shower, avoid dousing it under the water. The stitches will come out in a few days, but already the swelling is better. My face is a patchwork of scrapes and bruises, but the gash was the worst of it.

Robert did his best to protect me. I close my eyes and see the accident in slow motion. The other vehicle coming at us, hitting our car just in front of where I sat. The way Robert's arm banded across my chest as we careened into a ditch. We were weightless for a moment, and then it all came smashing down.

Glass.

Metal.

Blood.

My torso is speckled with bruises, and one nasty one that stretches diagonally across my chest—the seat belt as it locked, preventing me from falling through the windshield.

The backs of my legs are the most cut up, thanks to being dragged across the glass-ridden asphalt.

This has been the week from Hell.

I shower, scrubbing my scalp and avoiding the stitches.

I find the scar on the back of my head, and I hesitate. I remember the stitches I had to get for it, but I don't quite remember how it happened.

Falling backward, my head hitting the edge of... *something*.

A hand held mine in the hospital. The doctor didn't even have to cut my hair to put stitches in. Or maybe it was staples?

With sudden clarity, it dawns on me that I lied to Caleb. I don't have all my memories back. I don't know how I got the scar or how I told Dad about Mom's affair.

I don't know how she reacted.

How the blood got on my door.

Dad has a story to tell. He insinuated as much, but we ran out of time too fast. Maybe he can jog my memory. Maybe he can just *tell me* what I'm missing.

I rinse and dry as fast as I can. My body is sore, but I ignore it. After I pull on the loosest-fitting outfit I brought, I go seek out Mr. Black.

He's in his home office on the first floor, staring down at a file. It's the only thing on his huge desk besides a computer monitor tilted at an angle.

I knock on the door, and his head jerks up. His gaze goes

through me for a second, then he frowns. "Margo. You look a little pale. I expected you to be in bed."

He gestures to the clock above the fireplace. It's nearly ten.

"I didn't realize the time," I say as an apology. "I don't have a phone."

"Do you need to sit?"

I sink into the chair across from his desk. We sit in silence for a moment, and I try to think of the best way to word my question.

"I, um..." *Yeah, this is going well.*

Josh glances up, then slowly closes the file. "Why do I think you came in here for a purpose?"

"You're defending Caleb, right? In case Detective Masters tries to arrest him again."

"I am. I doubt Masters will do anything without solid evidence and a warrant."

I chew on my lower lip for a minute. "We kind of got off topic when it came to Masters."

He dips his head. "Right. Ben Asher was fearless in high school—but sometimes it made him cruel. Jim Masters didn't look like he does now. Back then he was scrawny, and a rule follower..."

"A good target for a bully," I murmur.

He nods.

"Ben has been gone for seven years, but some trauma doesn't go away. I suppose that's why, when Jim first saw your last name, then your relationship to Caleb, he doubled down. Like father, like son."

"But Caleb is nothing like his dad!"

He raises his hands. "I know. It's an archaic, simple way of thinking. And to answer your next question, the law allows them to hold suspects for up to seventy-two hours before charging them with a crime. When Masters was unable to bring any other evidence to the District Attorney, Caleb was released."

My eyes are huge.

He grimaces. "Once he gets his teeth into something, it's hard for him to let go."

"I told him Caleb was innocent."

He sighs. "You did. Doesn't mean the truth can't be twisted."

"Like... my dad's trial?"

"What makes you say that?"

I shift on the seat, suddenly nervous.

"Margo, stop." Josh rubs at his eyes. "I know this is hard. You just saw your dad, and I'm sure he professed his innocence. Then someone took you, which is traumatic. You were drugged—"

"Wait. Drugged?"

Drugged?

"The toxicology report came back. Your social worker got the results before they discharged you."

I swallow that information. It makes sense that they wouldn't let me leave without knowing what was in my blood. Still. I lean back and cross my arms over my chest. "What was I drugged with?"

"Margo..."

I'm beginning to think everyone in this damn town is keeping things from me.

"I deserve to know, Mr. Black," I say. "It's my body. Honestly, the doctors should've told me."

He nods. "We'll find out, okay?"

We sit and stare at each other for a moment.

"My dad did say he was innocent," I say quietly. "And I believe him."

I have so many questions, I can't begin to frame them in my mind. I can't help but think everything would be easier if all my memories returned.

"Margo?" He looks pointedly at my hands. "You're bleeding."

I release my wrist, where a thin line oozes blood. The rest of my wrist is covered in scratch marks. "Oh, um, I'm going to go put a... Band-Aid on it."

He says nothing, and I rush away. Instead of going back up to the safety of my temporary room, I go to the basement. Caleb's space.

He's not here—he went for a run with Eli about the same time I went up to shower—and the room is cold without him. I rinse off my wrist in his bathroom, determined to stop touching it.

The feeling of duct tape being wrapped around them comes back full force.

I thought I was knocked out.

It hits me hard enough to put me off balance. I grab the counter and stare at my reflection.

I should've kept Caleb's phone when he offered it, seconds before he left. Part of me thought I'd be happy with the freedom, but it just serves to isolate me.

A hysterical giggle creeps up my throat. Didn't I think that was *exactly* what Caleb wanted to do to me before? Isolate me. Single me out.

Turns out, all he had to do was mastermind a car accident, a kidnapping, and steal my phone. Oh, and put my foster father in the hospital.

Caleb could very well be the bad guy in my situation, pulling the strings. It's what he's wanted from day one: to break me. Destroy me.

He's not my knight in shining armor. While I've been

falling for him all over again, he never stopped playing the game.

He's the villain. I've known this from the beginning. And villains...

They'll do anything to win.

Chapter 10
Caleb

Past

Mom was gone. She didn't say where she was going before she left. One minute she was standing with me in the foyer of my uncle's house, kissing the top of my head, and the next...

I kept thinking she would come back. But it's been two days. Two days of moping, staring out the window, and avoiding my uncle's gaze. He was relentless, though. I couldn't seem to hide from him for long.

"You look like your father." Uncle David filled my bedroom doorway.

He was in slacks and an olive-green sweater. The collar of a white dress shirt was visible around his neck. He was even wearing loafers in the house, which struck me as odd. His expression was stoic. Not good or bad.

I slowly turned on the bed and faced him.

"I'm sure that's why she hasn't come back," he added.

I flinched. I'd been trying to stop but hadn't mastered my face yet. He liked it when I reacted to his words. He came out with these awful thoughts. He spoke them into existence and then watched the damage they inflicted. That happened before my dad died. But now...?

"Ben and I looked alike, too." He came closer and sat on the bed beside me. "Lydia... she's troubled."

"Mom?" I asked. "Troubled?"

"Always up to her ears in mischief." He grimaced. "It was what attracted Ben to her in the first place. Like a moth to a flame..."

"Mom was the flame?"

"Indeed," Uncle said. "Still is."

I didn't know what to make of that.

"Stand in front of me," he said softly.

Hesitation hurt. I learned that this morning. Now, I jump off the bed and stand before him. Uncle did look like Dad. He had the same mean glint in his eyes, too. But that meanness only came out in Dad after a few drinks. It was ever-present on Uncle's face. He was like a supermodel in the magazines Margo used to flip through. Beautiful and ice-cold.

There was no chair in front of him, but I already knew what he meant. We'd done this a few times—*lessons*, he called them.

I sank to my knees, keeping my eyes on Uncle's shoes. They were polished.

"Tell me again how it happened," Uncle urged.

"We were playing hide and seek." I glanced up. "Margo was hiding. She saw..."

"Your father fucking her mom."

I blinked. Mom never let me swear. She practically vibrated with anger when *hell* slipped out of my mouth. To say the *f* word seemed wrong on so many levels.

"She saw Dad..."

"Say it," he prodded. "It's just a word, Caleb. It's what they were doing. They were fucking. Right?"

I couldn't. Mom would be angry.

He exhaled. Disappointed.

The next thing I knew, I was flat on my back. He knelt beside me, his hand wrapped around my throat. The pressure was just enough that I could barely suck in air.

"Continue," he said.

Tears burn at the backs of my eyes.

"She came up to... tell me." It wasn't quite right, but the details were blending together. Did she find me or did I find her? "Her mom realized we saw her and begged her not to tell."

Uncle David leaned down. "But she did tell, didn't she? And then her father took matters into his own hands."

I shuddered.

"She should've listened to you, Caleb. If she had, your father would still be alive. Your family would still be together."

He squeezed harder, until white spots exploded across my vision.

"Say it," he repeated.

I knew better than to grab at his hands, but the urge was still there. The last time I did that, he backhanded me.

The easiest way to get out of this was to give him what he wanted.

"It's Margo's fault," I whispered. "She ruined everything."

"And what was your father doing with Amber Wolfe?"

"Fucking." The word was barely audible.

He released me and sat back, smiling. He was a bit maniacal, wild hair and a crazy grin. "That's it. One day, we'll demand justice. Action is the only way things get done around here. Trust me, son. It'll make you feel better."

I swallowed. I didn't believe him, but I would do anything to keep him calm.

"Yes, Uncle."

Present

What if everything I believed was... *twisted?*

"Wake up."

I open my eyes. I look up at Eli, my brows furrowing. How did I get in the car?

"You still have a concussion," he says. "In hindsight, we shouldn't have gone for a fucking run after dinner."

Right.

I touch the back of my head. The wound my uncle gave me is all but closed.

"I'm fine."

He grunts. "You're in denial, is what I think."

I don't bother with a response. He gets out, and I follow him up into the house. Mr. Black comes down the stairs as we're kicking off our shoes. Eli tosses his truck's keys into the bowl on the foyer side table.

"Margo's curiosity cannot be tamed," his dad says. "It's either a good talent or a dangerous one."

I pause. "She talked to you?"

He watches me with eagle eyes. "Wanted to get more information on Masters. And her father."

I grimace.

"Get some rest, boys. Caleb, you go back to school tomorrow."

I raise my eyebrows. "They're letting me back?"

Given the detective's interest in me and everything happening with Margo's family, I figured...

"Yes. Since no formal charges were brought against you, they can't expel you. Understand?" The expression he levels me with says I can't make any more mistakes.

I nod. "Yes, sir."

He exhales. "Goodnight, then."

He and Eli head up the stairs, but I hesitate. I should go see Margo, make sure she's okay. And yet...

Guilt overrides my decision. I can't see her, knowing I failed. I failed her in so many ways, I can't even count them.

I shove the emotion down and clear my throat. I'll see her tomorrow before school—or after, if she's still sleeping.

I get to the basement and stop. My bathroom light is on, throwing a warm, dim light across my room. I scan it, uneasy.

This wouldn't be the first time my uncle ambushed me. If Josh was upstairs, he could've slipped in without detection.

Instead, my gaze lands on my bed. My unmade... lumpy bed.

A knot forms in my chest. She was waiting for me in my bed while I was being an idiot. My headache suddenly seems very distant. Like it's not my head.

I go closer, and her hair fanned across my pillow becomes clearer. She faces me, but her lips are slightly parted. Eyes closed. She's beautiful and innocent in sleep, with no walls between us.

Well, none of *her* walls.

I sit on the edge of the bed and brush her hair off her face. She shifts, and I about die when her tongue pokes out, sweeping over her lower lip.

"You're back," she murmurs.

"You're in my bed." My chest tightens.

She sighs, reaching out blindly for me.

I catch her hand and kiss her knuckles.

Her eyes open, meeting mine. "I don't know if you're the best or the worst thing to happen to me."

Where is this coming from?

"Definitely the worst," I reply. "I went for a run with Eli and I think I passed out. He had to go back for his truck."

She huffs. "You have a concussion."

I roll my eyes. "I'm aware."

She watches me for a moment. I could sink into her gaze.

"You've been avoiding me," she accuses. "Minus, you know, being in jail."

She was kidnapped because of me.

She's been hurt, over and over, because of me.

And the worst part is, I haven't been able to prevent any of it.

Ian, our parents, her abduction.

"Stop thinking," she orders, pushing herself upright. "Caleb. I'm right here. I'm *okay*."

"But you..."

She touches my face.

"I couldn't save you," I mutter, and a piece of weight lifts off my chest. *See where honesty gets you?* "God, I didn't even know you had been taken until Detective Dickwad showed up—"

She pulls me toward her. Her hands are gentle on the back of my neck. I go with the pressure until our lips are inches apart.

And then I resist.

"Margo—"

She closes the distance between our lips and kisses me.

I'm shocked into immobility. She's not usually the pursuer in our fucked-up relationship. I've hunted her down, bullied her, broke her. But in the end, she turned out stronger than I could've imagined.

Her lips move against my frozen ones. It isn't until her teeth tug on my lower lip that my body thaws.

I slide my hands up her sides, over her shoulder blades and into her hair. She gives me the control. She broke the ice but now surrenders. I tilt her head back, and my tongue dips into her mouth. Her tongue moves along mine, forcing me out so she can explore my mouth.

She tastes sweet.

I lay her back down gently, cupping the back of her head even after it rests on the pillow. My body follows, hovering just over her. It was like this upstairs. Injured, wild. We're still fully clothed, and my skin is too hot. She breathes hard, too. The urgency is unmatched.

We're a mess, her and I.

Her leg hooks over my hip, drawing me closer.

I groan into her mouth, shifting so she can feel *exactly* what she does to me.

She tears her mouth away from mine, panting. "Caleb."

I shift to her neck, licking and kissing a spot just below her ear that drives her crazy. She wriggles beneath me, her head lolling to the side to give me better access. Her hands go to my pants and shoves them down.

She gets my boxers off next.

I bite her neck, and she shudders. I grin.

"I need to feel you," she whispers.

I roll my hips, the head of my cock brushing her panties. She's soaked, and it only makes me harder.

Her fingers find my erection, and she tugs her panties to the side.

I thrust into her. No hesitation, no *waiting*. We both let out a low groan.

Being inside her without a condom is dangerous. She feels so good. Her pussy grips my length while I stay still. I really want to just not fucking think for a little while. And getting lost in her is as good a place as any for my mind to go.

"If this hurts your head, tell me," I warn her.

"You have a head wound, too," she says. "So, ditto."

I chuckle. There is nothing on this planet that will stop me from being inside her right now. I've had a constant, minor headache for the last week. And this? Worth it.

My heart beats out of my chest. In the dim light, she appears ethereal. Dark hair, dark eyes, pale skin. So much pale skin. I grip her thighs, lifting her legs and locking them around my waist. I pull out, until just the tip is buried in her.

The muscles of her inner thighs flutter.

I slide her shirt up to her chin. No bra.

Her breasts are perfect, and her nipples harden. I pinch one between my thumb and index finger and push back into her.

She groans, her back arching off the bed. Her pussy clenches around me.

I almost explode right then and there. "You're going to be the death of me."

I draw back and slam into her, and she rises to meet me. I set a fast pace, ignoring the demons that've been crowding my head for as long as I can remember. She's beautiful splayed out beneath me, taking my length and begging for more.

"Touch yourself." My hand is still on her breast, and I tweak her nipple when she blinks up at me.

Slowly, her hand drifts down her body. Her finger pauses on her clit, and she shudders, then rubs in small circles. Her eyes flutter.

I roll my hips, hitting a new spot inside her. Her ass bounces on my thighs from the force of my thrusts, but her finger doesn't stop moving.

Her orgasm claws out of her.

I lean down and cover her lips with mine, swallowing her loud moan. She rakes her nails down my back.

I pound into her, hissing out a breath as I come. I still inside her and breathe sharply through my nose.

Our lips are still fused together.

She doesn't let me get away. If anything, we've broken through a barrier and she wants me *closer*. Her legs and arms wrap around me, and she tucks her head into my neck.

"You're not the worst thing to happen to me." Her warm breath hits my skin. "Far from it."

I slide out of her and roll us onto our sides. She immediately shifts again to face the same direction as me. My cock takes approximately two seconds of her ass rubbing it to slowly stiffen again. I push into her from behind, but not to fuck her.

Just to make sure she knows how close we are. How connected. Mentally and physically.

"Caleb..."

I hadn't realized my eyes closed. "You okay, baby?"

She sucks her lower lip between her teeth and contemplates my question. "I think I'm lost."

"Then I'll find you," I tell her.

"Why did everyone hate me? Shouldn't they have been mad at the people actually having an affair?"

"Apparently, everyone knew except your dad." It's time for a bit more truth around here.

She flinches. "What?"

"I don't know how, but Uncle David wasn't surprised. And at the funeral..." I grimace. "Mom didn't cry. She was more mad than anything else, and she left me with Uncle not long after. I think it was the betrayal..."

"Her husband was cheating on her," Margo says. "But you don't think she was more upset that he was..."

Dead. Or was she thinking murdered?

I lift one shoulder. "I was ten. I don't know."

"Dad said he didn't do it," she says softly.

"You can't be serious." The words are out of my mouth too fast. I should've held them back. But old, deep rage reignites in my chest. "He murdered my dad in cold blood. Of course he's going to lie to you and say he didn't."

My hips flex, burying my cock deeper into her.

"I shouldn't have said anything," she murmurs. She tries to scoot forward, but I hold fast.

"No way," I argue. "You stay right here. You feel me inside you all fucking night."

She stills.

I thrust into her again, more lazily. It's torture, though, to not pin her to her stomach and fuck her hard. Fast. Like she deserves.

She blows out a long breath. "I know."

"You know what?"

"That your dad's death still hurts. That your family blames the entire Wolfe family for it—including me." She cranes back to meet my gaze. Her beautiful lips tip down.

Maybe she's right. I do blame all of them.

It's what my uncle drilled into me from the moment I

stepped into his house. He liked shows of power. Cutting me down, making me feel small.

I did that to Margo when she arrived back in Rose Hill—but never again.

Chapter 11
Margo

I shoulder my bag and glance between Caleb and Eli. "I think I'll just have Riley—"

"Get in the damn truck, Wolfe," Eli grunts. "It's too early for this."

Caleb snickers. "He's not a morning person."

He puts his hand on the small of my back, guiding me to the passenger side of the truck. He opens the back door and slips my backpack off, tossing it in first. I follow.

While he went back to school immediately, I got an extra two days.

"What's the school saying about me?" I ask them once I'm buckled.

They look back. I chose the middle seat so I could see out the windshield, and also both of them.

"They're not saying anything," Caleb says.

I scowl. "Why not?"

"Do you want them to?" Eli questions.

"No."

"They won't because of us." Eli backs out of the driveway. "You're one of us now, Wolfe."

Right. Near-death experience will do that to a girl, I guess.

"You don't go anywhere without one of us," Caleb says. "We've been talking..."

"You've been talking?" I repeat.

"About your safety," he continues as if I didn't interrupt. "Ian is a wild card. I haven't forgotten what he did to you, and I don't think a little beatdown at a party is going to stop him if he has more shit to stir. Robert is still in the ICU, which means your stalker was fucking serious. Your stalker could be a classmate. Do you want me to go on?"

I sink back in my seat.

I guess he has a point... although I hate the idea of them babysitting me.

"Our next step is to uncover your stalker," Caleb continues.

He told me last night that Unknown texted him coordinates, and that's how he found me. Which makes it seem more and more like a setup for Caleb to get arrested.

"How?" I question.

He exchanges a look with Eli. "You're not going to like it..."

Great.

Chapter 12
Caleb

I can't remove my gaze from the sway of Margo's ass as she disappears into her second period class. Even with the cold weather, she's been sticking with skirts. Probably because I destroyed her other options, and she'd never admit it to Lenora.

"Lovesick, dude." Eli laughs. "I've never seen it so bad."

"I'm not..." *Lovesick.* It would explain why my chest doesn't feel quite right. Missing pieces and all that.

"Whatever. Hey, try not to give everyone hell at school."

I set my jaw. "I won't if they don't fucking say anything about Margo."

"We just need to get through hockey practice—"

"Fuck." I groan. "Coach is gonna ream me out for getting arrested."

Eli shrugs. "Probably."

Coach Marzden wins the Jackass of the Year competition every time. When we were freshmen, we admired the way he commanded a room. He was a role model for both of us.

However, it appears that even role models have a temper.

"Riley didn't come over," I say. "Last night? Would've thought she'd be like glue on Margo's skin."

He frowns. "She's avoiding the house."

"Did you do something?" I tilt my head. I didn't think they were that into it. Like, they'd fucked a few times to the best of my understanding. But maybe they didn't even do that much?

"This isn't a fucking psychobabble session," Eli snaps. "Leave it alone."

I scan the hallway automatically, making sure no one bad follows Margo into her science class. Unfortunately, our loitering catches some attention. Coach appears at the top of the hallway and immediately heads for us.

Anger rolls off Coach in waves. He's practically vibrating with it. Eli mumbles some hasty excuse and disappears before Coach reaches us.

Well, now *me*.

He stops in front of me, then motions. I follow him toward the athletic wing. He'll probably start the berating before we reach his office, just so some kids can hear that the great and terrible Caleb Asher has finally fallen.

Newsflash, I want to yell at them. It takes a lot more than one stalker to dethrone *me*.

Yet... I'm definitely losing my grip.

"In," Coach orders, holding the door open.

I sigh, then go to my usual chair in front of his desk.

"Did I fucking say you could sit?"

What the hell is his problem?

The arrest, probably.

I sprawl in the chair in defiance and force my body to relax. This isn't like a meeting with my uncle, where it could end with a glass thrown at my head—or worse. Coach may threaten and bluster, but he wouldn't even go so far as to remove me from the team. He just needs to yell.

It gives him some control he craves.

Then again, I like to fuck with control.

I watch him out of the corner of my eye. He circles around his desk and drops into his own chair, his glower firmly fixed on his face.

"You really made a goddamn mess of everything," he says. "Arrested. *Arrested.* What am I supposed to do with that? Let a felon stay on the team?"

"I'm sure Mr. Black would be happy to explain the difference between being held as a person of interest and formal arraignment," I say dryly. "Oh, wait, you should know. Didn't you major in pre-law? Before your life fell to shit."

He watches me. "Is that what you think?"

I shrug.

"You're a fool." He rubs at his eyes. "Honestly, Caleb. We all make choices. My life didn't *fall to shit.* It just changed."

"And you weren't angry about it?"

He sits back. "I was at the time. Now, not so much. What's your plan, son? You going to put this incident on your college applications?"

I grit my teeth. "Does it matter? I can get into any shitty old school. Dad—"

"Dear pops." Coach laughs. "Yeah, left you a fuck ton of money. Buy your way into any old school and tell me how it feels. Is that a stipulation for the trust fund?"

"Something like that." Or rather—exactly that. Until then, dear Uncle David has control of the accounts. He can't take money out, of course, but he manages it. Who knows what he's done since Dad died. I haven't been allowed near the books.

The bell rings, and I stand.

"Sit," Coach growls.

My smile falls away. "Why?"

"Because we have a visitor." He gestures toward the window.

The door opens. My uncle fills the doorway, looking down his nose at me. Nerves like snakes writhe in my belly. I tense, but subsequently, he blocks all the escape routes, too.

He closes the door behind him and takes his sweet time removing his coat, hanging it on the stand in the corner. And then he reaches over the desk and shakes Coach's hand.

He doesn't so much as glance my way when he sits, slinging one leg over the other. Proper, poised, in control.

I have to admire the way he takes over a room. Dad would be proud.

"You're keeping me from class for this?" I ask Coach.

"I was the one who requested the meeting," Uncle says. He adjusts his tie. "We're going to have a little chat about your future."

Looks like he's going into the office for once. Crisp white shirt, a navy-blue tie and sports coat. He's the picture of perfection and just as deadly.

"Why?" I'm immediately wary of his plan. Because I'm sure there is a plan hidden in there.

"I've come to request Coach remove you from the hockey team."

Silence.

My jaw drops open, and Coach... well, to his credit, seems equally flabbergasted.

I snap my mouth closed at the same time that Coach seems to shake off his surprise. He straightens in his seat, eyes narrowing at my uncle.

Well, this should be interesting.

"I hate to tell you this, David, but you can't come in here and demand—"

"Request," Uncle interrupts. "Very politely. Caleb has been learning some bad habits of late, and it cannot go unpunished. I had hoped his game suspension would do the trick. This is a stronger counter to his behavior."

"How's that?" I ask, unable to help myself.

Uncle glances at me. "Falling for a girl, acting ludicrously... it's only a matter of time before the girl turns up pregnant and ruins everything the Ashers have worked toward. At the end of the day, hockey is yet another distraction. Caleb needs to focus on what's important."

Fuck no.

"I hate to be the bearer of bad news, but Dad ruined everything *he* worked for when he sold the company. Right? The Asher name isn't even on the door anymore. What name is there to harm?"

Uncle's hand twitches. If we were home...

Well, I'll pay for this later.

Every action has an equal and opposite reaction, Dad whispers in my ear. Besides the points of inexplicable rage, he was actually a good dad. He taught me some valuable lessons before he was taken from us. Did I fear him?

A decent amount. Especially at ten.

Did he hit me?

No worse than Uncle... and there was always a reprieve. In those lulls, good things happened. It was almost better when he hit me and got it over with, because the following week was bliss.

Uncle has no such calm period after the storm. With him, the storm is always raging.

"You are under *my* supervision," Uncle snaps. "And I think—"

"Well, technically, the Blacks were awarded guardianship in court," Coach says. His eyes go back and forth between Uncle and me. "I do a lot for you, David. But this is over the line."

My stomach knots. Does he see what a monster my uncle actually is?

Worse than I've ever been. Worse than how Coach has ever acted.

"They sign all of Caleb's permission slips and are his emergency contact. Have been since..." Coach shrugs, but his eyes are gleaming. "Well, I suppose you know the catalyst of that decision better than most, right, David?"

Uncle leaps to his feet, his face turning a mottled red. "I will not be outdone!"

He storms out of the room.

A sick feeling coils in my gut.

"Why didn't you say anything?" Coach asks.

I stare at him. Is he asking what I think he's asking?

"I thought you knew," I say faintly.

For a while, Uncle's abuse was a rumor that flew over Emery-Rose like a flash fire. Everyone was talking about *poor little Caleb*. I had bruises and a cracked rib at fourteen years old. I'd already been living with the Blacks for a while, but it didn't matter.

Uncle picked me up from school one day. He had discovered my adventures all over the county. And honestly, as much as I don't want to admit it, that day is branded in my memory.

❄

Past

Uncle David waited for me at the curb. It was the first week of school at Emery-Rose Elite. The high school version of it anyway. I was expecting to go home with Eli and his parents, but they were nowhere to be found.

"In," he ordered.

I slowly climbed into his car. The door shut, and I just knew it was sealing my fate. He had a vicious temper, and I knew exactly what he had managed to find out.

He was quiet. He didn't drive away, not yet. He wouldn't until he'd said his piece. But right now, the silence was thick and cloying.

"Another home," he finally said. His fist lashed out, connecting with my mouth.

It surprised the hell out of me, but it also *hurt*.

Blood filled my mouth.

"You think we don't keep track of Ms. Wolfe?" he taunted. "Don't know every fucking move she makes?"

I didn't say anything.

He hit me again, and the blood sprayed out of my mouth. My whole body whipped toward the window. He grabbed my shirt collar, bringing me back toward him.

There was a dangerous look in his eye. Mostly crazy, but also... calculating.

"Because of the social worker?" I asked.

He released me.

I slumped against the door, watching him warily.

"You piece that together on your own, hmm?" he asked. His mouth made a straight line. "Smart boy. Maybe you'll be *smarter* and leave the girl alone. Someone is bound to get suspicious, and Ms. DeVine said she can't keep covering for you."

"Ironic, isn't it?" I laughed to myself. "Her name is literally *divine*."

Uncle fisted my collar again, pulling me forward and slamming me back. My head hit the blood-streaked glass, and white spots popped like fireworks in front of my vision.

"You're going to cut the shit," he ordered.

"Dear Uncle," I said, biting back a groan. "I'm just doing what you drilled into me."

He raised an eyebrow.

"Hating her." I sighed. "Hating her so fucking much, she can't be happy."

He reached around me, opening the car door. I fell backward, my back hitting the curb. Pain lanced through my torso, and a moan escaped me. Everything was flickering between numb and pain.

I picked myself up in time for him to chuck my book bag through the open door.

Then... he left.

And me? I had a loose tooth and split lip. Bruising across my jaw. A cracked rib. Fixable things.

Minor things.

If I spoke out, I'd be painted a liar. I'd never see a drop of my inheritance. He'd move me to the most remote boarding school he could find, just so that I'd never have the chance to get my hands on Margo Wolfe.

That was all I wanted. All I could focus on.

She made this my reality.

But... no one ever thought to stop my uncle. Not even the Blacks were successful, although they sure as hell tried.

He had my entire inheritance to use on lawyers, and he

liked to threaten to drain it before I turned eighteen. He had the upper hand *always*.

I picked myself up just as Eli's mom pulled into the school driveway. I did my best to wipe the blood from my face, but my jaw and lip were hot to the touch. There was no hiding that.

"Caleb!" she yelled. She left the car and raced toward me. "Oh my God. What happened?"

I was living with them, and it was a small blessing. Nothing more.

She touched my cheek, and I winced.

"Uncle David had some choice words," I mumbled.

She clucked. "He had more than some choice *words*. This is ridiculous. We'll fight it." She nodded, bolstering herself up. "You'll be safe with us."

Doubt it.

Guardianship would be as far as Uncle let the Blacks take it. I knew it already.

Up against him, it would always be a losing battle.

Chapter 13
Margo

Ms. McCaw is prompt, and I am exhausted.

She doesn't say anything about my messy hair or the dark circles under my eyes. I barely slept last night, and the school day was filled with stares and whispers. Inaudible whispers. It seemed like whenever I tried to overhear something, they moved along.

My shadows probably had something to do with that.

First it was Caleb. Then Theo. Liam. Eli. Caleb again, escorting me up the spiral steps to Robert's classroom. There was a sub—*of course*—who read from a basic substitute teacher lesson plan. There wasn't anything more in-depth, because the teacher in question has been unconscious since the accident.

We played with watercolors and called it a day, but even that was hard. The whole class was quiet, verging on forlorn. News had spread about Mr. Bryan. Everyone knew where he was.

Caleb brought me to the Bryans' house, where Ms. McCaw meets me. We sit at the kitchen table, and every blink is painful. My eyes feel like sandpaper.

"He's been moved out of ICU," my social worker tells me. "I talked to Lenora this morning, to make sure you'd be able to see him."

Caleb goes home. Ms. McCaw takes me to the hospital.

I watch the houses flash by from the passenger seat.

"You okay?" Ms. McCaw asks.

I shove away thoughts of Caleb and focus on her. She's the one who had me believing my dad went to jail for drugs, not *manslaughter*.

"I tried to look up Dad's trial coverage," I say, watching her reaction.

She doesn't flinch. "What were you hoping to find?"

"Anything," I answer. "But... apparently he wasn't sentenced for drug possession, or whatever you told me. He wasn't dealing... or even using."

Her lips purse, then smooth out. "I don't remember saying anything about drugs."

"What did he go away for, then?"

"Margo." Her tone is exasperated. She opens and closes her hands on the steering wheel. "You were young. I'm sure you're misremembering something. With your mother's drug addiction, it would've been easy to transpose that onto your father."

She's trying to make me think I'm crazy.

I slowly nod. "You must be right."

We're quiet for a minute, and then she says, "It's sad, really. Your parents... The whole thing is unfortunate."

"Lydia came to see me, didn't she?"

Angela hesitates, but only for a split second. "Lydia Asher? Um, yes, I think she did. She was like a second mother to you."

I focus back on the road. We're nearing the hospital.

I wonder what she'd say if I told her I went to see Dad. She'd probably freak out on me and the Bryans.

But... she never asked where we were coming from when the accident happened. So maybe she knows the only way we'd be out on that side of town would be if we were visiting the prison.

I shift. My hand feels for the knife in my pocket, and the knot in my chest loosens.

She stops in front of the hospital. "Lenora said she would take you to your therapy appointment, okay? Call me if you need anything."

Need anything.

I need answers. The truth.

But I can't really say that, now can I?

I get out and walk toward the entrance, but her voice calls me back. "Margo, sorry, I forgot! Here."

She reaches toward the open passenger window, extending a cell phone toward me. "To replace your other one. It was recovered in the car at the scene of the accident, so the insurance covered the new one. Isn't that great?"

It's an upgraded version of my previous one.

I smile because that's what I'm supposed to do. Thank her. The phone reminds me of the collision. Weird how these little things can be so triggering. But even so, it'll be nice to be back in contact with Riley and Lenora. And Caleb.

She pulls away while I'm still looking down at it.

As long as Unknown hasn't messaged me... But why would they? Their master plan succeeded.

Or did it?

I mean, Caleb is still a free man.

Taking a deep breath, I slip it into my jacket pocket,

turn on my heel, and go into the hospital. I can deal with that later.

I have the room number on a piece of paper in my pocket. After helpful direction from a nurse, I step into a busy wing. Lenora sees me almost immediately and jogs toward me.

She throws her arms around me, hugging me close.

I breathe in her scent—a mix of lavender shampoo and perfume—and relish the fact that it's become familiar already. It reminds me of safety. And while I just saw her yesterday, it feels longer. More than just wanting to settle back into normal... I want to go *home*.

"I'm glad you're here. How are you feeling? How was school?" She brushes my hair back, scanning my face. Worry creases her eyebrows, and she briefly touches my forehead, near my stitches.

"It was fine. Caleb and his friends were being protective."

She smiles. But while she's concerned about me, she looks like she hasn't slept in days. Her eyes are puffy, and she wears leggings and a baggy sweater. Clean clothes is a good sign.

"They've been letting me stay in his room on a cot now that he's out of the ICU, but..." She tries to smile, but her chin wobbles.

Impulsively, I hug her again.

Her lips brush the top of my head, and I close my eyes.

"He's going to be okay," she whispers. "You're safe. He's safe."

I blink back tears. "Okay."

"He was asking for you."

I pull back slightly. "He's awake?"

"Yes, they just gave him breakfast. It's the first meal he's had…" She covers her mouth. "I'm just so thankful you both got through this."

I don't know how to respond to that, so I say, "I'm glad Caleb found me."

Her face falls. "God, Margo, the police took him out of here so forcefully, I didn't know what to think."

"It wasn't Caleb," I say firmly.

"I believe you." She wraps her arm around my shoulders and leads me down the hall. "And I know the detective was rather critical, but I wouldn't let you stay in the same house as Caleb if I thought he had something to do with it."

I tilt my head. "But… you did point the detective in Caleb's direction while I was gone, didn't you?"

"He asked if you were dating anyone. I didn't realize he was going to single him out."

Yeah. I wouldn't have guessed it either.

We stop in front of a door to a private room.

"Are you ready to see Robert?"

We enter. He's propped up in bed, a rolling table in front of him with a plate of food on it, and… so much medical equipment surrounds him. Wires disappear under his gown, there's an IV taped to his arm. He has a tube under his nose for oxygen.

How can a person go from strong to so frail in days? His skin is pale. His face is covered in healing cuts and fading bruises, and his right arm is in a cast, slung to his chest.

This is my fault. I put him here.

I can't move.

But I still catch his eye—or maybe it's the *snick* of the door closing.

His whole damn face lights up.

And me? I burst into tears.

"Come here, sweetheart," he says, reaching for me. He pushes the table away.

I'm stuck in guilt, my shoes glued to the floor. How do people overcome anguish?

"Margo." His hand is still stretched toward me.

I finally move, venturing closer. They had intubated him for a collapsed lung, sedated him. And now…

"Come here," he repeats. He scoots to the edge of the bed, patting the space next to him.

I wipe at my face, but the tears keep coming. I finally sit next to him. Take his hand.

He lifts my hand and kisses the back of it. "I'm so glad you're okay."

There's a thousand-pound weight on my chest. Slowly, I lie next to him. I curl my arm over his chest and lay my head on his shoulder.

He smooths my hair.

Wipes my cheeks.

He brushes my hair back from the cut on my forehead, and I feel his sharp intake of breath.

"That's nice stitching," he says. "Good as new, yeah? Both of us."

"You—" I close my eyes. "No. You're not good as new. You're in a hospital bed. Your arm, your lung—"

"All will heal."

"It's my fault," I whisper. "And I'm sorry. I'm so sorry—"

The guilt overwhelms me, and I choke on a sob. He hugs me closer. I fall apart, but he keeps whispering words I can't make sense of. *It's okay*, and *We're all right*. But those are just things you say to make someone feel better.

I deserve to feel bad about this.

To be shipped off to a different foster home. To never see them again.

It would be a just punishment.

Fair.

So this? This is a goodbye.

This is putting my heart in a blender because I deserve pain over any form of happiness. Caleb knew that, made sure it was drilled into my head. Even my mother knew it—it's why she left instead of choosing to fight for me.

He lets me cry into his chest without complaint. Eventually my tears will run out, but the grief is endless.

I sit up. Lenora comes farther into the room, a box of tissues in her hand. She offers me the box, and I take a few, dabbing at my eyes.

And then I force myself off the bed and go to the window, then suck in a deep breath. The weight is still there, crushing me.

"You should get rid of me," I say to the glass. We're on the fourth floor with a decent view. The hospital is the tallest building around. There's the neighborhood, then a stretch of forest, and there my line of sight ends. "I'm no good. A danger, even."

"Why would you say that?" Lenora asks.

"For the past three months, I've been..." I close my eyes. "Harassed? Stalked? I don't know. By someone I don't know. But then on Sunday, they—"

"Margo—"

I spin around. "It's my fault. They hit our car to get to me. And you were hurt because of me."

I rub my chest. I can't breathe again. My heart takes off, galloping out of control.

My fault, it chants with every beat.

Lenora guides me into a chair. "I think you're having a panic attack."

My fault. My fault.

I gasp, but I can't seem to get any air. Black spots flash in front of my vision.

—what did you do, Margo?—

This wouldn't the first time you destroyed a family.

"Breathe, honey," Lenora says.

And then Robert is on his knees in front of me, his hands on my cheeks.

"With me, now," he says. "In and out."

"You shouldn't be out of bed." Lenora strokes his hair back. Her other hand is on my shoulder.

I take a moment to appreciate them both.

They're grounding.

"Margo," Robert says firmly. "We're not sending you away. Len said you're staying with the Blacks until I'm well enough to go home. It should be any day now, right?"

He sucks in a noisy breath, holds it, then blows it out.

I mimic him, and cool, sweet air rushes back into my lungs. We keep going until my heart has slowed. My hands shake, but I mask it by smoothing out my pants.

"We're not giving you up," he repeats. He uses the arm of the chair to lift himself off the floor. He makes it almost all the way straight before he doubles over.

"Robert!" Lenora yells, grabbing his arm. "What's wrong?"

"My chest is on fire." He coughs into his hand, then grimaces at it. One of the monitors behind his bed starts beeping.

I hadn't realized he was still connected to them.

A second later, a nurse rushes into the room. "Robert, what are you doing out of bed?"

She guides him back into it, making sure everything is in place. The monitor is still going crazy. He rubs at his chest, shaking his head. He coughs again, and blood sprays across his blankets.

The nurse hits a button at the head of his bed while Lenora and I watch in horror. The air seems to be sucked from the room. His face goes deathly pale, and his eyes roll back a moment before he seems to go unconscious.

A team pours into the room, and Lenora and I are shuffled back against the window.

Robert jerks, surrounded by nurses, and they quickly flatten the bed.

"Get them out of here," someone orders.

A nurse separates and herds us out, down the hall. I clutch at Lenora's hand.

"What's happening?" she demands.

"Looks like a complication with his chest tube," the nurse explains. "Please wait here, I'll be right back with more information."

She leaves us in a waiting room.

Lenora drops into a chair and covers her face with her hands. "Death can't take him, too."

Oh God.

Why is it only just now occurring to me that her daughter died in a car accident?

I slip my arm through hers, drawing her hands away from her head. Slowly, as if I not to frighten her, I thread my fingers through hers.

She squeezes, turning away from the doorway and toward me.

"He'll be okay." It's me this time, reassuring her. It's a bravado.

He might not be. He might...

I close my eyes and hold on tighter, hanging on to my apology.

Cindy and Jeff, my last foster parents, would've urged us to pray about it. They thought God could fix everything He wanted to—and if things had a shitty outcome, well, at least we learned a lesson.

Utter bullshit.

I take off my jacket—I had forgotten I was even wearing it—and fold it over the arm of a chair. I sit and contemplate reaching for my new phone, but my hands are trembling too badly. Caleb is at hockey practice, I think. Riley might be home.

If I was in a better state, I'd reach out. Ask them for support. But it seems like an unnecessary burden, so I stay still.

Lenora paces by the door.

Finally, minutes or hours later, a doctor comes to see us.

"Robert was rushed into emergency surgery," she says. "He has a pulmonary embolism. In other words, a blood clot in the lung. This particular kind he has can be quite severe."

"Was it because he got out of bed?" I ask from the corner of the room, covering my mouth with my hands. Still, the words slip out before I can stop them.

Lenora shakes her head. "No."

"The PE could've been caused by a number of things. We also discovered that the site of the chest tube had become infected." The doctor clears her throat and focuses on me. "Was him getting out of bed the cause? Probably not. There's no way to know for sure, so you shouldn't think it was because of you."

I bite my lip. Part of me doesn't want to accept that dismissal of blame.

I can't let it go.

"How long is the surgery? Is he... did you catch it in time?" Lenora asks.

"Removing the blood clot is a minimally invasive surgery. The surgeon is going to remove it and also clean out the infection. We'll update you once we know more, but we caught it. That's the important part."

Lenora lets out a long breath at the same time my entire body shudders.

As soon as the doctor leaves, she falls into the seat next to me. "He can pull through this."

"How do you do it?" I ask.

She tilts her head and raises her eyebrow.

"I mean... the emotions. Everything in the past week. How are you still standing?"

She lets out a little laugh. "I'm still standing?"

We're quiet for a moment.

"No, I'm functioning. You'll be surprised at how much you can endure before you shut down." She blinks at the ceiling. "But, I can't tell you how many times I wanted to scream. Every single moment he was in the ICU. Even now."

I understand that.

"Love can be beautiful. But it can also be a terrible burden."

My eyes burn. My thoughts jump to Caleb. Of course they do.

"Is it better to be alone?"

She considers my answer, and in this moment, that's what I appreciate the most about her. She doesn't bullshit me—I'm practically an adult. She's never tried to make me feel younger than I am. Sure, she's still a parent. But it's different.

"There are epic love stories that end in tragedy," she

finally says. "And then there are people who just float at the baseline of emotion. No love, no loss. I think it's better to experience it all. Everything good and bad and terrifyingly ugly in this world. Otherwise, we'll just walk around numb, and what kind of life is that?"

Love, loss, tragedy.

"And besides, who's to say every story ends in a ball of flames? Some surpass time." She wraps her arm around my shoulders.

I surprise myself by leaning into it, resting my head on her shoulder.

"I'm scared."

"Why do I think you're not just talking about Robert?" She hums.

"I don't want to fall in love with Caleb if he's just going to break my heart," I whisper. "I don't want him to... string me along or mess with me."

She taps my bracelet. "What's the story with this, if you don't mind me asking?"

I snort. "When we were eight, I basically talked Caleb into pretend marrying me. It was just braided thread back then, nothing substantial." I twist it around my wrist. "I lost it at one of the foster homes, but I think Caleb somehow stole it. It was my own fault for not wearing it, but I didn't want it to break. He fixed it up and gave it back to me at the masquerade ball."

"Before he told us the lies about our daughter."

"Yeah."

"The eight-year-old Margo was ready to commit." She chuckles. "If only we all had the courage that kids do."

"Well, that was before I broke his heart, and he broke mine."

She twists toward me. "If you listen to anything I say, I

hope it's this. Hearts heal. Scars fade. Memories of the past... they don't last very long either. If you love him, love him with everything you have, and I promise it'll be worth it."

I blink back tears. "Is that how you feel about Robert?"

"Absolutely. We may not seem like it at times, though." She wipes at her own cheeks. "Time has worn us down. But we put work and love into our relationship every day."

"It's funny... I never got to have a conversation about relationships or sex or love." I roll my eyes. "Mom and Dad had a weird, angry relationship. The Ashers weren't the best role models either. And the foster families..." I laugh under my breath. "None of them really had their shit together. Some pretended, of course, but we saw through it."

"I'm sorry you've had to go through that," she says. "I need to make a phone call, okay? How about you get us something from the vending machine."

She hands me a few dollars and shoos me into the hall.

My body is numb. I walk down the hall and around the corner to the little alcove of vending machines. I get each of us a coffee and a granola bar, then trudge back.

The hairs on the back of my neck stand up, like someone is watching me.

I spin around, but the hallway is practically empty. Just a nurse walking away from me, pushing a cart, and another woman in scrubs at the nurses' station.

I back away from that spot. I get the same feeling again and turn, coffee sloshing through the little hole in the lid.

"Fuck, ow." I set down the coffee and shake out my hand, wincing at the red spots that already appear on my skin.

The hallway is empty.

Thoroughly spooked, I grab the cup and rush back to the waiting room.

How was it so busy not too long ago and deserted now?

"Angela told me she got you a new phone?" Lenora asks when I've retaken my seat. Angela—better known as Ms. McCaw.

"She gave it to me when she dropped me off. I haven't looked at it."

Lenora's eyebrows lift. "Well, maybe you should set it up and see if someone wants to come by. Riley or Caleb..."

"Is that okay?" I ask. "I don't want to intrude."

"It isn't intrusive for you to have someone to support you," she says quietly. "God knows the whole family was here when Isabella—"

I watch her out of the corner of my eye. I don't want to ask, but at the same time...

"They brought her here?"

"She was cold," she whispers. "By the time they found her. It was an unusually cold night, so her temperature was too low. I guess you can't declare someone dead until they're..."

Warm and dead. I'd heard that on a television show or two.

"Yeah," I mutter, just so she doesn't have to say it out loud.

How awful? Knowing they were warming up your frozen daughter just down the hall, and she probably is already dead—but who really knew?

"I'm sorry you've had to be back here," I say.

She waves me off. "It was a long time ago. Robert and I were very different people."

"Funny, I used to say that about Caleb and me."

"You should call him." She presses her lips together. "You've been staying with his..."

"Friend's family," I supply. "Is he technically a foster, too?"

She shrugs. "Benjamin Asher left behind an odd will, I heard once. It was all Rose Hill could talk about. His disgraced wife and scorned brother."

My eyes go wide. "What?"

"I'm not too sure about the details—Robert and I were still getting our feet wet in town. My first big job was transitioning the Asher firm over to Prinze Industries, but we were still in the city at that point. After a successful merger, my company paid for our relocation."

"Oh, wow. So, you knew Caleb's dad?" *And you never mentioned he was dead?*

"I only met him twice. Once to discuss his future at Prinze Industries, and the second time when he signed the paperwork." She shakes her head. "That wasn't long before..."

"But back to the will..."

"Oh, yes. It was all over town—especially my coworkers, honestly, they're gossiping fools—that Benjamin had left everything to his son."

"Are you sure?"

She laughs. "Not in the slightest."

I mull it over. Taking it with a grain of salt, even if Caleb's dad had left him *most* of what he owned, it was still a sizeable chunk. And it would explain his uncle's fury. And his mother's... His mother's *what?* She's been missing from the story this entire time.

"I think... I will make that phone call."

She nods.

I fumble with the phone. My hands are steady now,

thanks to the granola bar, and I unlock it with my usual password to find that everything from my previous phone has already been loaded onto this one.

Suspicion gnaws at me, but nothing seems unusual about it.

I dial Riley's number, not trusting a text message.

"Margo?"

"Yeah, hey." I clear my throat. "Um, could you come to the hospital? If it's not too much trouble?"

"Of course," she says immediately. "I'll be there in ten."

Lenora has resumed pacing.

"It's getting dark out," she comments. "Nice of them to give us a window."

I shiver. "I'm glad I'm not learning to drive anytime soon."

She squints at me. "Huh?"

"Driving in the snow... doesn't sound like a good time."

"You don't—" She smacks her forehead. "We're idiots!"

"What..."

"Margo, what a complete, total, awful oversight on our part." She winces. "I'm sorry, I should've realized it when your foster sister came by and boasted about her learner's permit."

"It's not a big deal." My fingers find their way to my wrist, and I have to stop myself from scratching at the scab. "I just, you know, plan on learning eventually. Or at least taking the test and hope I pass."

She scoffs. "No, absolutely not. As soon as this is all sorted, we'll put you in driver's ed. And we'll practice once you've had a few lessons."

My eyebrows go up. "Just like that?"

"I've seen your reckless tendencies. I don't even want to

know what that'd be like with you behind the wheel," she says, and it takes me a moment to realize she's teasing.

Lenora.

Teasing.

Who would've thought?

I cough over my laugh. "I wouldn't be *that* bad."

"You sure?"

She giggles, and it breaks the dam. I laugh, too. We both howl with laughter, clutching our stomachs. Tears—happy ones, I think—stream down my face. My abs hurt by the time we finally stop.

"Oh God," I say, the happiness draining away like someone just pulled the plug on it. "We're laughing while—"

"Stop right there," she says, reaching out and taking my hands.

For the first time, probably ever, I hold her hands back.

"We're allowed to laugh. He'd probably be happy we weren't crying without cause."

"But..." *He could still die.* It's late, almost six o'clock. Two hours since Ms. McCaw dropped me off.

Hours or minutes. Time swung away from me when I wasn't paying attention.

I'm still contemplating that when Riley appears, breathless. She looks between Lenora and me. We must be quite the sight—red-faced and winded ourselves—but she doesn't comment. She squeezes the daylights out of me.

I grasp at her, letting the rib-crunching hug put me back together.

Chapter 14
Margo

I feel him before I see him.

This time, at least, I know it's him. My neck prickles, and goosebumps race up the backs of my arms. I straighten with the pack of candy in my hand and turn to face him. The vending machine hums beside me.

He walks toward me with his hands in his pockets. His dark hair is brushed away from his face, and his light eyes are tracking my movement. I scan his body just as he does the same to me.

White shirt, black jeans, a black shell jacket.

His expression is serious. Befitting a hospital, I suppose. I shiver, suddenly wishing I was back in the waiting room. There are witnesses there, and...

He's been weird.

I've been weird, too, I know. We've been under the same roof, and we only shared a bed the first night. Is there something wrong with me? I want him—just looking at him, right now, I *want* him. But I haven't been able to act on it.

"You okay?" He stops in front of me, close enough to touch, but not. "You're pale."

"Robert is in surgery."

His hand tightens on mine. "You're running away."

"Just mimicking you." I glare at him and tug.

He releases me. "It's because I don't know how to help you."

I blink.

"You're hurting, for fuck's sake, and I don't know—" He turns away and runs his hand through his hair. "I'd like to think I know you. That you don't want coddling. But if not that, what?"

I sigh. "A hug would be nice."

He yanks me forward, into him, faster than I expect. He wraps his arms around me, bone-crushingly tight. I'm enveloped in his embrace, yes, but also his warmth and his spiced scent. I lean into him, knowing that no matter how hard I push, he'll stay standing.

"Like this?" he whispers into my hair.

It's tight enough to hold me together for a moment. Just like Riley's hug, but this one...

I relax, and his hand cups the back of my head.

"Now, if only we could stay like this," he teases.

I don't say anything but slowly bring my arms up and circle his waist. My breath shudders out of me. *Yes*, I want to say. *This could be a forever kind of thing.*

"Do you remember what I said?"

I pull away just enough to meet his gaze. "You say a lot."

His smile is faint. "I'm always going to find you, baby."

"I believe it." It scares me as much as it comforts me. "But what if you find me and we *both*..."

"Go dark?"

I nod. I can feel it crawling through me. It's a slippery feeling, addictive. And the worst part? It pushes out all my other emotions. I know he feels it, too. The rare times his demons have come out full force.

He lifts one shoulder. His grip on me eases, allowing me to take a small step backward. "So what if we do?"

I contemplate that.

"Ah, Margo, are you—?" Lenora stops in the middle of the hallway. "Caleb, glad to see you could make it. The doctor is going to talk to us, honey." She holds out her hand to me.

I release Caleb and go to her. She squeezes my fingers.

Nerves flutter through me, and I realize this is the moment. The one where we find out if Robert made it or not. If he's alive or...

I take a deep breath. Breathing is important. How would it feel if one lung stopped working? If I started coughing blood?

I close my eyes for a heartbeat, and I replay blood spraying from Robert's lips. The way he rubbed at his chest, like he couldn't get enough air.

The car.

—What did you do?—

I don't realize I've stopped moving until Caleb puts his hands on my shoulders, propelling me from behind.

"This is a fear we need to face," he whispers in my ear. "But you're not in this alone."

I shake my head. "If he dies, I'll never forgive myself."

His lips touch the shell of my ear. "It isn't you who holds the blame."

No, he's right.

It's the freaking stalker.

The doctor is in the waiting room, Lenora already in front of her. I stand beside her, leaving Riley and Caleb behind. There's another woman in the room, dressed in scrubs, who hangs back, too. I recognize her as Lenora's doctor friend.

"He's out of surgery," the doctor says. "He's in recovery right now, but we're hopeful that everything looks good. He's off the ventilator and should be waking up in a little while."

"Can we see him?" Lenora asks.

"Yes. I'll have a nurse come get you when he's back in his room, although he'll be quite groggy. We're going to keep him here for observation for another few days."

Lenora shakes her hand, and then the doctor leaves us.

I let out a long breath. "He's going to be okay."

"Sounds like it," Lenora says. She smiles.

We've been full of hugs today. Hugs and sadness and panic and worry. Too much worry.

The exhaustion hits me like a ton of bricks to the face.

"Do you want to head home?" she whispers. "You've had a long day."

"You've had a long week. I..." I can't go without seeing him one more time. To confirm with my own eyes that he's okay. "I'll get a ride home with Caleb or Riley after we see him."

She nods, stroking my hair. "You have an appointment to get these stitches removed soon."

"Monday." Thank goodness, because they're driving me nuts. I try not to focus on it. On what it symbolizes.

How did I walk away with just a gash and some bumps and bruises, and Robert...

I cross the room and sit between Riley and Caleb. There are things I need to say to Riley... preferably without Caleb eavesdropping. So instead of speaking, I just let both of them take a hand, and I close my eyes.

"Wake up, baby."

I groan. The first person I see is Riley. Her phone is in one hand, her lower lip sucked between her teeth. My hand is still caught in hers.

Caleb has my other one. But he also...

I grimace. "Why am I sitting on your lap?"

"Because you started snoring about two minutes after you closed your eyes."

"I did not."

"You did," Riley confirms. "And you looked so uncomfortable, Caleb just *had* to fix it."

"Ha, ha." I slip free of their hands and put my palm on his shoulder. I stand, ignoring the creaking feeling in my bones. "Is it time?"

Lenora and her friend are near the door, talking in low voices, but Lenora glances up at the sound of my voice. "Yes, he's back in his room."

I smile, then frown. Fear lances through me. *Oh God, what if he's...*

"Come now, honey," she says. "The sooner you see him, the sooner you can get back to snoozing."

"Very funny."

She grins. "I thought so."

We leave our friends behind and go down the hall, into Robert's room. The television is on, muted. The lamp in the corner burns dimly, casting deep shadows around the room.

"There's my girls," Robert mumbles. His eyes are half closed, but his head lolls in our direction. He smiles. "What an adventure we're on, huh, Lenny?"

"An adventure? You nearly gave me a heart attack." She goes to his side, brushing back his hair and kissing his cheek. "How are you feeling?"

"Dandy, dandy." He smiles. "Had a nice chat with Isabella."

I freeze.

"Ah, there she is." He looks right at me, and everything in me locks up.

Does he think you're his dead daughter? No, no, no.

Can surgery cause amnesia?

Am I going to have to tell him that I'm not his daughter?

"Margo-girl, you had me worried," he continues. "But you two stuck together, right?"

"We did." Lenora straightens his blankets.

I venture closer. "I'm sorry for worrying you."

He takes my hand once I'm close enough. "You're okay?"

I'm really sick of crying. A lump forms in my throat at his blatant concern.

"You were just in surgery, and you're worried about me?" I clutch at his hand with both of mine. "It's..."

"My job as a dad," he says. "Isabella would expect no less of me and neither should you."

I glance to Lenora, but her gaze is fastened on him. Her hand covers her mouth.

"It's late," I say, pretending to check the clock on the wall. I already know that it's well past nine. The surgery went on for a long time, and I don't think I can take much more of this hospital. "I'll come see you tomorrow."

I lean down and wrap my arms around him, gingerly. He rubs my back, then I stand back up.

"I'll walk you out," Lenora says. We go to the doorway together. "You'll be okay with the Blacks?"

"They're very nice." I shift. "Once Robert comes back, I get to...?"

"Yes," she answers immediately. "You'll come home, too. I'll be relieved to have you both under the same roof, trust me."

Caleb's attention is on me—I can feel his stare from here. I hum my agreement about being under the same roof and give Lenora one last hug before I go.

I pause in front of Caleb. "Riley's bringing me home. We have things to discuss."

"Things," he says. "Things you don't want me to hear?"

"Yes." I raise my eyebrows. "You don't trust her?"

"I don't trust anyone around you, baby. Not anymore."

I trace my bracelet. "But you trust me?"

He puts his finger under my chin, lifting it. I meet his gaze and frown.

"I do trust you."

My heart skips. "Oh."

"You don't sound happy about that." He smirks, then leans down and steals a kiss from my lips. "Little wolf doesn't know what to do with trust?"

"Not in the slightest." I shake my head, backing away from him.

I've seen Caleb possessive. Angry. Hostile. Ruthless. But... trusting? Not since we were kids. Not since we were young and innocent.

Look how far we've come.

How far we've fallen.

Riley waits for me at the end of the hall. She passes me my jacket, and we quickly make our way to her car.

"I've been worried about you," she says.

"Well, you might still be worried when I tell you..."

She starts the car and fiddles with the knobs. After a moment, heat pours out of the vents.

"Spill."

I fill her in on Caleb and Eli's plan to lure Unknown out. After the brief synopsis this morning, they didn't bring it up again. I think they're waiting for me to accept it. After all, they said I wouldn't like it. And I don't. It involves using me as bait.

I am not good bait.

Hell—the argument could be made that I already *was* bait, and they totally failed in uncovering their identity.

"You're shitting me." She gapes at me when I finally stop talking. "Are you going to do it?"

I smirk. "Well... yeah. But with a little twist."

Chapter 15
Unknown

You've gotten bolder, Margo. It makes me wonder: is this Caleb's fault? Or a stable home environment? Has courage given you a new pair of wings?

But you're forgetting about the cage. The thing that traps you. Holds you hostage.

While I dance around, you're locked into place. Sometimes I wonder if it even matters. Things are fraying at the seams, and nothing is as it appears.

Certainly not me.

And I'm guessing not you either.

That leaves me to ask: Will you find me? Will you succeed in your *trap?*

There's so much more to us than you know. We're in this together, Margo, to the bloody end. And I think the end will most certainly be... *exciting.*

Will you tell me when you've had enough? When I can finally stop messing around and just show you what I've learned?

Evil doesn't always wear a devil's mask.

Even good people have a dark streak.

And anyone can break.

So just know this: I'm coming for you.

This started a long time ago.

Beat your wings against the bars, pretty little bird. It won't make any difference in the end.

Chapter 16
Caleb

Monday is cold and bleak.

There's a fresh coat of snow on the ground, giving the world a black-and-white quality.

But there's still a substitute teacher at the front of Mr. Bryan's painting class. Margo is out today because her foster dad was being discharged. How nice, right?

The weekend had passed quickly. We made popcorn and watched movies. Riley joined us grudgingly, at the behest of her best friend. Eli and Riley barely looked at each other, even though they were in the same room.

Note to self: find out what the fuck is going on with them.

As soon as the dismissal bell rings, I head to the parking lot. Liam, Theo, Eli, and I have somewhere to be before we head to practice. They're gathered between Theo's car and mine, laughing about something.

"Everyone in the truck." Eli claps, grinning. "We're gonna go fuck some shit up."

"Excuse me?" Liam questions. "You didn't say we were gonna have fun on this errand."

I snort. "We're going to find the vehicle that hit Robert and Margo. Our best guess is the junkyard. You should feel right at home there, huh, Liam?"

Liam shoves me.

I laugh and climb into the front seat.

Chapter 17
Margo

"This is foolish," Riley says for the tenth time.

I roll my eyes. "Caleb's going to regret telling me about this place."

When we discovered the mermaid figurine—and, more importantly, that it was transmitting a video feed—Caleb brought it to his old friend, Matt.

That friend did some tech-whiz shit and led him to this place.

Lucky's Diner.

Caleb mentioned... well, he mentioned that there was a twenty-four-hour diner that was a hotspot. It took some narrowing down, but *surprise, surprise*—this place is the only one in Beacon. Only one in Hillshire County, actually.

Riley kills the engine, and we sit in silence. "It looks shitty."

The diner across the street is... not someplace I would expect Caleb and Matt to go. The sign's lights flicker on, even though it's the middle of the afternoon.

Riley graciously decided to cut class in order to accompany me on this adventure, but from the expression on her face, she's regretting it.

"Lucky's Diner," I read. "I just... expected something fancier."

"Who do you think is in there?" she asks. "Are we going in as like, 'Oh, just coming in for a meal, don't pay us any mind!'"

I laugh. "You'd make a horrible spy."

She flips her hair. I have a flashback to Amelie and Savannah doing similar moves, but I shove it out of my head.

"You know what's horrible?" she asks. "That you're graduating in a semester and I'm going to be stuck there for another year."

"Yeah, that does suck. But I'll probably still be around. Maybe I'll get a job as the school janitor's assistant. Then you'll still see me every day."

She snorts. "You're ridiculous. You're going to college, remember?"

I shrug. If I wanted to go, I'd have to apply.

And then get accepted.

And then come up with the money for tuition.

"Robert comes home tomorrow," I say. "Today's my last day to figure this out."

She groans. "Okay, fine. Let's go into *Lucky's Diner*—which, for the record, looks pretty damn unlucky."

We're the only car front and center in the parking lot. There are a few parked in the back corner, but those are probably employees. In the few minutes we've sat here, no one has come in or out.

"Okay. Yeah." I unbuckle and climb out.

Riley follows suit, and together, we walk toward the diner.

The back of my neck prickles, and I pause, glancing behind me.

"Catch up, tomato," Riley calls.

I wrinkle my nose, scanning the area.

Nothing except for a deserted lot.

"'Catch up, tomato?'"

"Like ketchup?" She elbows me. "Dad used to say that to me all the time."

I shake my head. "Absurd."

"Gladly so."

I let her go through the door ahead of me, hesitating before I enter. The niggling feeling of someone watching me hasn't gone away. I look behind me one last time.

The paranoia is really getting to me, but I'm glad I don't see anyone. I don't need any dark figures lurking around corners, waiting for me to misstep.

"Welcome to Lucky's," the hostess says.

That voice.

I slowly turn back around, pushing past Riley.

Lydia Asher?

Caleb's mom's mouth drops open. "Margo?"

First thought? Horror.

Second thought? Nausea.

I guess those two kind of go hand in hand. And if we weren't here for answers, well, I'd be out the door before she could say another word. Instead of running, I lock my muscles and really try to see her.

Because what happened to her after her husband died?

Riley squints at me, then her. She'd be unfamiliar with Lydia Asher, having moved here after the trial and town-wide publicity.

"You know Margo?" she asks the older woman.

"It's been a while." Lydia's voice is faint.

I can't quite decide on her tone. It could be soft—it certainly sounds it. But there are blades that are so sharp, they slice without pain. Not until after. And maybe that's her—honed too sharp by time and anger.

"Not long enough," I find myself saying.

"Then why are you here?"

"Hold on," Riley interrupts. "Huh?"

"Caleb's mom. Lydia Asher." I finally tear my eyes away from her and look around. The place is deserted. "Why do you work here?"

"Excellent food." She picks up two menus from the host stand. "I assume you ladies are here to eat?"

"No—"

"Yes." Riley smiles sweetly. "Can we have that corner booth?"

Lydia watches her for a beat, then nods. "Of course."

She leads us down the aisle. It's a long and narrow diner, with a bar and bolted-in stools on one side, and a row of booths against the windows. The booths wrap around and end at the kitchen doors. Behind the bar, there's a window into the kitchen. It seems deserted back there, too.

"Busy day?" I run my hand over the counter.

I've never seen a restaurant so quiet.

"It picks up around brunch," she murmurs. "Here you are. Water?"

"Yes, thanks." Riley takes a seat.

Lydia hesitates next to me. "Why are you really here, Margo?"

I shrug. "Just hungry."

Is Lydia—or one of the other Ashers—my stalker? We've been thinking that it was someone around my age. They knew things from parties and school. There's no way Lydia would have been able to get that information.

But this is just too high of a coincidence.

"All the way in Beacon?" she questions.

I don't like the way she's watching us. She thinks we're up to something. We *are* up to something, but I don't like that she's automatically suspicious.

"We were in the neighborhood. And I guess we were just feeling... lucky."

She narrows her eyes. "All right."

I sit across from Riley once she goes.

"What are we doing?" I lean across the table. "Are you crazy?"

"She's the one who left him with his uncle, right?" Riley tracks Lydia's movements across the diner.

She hasn't forgotten our rescue attempt from Caleb's uncle's house. Neither have I. To know she willingly left her son—her *ten-year-old* son—with the monster is more than I can stomach.

Something crashes, and we both jump.

I twist around and catch a flash of dark hair through the window into the kitchen.

When Lydia doesn't reappear, I glance at Riley. "Should we check on her?"

"Honestly, I'm not sure what we're even doing here. I was hoping she'd give us some clue. So we should stay longer, right? Just eavesdrop."

Right. That's what we do.

Meanwhile, Lydia's probably on the phone with the *real* Unknown, and they're going to stage another attack. Maybe they'd hurt Riley this time.

My skin is too tight.

There's another crash, and then the sound of voices.

"This is weird." My skin crawls. "I have a bad feeling about this..."

Riley leans toward me. "You said your dad didn't kill her husband. What if she had something to do with it?"

"Then... we're alone with a dangerous woman."

"No!" Lydia yells from the back room.

We both shoot to our feet, grabbing our stuff.

Riley yanks me toward the entrance. "Move, Margo. Come on."

The kitchen door flies open, and my mouth drops.

I stop.

Stop breathing.

Stop thinking.

Because my mother is finally in front of me.

It's almost weird how she looks exactly the same and completely different at the same time. She glares at me— familiar. Her hair is pulled back, mostly covered by a black bandana—familiar. Chef's coat—*familiar*. Wrinkles across her tanned face—new. Thin. Angry.

I shudder.

Riley grabs my arm and hauls me toward the door. Maybe she can see the family resemblance, or maybe she's just freaked out about this woman's sudden appearance.

Mom opens her mouth, but my shoulder hits the doorframe.

It knocks some sense into me.

Spinning around, I finally go with Riley. My feet move fast, almost outrunning my friend. We sprint to her car and fall into it.

"Go, go, go." I stare at the entrance.

Mom bursts out just as Riley turns onto the street, and we fly past her.

Around the corner.

Shit.

"Who the hell was that?" Riley yells.

I laugh. I can't help it.

Three *fucking* years, and I stumble upon her by accident. What kind of insane irony is that? Whoever is controlling my fate must think themselves a comedian.

"My mother," I say through my giggles. But then the laughter falls away. "Caleb must've known she was there."

When we're far enough away, Riley pulls onto the shoulder of the road. It's one of the back ways to get between Beacon and Rose Hill, and it's deserted.

"That was your mom?" She cranks the heat again.

Now that I'm sitting still, my hands tremble. "I'm so sick of surprises."

She sighs. "I thought we were going to find Unknown. You know? Like in *Pretty Little Liars*."

"I never saw that show." I shake my head. "Were they threatened by a mysterious texter, too?"

She chuckles. "Yeah, they were."

"Huh."

She types on her phone. "I'm going to make a list. We've got to narrow this down." She taps her chin. "Okay, so... Unknown texted you before you started school. They had to have your number somehow. Before anyone else got it."

I sigh. "It was a new number, too. My social worker got it for me."

"The social worker who lied about why your dad went to prison?"

Yikes. "That's the one."

"They also had to see Ian dragging you off at school," Riley points out. More typing. "That was in the middle of the school day, and kind of a random day to be there. It would've had to be pure coincidence."

I put my hand over my stomach, getting phantom pains just from thinking about what Ian did.

"Unknown said that was the only nice thing they would do for me." I sigh. "Amelie and Savannah were involved in that one. Amelie said Sav sent it to her, and when she didn't care, she sent it on to Caleb."

"Confusing." Riley frowns. "We kind of ruled them out, right? I mean... not the two of them together. That was a working theory at one point. And... there was the party. With the video."

"Ugh."

"What else?"

"They seemed to have insider knowledge. But... not inner circle stuff."

Riley grins. "You've ruled me out, then? Because I'm totally inner circle."

"Unless you have a secret phone I don't know about..." I quirk my lips.

Her smile drops. "I didn't even think of that. It could be literally *anyone* who picked up a disposable phone at the store. Paid minutes in cash..."

"Yep."

"So you haven't seen your mom since...?"

"She'd stop by to check on me in foster care, but it was more about money than anything else. Quick visits on the sidewalk. That finally stopped when I was fourteen."

Riley frowns.

"Please don't pity me," I beg. "She's a terrible mom, asking her teenage daughter for money. She gave me a present once, when I was... twelve, maybe? A little stuffed bunny for Easter."

"That was nice," she says.

"Yeah, nice. One of the other foster kids at the time stole it before I'd had a chance..." I sigh. "I just wanted something to hold on to that let me know she was thinking of me, but even that got taken away."

"Maybe that's why she's back."

"To hug me?" I scoff. "Doubtful. Did you see the anger in her eyes? She always held a grudge for the secret I let slip."

I fill Riley in about catching my mom and Caleb's dad together. How Caleb told me he knew, begged me not to tell, and then we got caught leaving our hiding place. Mom said it was nothing, but...

That's not quite accurate.

"So you went home and told your dad," she finishes.

I lift one shoulder. "I think so."

"You don't remember that part?"

"Not yet. It's coming back in pieces."

She pulls back out onto the road, heading home. "You haven't got any new texts, right?"

"Nope." My phone buzzes, and I groan. "I jinxed it."

UNKNOWN

Secrets are coming out...

Chapter 18
Caleb

It only took fifty bucks to bribe the junkyard attendant. He showed us to the cars involved in recent accidents, then ambled away with his hands in his pockets. I honestly didn't think it would be that easy, but then we see how many cars there are.

I guess Hillshire County drivers suck?

Or it's been a tough week.

Eli kicks at the ground. We've been staring at the wrecked vehicles for the last hour, trying to figure out which one collided with Robert's.

I go closer to Robert's car. What's left of it anyway. My friends trail me.

All the glass is broken. The windshield is still there, severely cracked and only attached in one corner. There's glass everywhere. All the windows are gone, and the roof is crumpled.

"How did they survive this?" Theo asks.

He leans down on the driver's side, peering in. It's streaked with blood. Most of the door is gone, cut away by the rescue team.

"The car was upside down," Eli informs us, reading from his phone. "Hit from the side, just in front of the passenger door."

I wince. Margo was *right there*. She could've been killed if they were off by a fucking fraction.

There was a little article about it in the paper, but I wasn't able to read it. Couldn't stomach the thought. And now I'm staring at the actual evidence, and I think I might puke.

"Margo was in the passenger seat," he continues. "And she wasn't found at the crash. When her foster mother and case worker couldn't locate her, she was reported missing."

I shake my head. "They dragged her out and left Robert behind."

I like the Bryans. They're good for Margo, even after I tried to ruin it. They're good people in general.

And someone tried to—

"Don't spiral," Liam says behind me.

I find him watching me instead of the totaled cars.

"I'm not."

"You are," he argues. "Going down the wormhole. This close to letting the anger take over. Well, just—don't."

I grunt and try to listen to him for once. I take a deep breath, then another.

"Margo and Robert both survived this," he continues. "Got it?"

"I fucking got it," I growl.

I leave Robert's car behind—I can't look at it anymore— and go to examine one of the others.

"There's barely any paint on Mr. Bryan's car," Theo muses. "Black."

I raise my eyebrow. Only one of the cars here is black, and its back end is crunched in. Not likely to be the culprit.

"Check this out," Liam calls. He's across the lot, standing next to a maroon van that was not part of the cluster the worker showed us. "Could there have been a brush guard on it or something?"

There's nothing on there now, but there are marks where some sort of apparatus was clearly removed in a hurry. Its front isn't damaged at all. My anger flares, white-hot, but I push it down. There will be a time to deal with this later. When I have a body in front of me that can hold responsibility.

"That isn't cheap. And not typically a rental."

"I doubt it was a rental." Liam circles it.

His dad has always been into cars. I heard he once thought about opening his own shop. The family restored a few cars and sold them to folks in Rose Hill with too much money to burn, and I know for a fact Liam was just as involved in the project as his dad and brother.

He opens the van's passenger door and leans in. He cracks open the glove box. His hands, thankfully, are gloved. We've all seen too many crime shows to do any different.

"What are you doing?" Eli asks.

"Looking for the registration," he says. The *jackass* he'd normally tack onto the end of such a statement is implied this time.

I roll my eyes.

He pulls out a piece of paper, grinning. "Not the Power-ball, but no small potatoes either."

"Sorry, is that a lottery analogy?"

"Shut up." He scans the paper, then tosses it across the driver's side to me. "They were trying to hide this piece of shit in plain sight."

I open the page slowly. It's a receipt for an oil change, with the owner's name printed neatly in the upper corner.

Lead stones drop into my stomach.

"Do you know who it is?" Liam asks. There must be something alarming in my expression, because he whistles for the other guys and comes around the vehicle.

He pries the paper from my hand and shows it to Eli and Theo.

"That name sounds vaguely familiar," Eli comments.

"It should." I take the paper back and stare down at it, just to make sure I didn't hallucinate.

This situation just got a whole lot more fucked up.

"Tobias Hutchins," I say, staring at the name. "Also known as Keith Wolfe's public defender. The one my mother bribed to botch his plea deal."

Chapter 19
Margo

I pace in my room, practicing flipping open the knife I found. It's a folding one. I was lurking in Caleb's basement room, trying to wait to surprise him, but then I got bored.

And then I found the knife. It would be so much better to be able to protect myself, right? Imagine my stalker came after me, and I had *this* in my pocket?

I jab the air, slice it, twirl around and pretend to stab it into someone's eye.

I debate practicing on a pillow but quickly dismiss it.

My actions slow when the garage door rumbles open. Josh and Norah are in the city. Although they're due back tonight, I doubt they'd come back so soon. Which means Eli and Caleb have returned. The door downstairs slams shut. Voices drift upstairs. More than two.

I flip the knife closed, sliding it into my pocket, and drift into the hall. I was hoping to catch Caleb alone, but now... I smell food.

My stomach growls, and I head downstairs without delay.

Caleb is the first to see me when I walk into the kitchen. They're raiding the fridge for drinks. There's a stack of pizza boxes on the kitchen island. Eli is half hidden behind the door, tossing out cans of soda.

Caleb's eyes narrow, moving up and down my body.

Oh, right.

I should've put something on over my tank top, but I'm too heated. *Literally.* It's work keeping the frustration off my face. And I was kind of working up a sweat pretending to fight people off like a fencer.

Caleb should've told me about my mother.

"I need to tell you something," he says to me.

"It's a little late," I snap.

I march up to him, stopping a foot away. Close enough to touch, but I don't dare reach out. Neither does he.

"Margo—"

"No. We went to the diner Matt took you to, okay? I saw—"

"You *what?*" Caleb's face pales.

It's not often that I catch him by surprise. Almost never, I'd say. But today—today is the exception.

I set my jaw. "You should've told me that my mother was there."

"Oh shit," Eli whispers.

I ignore it and focus on Caleb. The churning feeling in my stomach, that's been with me since we left Lucky's, only worsens.

"I didn't know." He reaches for me. "I only saw my mom."

I keep out of range. It would be too easy to let him placate me with touch. He knew his mom—his high and mighty mother—was working there? Didn't think to mention it along with the brief mention of the diner.

My stalker frequents that place. She's got to be a suspect, right?

"She's working where?" Liam asks.

"Lucky's Diner," Caleb and I say together.

My face heats. But then, when no more questions come, I look harder at Caleb. Then his friends. They're all being a little... cagey.

"What did you do?" I ask.

Eli smirks. "We went to the junkyard."

"The junkyard," I repeat. "Why?"

Theo clears his throat. "Maybe we should take this to... anywhere else."

Eli snaps his fingers. "To the couch!"

Liam and Theo gather the pizza boxes and follow Eli. I start to go, too, but Caleb holds me back.

"How was it?" he asks.

I tilt my head. "Which part?"

"Seeing them. I should've known Mother knew where your mom was, but I... believed her when she said she didn't." His expression darkens. "I wish you hadn't gone alone."

"Riley was with me."

That doesn't appease him.

"It was weird to see your mom. She was definitely shocked to see me, too. I think mine is working as a chef there, which makes sense... It's what she knows, after all." I look away.

He grips my chin, twisting my head back around. "Don't hide from me."

"Seriously? After all your hiding?"

"I can see you leaving as we speak."

I push at his chest. "And where have you been? Lurking in the shadows. Following me and so-called *leads* around town." My voice drops. "We should be doing this together."

His face softens. "Is that what you want?"

"To work with you on this? To spend time with you actually doing shit instead of avoiding each other?" I roll my eyes. "Of course that's what I want."

He smiles, and it lights up his face. The times Caleb Asher truly smiles are few and far between. But when he *does*, he's easily the most handsome guy I've ever seen.

My heart skips a beat.

Damn you, heart.

"Let's go solve this thing, then," he says.

The guys wait for us in the living room, all of them expecting me to have all the answers. Or maybe I'll just have the most dramatic reaction to whatever they uncovered.

Who knows.

Caleb drops into a spot on the couch.

I take a seat in the armchair closest to him, draping a blanket over my lap. I'm not quite over my anger enough to sit thigh to thigh with him. That would make me too aware of his body heat, and then I'd get distracted by thoughts of his body, and...

Well, see? I don't even need to be seated beside him to get distracted.

Caleb opens his mouth, and I hold up my hand.

"Is this bad? Like, really bad? I just need to mentally prepare myself."

"It could be better," Liam says.

Not super helpful.

"Tell us when you're ready," Caleb urges. He grabs a slice of pizza, my favorite kind, and sets it on a plate. Then puts the plate in my lap.

I hold on to it while I struggle to calm myself.

"No time like the present," I eventually say.

I fold the pizza and shove it into my mouth.

"We went to the junkyard to get our hands on the vehicle. It wasn't impounded by the police because it wasn't ever found, which seems kind of like a loose end. The thinking was that the car that hit you ended up there anyway, just not connected to Robert's car."

Eli growls. "Because Masters was after Caleb like a hound after a fox."

My eyes go wide. "So, wait a minute. You're saying you were able to stroll right into the junkyard and find the vehicle that hit us?"

Caleb shifts. "Right. Well, we have a suspicion."

"And whoever owns the vehicle probably had something to do with it," Eli adds.

"Supposedly," Liam says. "Assuming it wasn't stolen."

Ugh. I focus on Caleb. "And was it stolen?"

Eli perks up. "We didn't check."

I facepalm. "You didn't check."

"It's a quick search in the public records," Eli mumbles. "Don't you ever look at those?"

I shake my head, not bothering to ask why the hell I'd do that. Instead, I turn back to Caleb. "And? Who did it belong to?"

"Listen, Margo, before I say it—"

"Aha!" Eli yells. He lifts his phone. "It was reported stolen about three hours before the accident."

"Why are you cheering?" Theo shakes his head. "That's not a good thing."

Caleb clears his throat. "Margo, I'm just gonna blurt this out."

I wave him to proceed, my throat suddenly tight. It's

better if someone would just tell me the damn truth, right? I don't think I can do this any longer. The suspense, the mystery.

"The car belonged to Tobias Hutchins."

I blink. And then... blink again.

My mouth gapes open and closed.

What?

"He was your dad's—"

"I know who he is," I snap. "I... Riley and I..."

Caleb narrows his eyes. "You *what?*"

I take a deep breath. All my sleuthing is about to come out into the light.

"We ran into him in New York City," I remind him, "and you told me who he was later."

Caleb's eyes narrow. "I told you his name was Tobias, and that he was your dad's lawyer."

"Right."

"And I know for a fact that there aren't any online articles about it—"

"Correct," I interrupt. "I know. *But,* there can only be so many Tobiases in New York City. And a lot of law firms actually list their lawyers on their websites with nice headshots, so..."

"You found him, I take it," Caleb says drily.

"Went and visited him," I admit.

His hand curls into a fist. "You did *what?*"

Eli laughs, waving the vodka at Caleb. "Want this? Might make the bad news easier to swallow. Pun totally intended."

"Shut up," Theo hisses.

"*Anyway,*" I continue, "he was pretty fucking shady."

He doesn't really seem *mad,* just irritated. And appalled. And... stumped. I, Margo Wolfe, have rendered

Caleb Asher speechless. It's about damn time I've had the upper hand.

"Obviously you didn't just stop at finding the car's registration or whatever—"

Caleb winces. "Tobias might not know a teenage stalker, but he certainly knows my mother."

I go still. "From seeing her in court?"

"From before that," he admits. "He and my mother have been friendly over the years. I think they went to undergrad together."

"That had to have been a conflict of interest."

Caleb sighs. "I think my mom paid him off."

It takes a second for his words to register. He thinks his mother *paid off* my dad's lawyer? Why the hell would he keep that to himself? That should be proof enough of Dad's innocence. Even if it's not enough for him, it's *something*.

Horror courses through me, and I shoot to my feet. "How long have you known?"

His expression is open. Sincere, even.

"I overheard them," he says. "They often had conversations in my parents' bedroom, just the two of them."

He waits for my realization to dawn.

The Ashers are wicked, wicked people.

How we ever got caught in their web is almost inconceivable. Dad should've known Ben wasn't the same person he went to school with—that money had corrupted him. But it seems to stand that Lydia Asher is just as bad.

A memory filters back to me. I was looking for Caleb—another game of hide and seek in his huge house—and overheard them. I didn't recognize him at the time, didn't have any idea who he was except that he wasn't Caleb's dad. But they were in the bedroom...

What kind of conspiracy were they discussing? That was before Caleb's dad was murdered.

"Were they planning something?" I ask woodenly.

Caleb's expression closes.

If they were planning, would it be horrible to blame them?

For Ben's murder.

Dad's arrest.

Mom's addiction.

And Lydia... well, she became an outcast. That couldn't have been part of the plan.

"Did your dad cut your mom out of the will?" I ask.

Caleb stops short. "How do you know that?"

I hum. So the rumor Lenora heard was true. It made sense, what with everything we're learning. "Lydia and Tobias were in bed together—figuratively *and* literally. She left you with your uncle and went where, to work in a shitty diner for the rest of her life?"

Theo whistles. "She's finally asking the right questions."

"Assuming Tobias and Lydia are still relatively close... how is Matt related?"

Caleb pauses. "What do you mean?"

"You went to him," I say slowly. "He knew the diner. Did he see your mom? Did he figure out who my stalker is?"

Liam and Theo are standing now, too, creeping closer. Our voices are getting softer. This type of thing, it's too big to talk about loudly.

I look over my shoulder, toward the front door. I closed it, but... maybe I should've locked it, too.

"Mom knew Matt," Caleb says. "He was my friend, she had seen him around."

"But does she know him currently?" I prod. "Did she recognize him?"

He stares at the ceiling, blowing out a breath. "Fuck."

"That's not an answer," Eli calls from the couch. He's still got the vodka in his hand, and his cheeks are red.

Besides Eli, they're all focusing on me. Caleb seems to be concentrating. Maybe trying to read my mind. I take in his expression: slightly furrowed brows, searing blue eyes, his lips pursed.

Then he says, "I don't know if he kept digging. Matt took me to the diner, and my mother recognized him. Greeted him by name."

"The plot thickens," Eli sings. "You think that means he's involved?"

Liam stomps over and snatches the bottle from Eli's grip. "Let's take this seriously."

Eli tsks. "I could punch you for that. And I *am* taking it seriously. But this is all conspiracy shit. We've got no proof except that car, which is circumstantial at best."

"You've been hanging around your dad too much," Theo mutters.

"You explain to me how the car of the lawyer who talked my dad into accepting a shitty plea deal ends up in the same junkyard as Robert's?" I scowl. "It doesn't matter. Matt's a dead end."

"He could give us answers," Liam suggests. "If we pay him a visit."

Great.

I raise my eyebrows at Caleb, who only seems intrigued by that idea. He kisses the top of my head, then smirks. He *likes* the idea of confronting Matt.

Eli's sudden snore rips through the room.

We're falling apart here. But besides the unanswered questions, no one is in immediate danger. Well, I might be, but that's another matter.

Theo slaps his hand over his face, while Liam snickers. They both go to Eli and hoist him up. Liam slaps his cheek, but Eli barely cracks an eye.

He nearly finished the bottle of vodka on his own.

"Gonna put him to bed," Liam says.

They guide him out of the room. The muffled thumps of them trying to get Eli up the stairs together reaches us, and I giggle.

Caleb faces me. You leave tomorrow. Which means..."

Last night together.

"We should make it count," I manage.

Theo and Liam come thundering back down the stairs. "Boy's passed out."

"Good," Caleb says. "We'll see you guys at school tomorrow."

It's a dismissal, and everyone knows it.

They leave, closing the door behind them, and Caleb smiles at me.

"Hi."

"Hi," I laugh.

"You're not mad at me?"

I take a closer look at his face, surprised when I discover that he's being vulnerable. Open, for once in our lives. Well, recent lives. I used to be able to read him like a book.

"I'm not." I run my hand up his arm, to his neck. "And I'll be less inclined to *get* mad if you kiss me."

He leans down. "I think I can oblige."

His lips touch mine softly. Butterflies erupt in my chest. We're used to being greedy with our kisses, always demanding more of each other. Now, it stays honey-sweet. His tongue runs along my lower lip, but it isn't demanding. It's slow, and I feel it so much more, down to my toes.

Whoever said kisses could be toe-curling was clearly talking about *this* kind.

My phone buzzes in my pocket. I pull back just enough to look at it, and Riley's name scrolling across the screen.

"I should get this."

Caleb moves down to kiss my neck. He hovers over my throat, expectant.

"Are you—?"

His teeth nip my skin.

I laugh, but it's more of a breathless sigh, then hit accept on the call.

"Hey! You okay?"

"Why do you think something is wrong?"

"I don't think you've ever called me."

She pauses, then laughs. "Yeah. Fuck. No, I'm not okay. Mom's having... issues. My brother is having separate issues. I feel like I'm crawling out of my skin with worry for both of them."

"Do you want me to come over?"

Caleb resumes his attack on my neck, and I bite my lip to keep from moaning into the phone.

"I'll be okay." Her voice is hoarse, and it tugs at my heart. "You have a lot going on, and I just wanted to hear some sanity."

"I'm sane," I assure her. "Tomorrow. My house. Ice cream and action movies."

Caleb's tongue touches my neck, and I jump. I try pushing him away, but he just latches on with his teeth. *Evil man.* Each touch is an electric zap bouncing through my body. I'm ready to tear his clothes off right here in the living room, in front of the windows—

"Sounds good," Riley says.

My mind is already a mile away.

"I'll see you in school? Unless you're skipping... in which case, tell me so I can skip, too.

She manages to laugh, which I consider a win. "You got it."

As soon as she's off the phone, I push Caleb away. "Stop, stop."

He smirks at me, but it slides off his face when he sees my expression. "What's wrong?"

He follows my gaze to the window.

"Margo. Do you...?"

I get goosebumps.

And I swear, it isn't because Caleb most likely gave me a giant hickey on my neck.

I race to the front door, flinging it open and bounding out onto the porch.

A car screeches down the street.

"What was *that*?"

"I keep feeling like someone is watching me," I say. I hate, *hate* the fear in my voice. I thread my fingers with Caleb's and hold on tight. "And that—"

"Unknown. You're sleeping in my bed tonight," he says firmly. "I don't give a fuck if the Blacks have an objection, or if they find out. You'll be safe with me."

I blink back tears. "Thank you."

"No thanks necessary." He holds me close. "We'll find them. I promise."

Chapter 20
Caleb

Margo is freaked out. Information overload, plus Robert in the hospital and learning that her mom is only a town away...

Yeah, I'd probably find any excuse to lose it.

But she doesn't. She holds on to my hand hard enough to crush my fingers, and she sure does sound scared, but... she doesn't look it.

On the outside, she's strong.

I scoop her up and carry her down the stairs, and it's then that I feel the way she shakes. It's more of a shiver than anything else, but it doesn't stop even when we're downstairs.

Dusk has set my room in strange blue hues, making it seem all the more eerie. I turn on the lamp by my bed and lay her down.

"You always go straight to bed," she comments.

"Seemed the most logical," I answer. I pull the blankets up over us. "It's your safe place."

Her eyebrow goes up. "Is it?"

"After every incident, you come here—whether my choice or yours. It's just habit now. You'll relax."

"It's not your bed," she mumbles.

It has to be. After I found her in the woods, and then when I was out with my friends instead of being here for her—

"It's *you*." She lifts herself up. Defiance flashes in her eyes. "It's not this bed, Caleb. It's you and your presence and knowing that if you're gone, you're coming back *here*—"

Those words unravel my self-control.

I slam my lips on hers, pushing her into the mattress. I bite her lip, eliciting a fierce groan from deep in her throat. She fights back, surprising me by getting leverage under her and rolling us over.

I love the feel of her weight on me. Her hair falls around us, creating our own privacy curtain as she kisses me again. Deeper.

Her hips move against mine ever so slightly, calling my stiff erection to attention.

God, I need to be inside her. Right. Now.

She kisses my jaw, my cheek, up and over my eyelids and forehead. "You're incorrigible," she whispers. "And you aren't perfect. So far from it."

"I know."

"And I hate that you keep secrets."

"I know."

She's still peppering my skin with kisses, dragging her lips around. Her hands bury themselves in my hair, tugging my head back. She nips my earlobe.

"But there's something you don't know."

I exhale in a huff when her tongue touches the shell of my ear.

"And that..." She stares down at me. "Is that I'm in love with you."

My heart... yeah, it does something funny. Skips, twists, jumps for joy. Love? Me?

Sure, when we were kids. When my heart was whole. But that was innocent love.

This is... dirty. Raw. So painful I might just burst.

Fuck. Me.

She touches the corner of my eye. "Never thought I'd see the day when Caleb Asher shed a tear."

I roll my eyes. "I'm just..."

"If you say you don't love me back, I'll call you a liar," she threatens. "No other emotion would explain the psychopathic tendencies you sometimes exhibit."

I flip her over onto her back, hovering above her. My weight settles onto her, showing her exactly what I think of this situation, and she exhales.

Carefully, I lift her hand. Kiss her palm, then down farther, to where her skin is so white it's almost translucent. And the bracelet.

"I'm possessive," I admit. "It's a flaw."

"The first step is admitting you have a problem," she whispers.

I smirk, but it slips away rather fast. "I don't know how you can proclaim love when there are so many missing puzzle pieces."

The palm I just kissed cups my cheek. "What else could there possibly be to ruin this? Ruin us?"

I shake my head.

I don't know, but I wouldn't be surprised if something did.

Wouldn't be the first time... and it's just our luck to be

torn apart. I think of my dad and her mom, the way they were drawn together and ripped brutally apart.

Maybe Asher men are destined to fall for Wolfe women.

It can't be helped. And it can't be stopped.

I'm following in my father's footsteps—minus the wife.

And this time, I'll just have to hope we have different endings. That I won't ruin every good thing.

"If you're not going to say it, show me," she says.

I smile. Her hands are already on the button of my pants.

"That, I can do."

Chapter 21
Margo

D r. Sayer is... not quite how I pictured her.

Long black hair in beautiful, intricate braids, dark eyes and skin. She wears a long flowing dress that isn't weather appropriate, but it's warm in her office. There's even a fireplace behind her.

The whole office has a cozy vibe. Dark wood walls and furniture, a cream-colored rug on the tiled floor. One whole wall filled with books and baubles. Some related to psychology and talk therapy, plus a healthy mix of classics.

I spend the first fifteen minutes of our session standing by those books, running my fingers along the titles.

"*To Kill a Mockingbird?*" I ask, the first thing I've said besides our introduction.

"Do you not like that one?"

I shrug. She's at her therapist chair, which faces a couch and a chair. I guess I could've got my pick of the two, but instead... here I stand, silently counting down the minutes.

"I found myself drawn to Scout's attitude," she says quietly. "There's a lot we can learn from a girl like her."

My finger travels next to *The Bluest Eye* by Toni Morrison. "Envy is dangerous."

"Are you envious?"

I sigh. "Isn't everyone?"

"Probably," she agrees. "It's why the book is so widely regarded. But it strikes each person differently."

"I've always been labeled the foster kid. And before that, the poor scholarship kid." I pull the book out and flip through it. There's writing on a few of the pages, tight cursive that I don't bother trying to interpret. "Isn't that... well, obviously it's not racism. But being followed around shops just because I don't really fit in, that's not fun."

Dr. Sayer stays silent.

"That's not why I'm here, though," I say. "I'm here because I was kidnapped."

I put the book back on the shelf.

"We can discuss whatever you'd like."

I exhale. "How many foster kids do you talk to in a week? Six? Ten? Thirty?"

She just watches me.

"I'm just the same as them."

"I'm sure you share some qualities, but that doesn't mean you're the same. Isn't that kind of like erasing your own identity?"

I finally sit. "I don't think I really have my own identity."

"Is that your own standpoint or one you might've had put on you?"

How did we get talking about this? Instead of thinking about the answer—a painful consideration—I shake my head. "You don't want to know about me being kidnapped?"

"We can talk about it."

I regard her. "I feel bad about it."

"Why?"

"Lenora, my foster mom, shouldn't have had to deal with that." I rub my wrist. "Her daughter died in a car accident. And then I just imagine what she had to go through with her husband... Robert was in the car with me."

"How is he doing?"

I brighten. "Good. He's going home today, which means I get to go home, too. It'll be nice to be back in a routine."

"You were staying with a family friend? Your social worker mentioned they had been registered as a respite home a few years ago, so they were eligible. And your boyfriend lives there."

I slowly nod. "Yes. Is that bad?"

"Perhaps he offered you a bit of stability that a different respite home wouldn't have been able to."

"Right."

"So, you feel guilty because Lenora was going through all of that alone."

"Right," I repeat. "I shouldn't have gone to see my dad. That was where we were coming back from... The prison. It's my fault we were out on that street in the first place."

"But you were taken?"

"I was, but I don't remember a lot of it. I was drugged with something, and... I don't know. I think the detective brushed my case off when Caleb's alibi held up."

I wait for her to say something like, *And how do you feel about that?* For once, I have an answer: angry. Angry that I'm forgotten about yet again, tossed to the side. We're well on our way to figuring this out ourselves—shouldn't a detective, with more resources, be able to do far better?

She doesn't ask. She instead stands, crossing to her desk. "Have you talked to your foster parents about how you feel?"

I frown. "No. There's been a lot going on."

"Understandable." She comes back with a composition notebook in her hand. She extends it toward me, and I reluctantly take it. "Maybe you feel like people don't listen."

"It isn't that they *don't* listen, it's that they *won't*."

"Can you try something for me?"

I lean back, setting the notebook beside me and folding my arms over my chest.

"Hear me out," she says, smiling. "I've found it's easier to be heard when the words can't be ignored. When it's in black and white in front of them."

"You want me to write down my feelings." *I should've known.*

"Maybe put it in a letter," she suggests.

"To who?"

Mom? Lenora and Robert? Dad?

"Whoever you want."

I chew on that request for a moment. Bounce it around. Are there people who I could write a letter to, get the emotions off my chest, and move on from it? Sure.

But right now, that's at the bottom of my list of priorities.

"It was scary," I finally say. "Knowing someone had taken me away from Robert. The second before they knocked me out, they kept apologizing. Even when I was in the barn, and they were arguing..."

I press my lips together.

"How are you sleeping?" she asks.

"I'm... barely." Every night is a struggle, although I haven't told another soul that. I've scarcely admitted it to myself—that my sleep troubles might be a result of being taken. And the accident.

It doesn't help that every time I close my eyes, I feel

Robert's arm across my chest, protecting me as we careened toward the ditch.

"I told my boyfriend I love him," I blurt out. "Because I definitely do. But he didn't say it back. I know he does, but I was really hoping to hear him say the words."

She takes the subject change in stride. "First love?"

"Only love," I say firmly.

She smiles. "When you know, you know. And maybe, since he didn't just automatically say it back to you, it'll be more special when he does."

I hum. "That... makes me feel better, actually."

"That's what I'm here for."

I raise my eyebrow. "Pep talks?"

Her smile turns into a grin. "Perspective."

"Ah."

She glances at her watch. "And now, unfortunately, our time is up. Try writing in the journal. Bring it back with you on Friday."

My cheeks heat up. "Am I going to be reading it out loud?"

She shrugs, and I catch a mischievous gleam in her eye.

Honestly, I need some personality other than serene from her. Still, I take her expression to mean, *maybe*. Maybe I'll read it aloud. Maybe we won't even crack the notebook open.

Lenora is parked at the curb, waiting for me. She looks at me expectantly when I slide in, but I just shake my head.

"Right, right, I shouldn't ask."

I laugh and tuck the notebook into my bag. "It is supposed to be confidential."

"Well, fine. But did you find it helpful?"

I think back on my conversation with Dr. Sayer. The more I think about it, the more I like her definition of her job: to give perspective. She's not out to heal or fix me—not that I can tell anyway.

"It was," I decide.

"Good. Robert is home, eagerly awaiting our arrival."

I straighten. "He is? Already?"

"Yep. He got a clean bill of health from the doctors. As long as he takes it easy, he should be okay to return to work next week."

I touch my forehead. The stitches came out this morning, before therapy, but they said to keep a butterfly bandage on it for another day. Under it, though, is a new pink scar.

And I've never been so excited to wash my hair without inhibition.

It starts snowing when we're almost home. My muscles tense, and I grab on to the door.

"Margo, are you okay?"

It was snowing when Robert and I crashed. It was easy to push down the fear of vehicles when it was Riley driving me, or Ms. McCaw. Or Eli. The skies have been clear, the roads dry.

I lean forward, eyeing the side streets. A car could come out of nowhere and sideswipe us.

She slows our car until we're crawling down the street. "Honey, breathe."

I take in a ragged breath. It's snowing hard and fast. I close my eyes.

"Can we just get home?" I whisper.

"Absolutely."

She reaches over and holds my hand the whole way back, and it helps. It's her form of a lifeline—and maybe she understands my sudden anxiety.

I wonder how long it took her to get into a car after Isabella died.

"We're here," she announces, turning into the driveway.

I open my eyes and release her hand, embarrassment flushing my cheeks.

"I'm sorry."

Her eyebrows furrow. "You don't have to apologize."

Nodding, I get out of the car. The embarrassment is replaced by anticipation, and I rush ahead of her to get in the house.

"Hey, kiddo," Robert calls. He walks back toward the living room with a glass of water. "Let me just put this down..."

He sets it on a side table, then holds out his arms.

I dive into them, holding back a fraction for fear of hurting him. He wraps his arms around my back.

"There she is," he says into my hair. "Good as new, the both of us, yeah?"

"You said that exact same thing before," I mumble into his chest. "And then you almost died."

"Ah, well. Old habits die hard. My father used to say that to my brother and me. We were always getting hurt." He chuckles and pats my back.

I pull back, wiping at my cheeks. I'm ashamed of the tears there, but they're more happy than sad. He's home. I'm home.

It isn't just a house anymore.

My heart swells.

"Len, we should order Chinese and watch some movies."

She laughs behind me. "May as well. I don't have any food in this house. Margo, want to take this up to your room?"

I turn. She holds the bag I had packed for the Blacks'.

"Oops, sorry."

"I know you were in a rush to get in here." She winks at me.

I loop the strap over my shoulder and hurry to the stairs. Up to the second floor, where pictures of the Bryans stare at me. They've replaced some of them with new pictures, doing their best to make me feel welcome. Pictures of me and my friends, Caleb and I from the ball, a selfie I took with Robert and Lenora on Thanksgiving.

I smile at that last one, the three of us with our faces so close together. They frame me in, their arms looped around me. It's easy to see why they picked that one to display in high-definition color. We're so happy.

My first stop is the bathroom, unloading my toiletries and makeup bag, then I push open the door to my room.

It meets some resistance, like it's caught on something.

I frown, pushing harder, and manage to get it open most of the way.

But my room...

Horror radiates through me. Horror and disbelief.

I can't help it.

I scream.

Chapter 22
Liam

Theo jostles my arm.

I smirk at him and slide open the window. As soon as it's up, I hoist myself through the opening and into the dark, quiet house. I land almost silently and glance around while Theo climbs in after me.

"Spare room," I mouth at him.

He gives me a *no shit* look.

We leave the room and split up. We're kind of winging it, here, and it's a game to see who will find our prey first. I open one door, wincing when I spot two lumps in the bed.

Parents' room.

I close it as quietly as possible and move on. The house is too big. An office, another guest room, and finally Theo flags me down.

My adrenaline immediately kicks into high gear.

We enter the bedroom. He takes one side, I take the other.

I stare down at the slumbering Matt Bonner.

Theo and I discussed the plan only briefly. Margo pointed the finger, and Caleb couldn't proclaim his innocence. So we're taking matters into our own hands. We'll see what Matt has to say.

Theo holds up the roll of duct tape. It makes a noise as he rips a few inches off, and we both lean forward. The first touch is Theo slamming the tape down over Matt's mouth. I grab his arm, Theo takes the other, and when Matt wakes, we're ready.

He thrashes in our hold, but we keep him pinned to the bed.

I punch him in the gut.

He groans.

We get him off the bed and toss him to the floor. He makes a *thump*, but we wrestle him into position to tape his ankles and wrists. Finally, Theo pushes him onto his back. Matt's wild eyes take in our faces, and his nostrils flare.

Of course he recognizes us.

We're not trying to hide.

"It's your lucky day, Matty," I whisper. "You've won a free trip to Rose Hill."

He shakes his head, but Theo and I are moving again. We pick up Matt, who immediately starts thrashing. I wrinkle my nose.

"Maybe we should knock him out," I suggest.

Theo sighs.

Matt stops.

"We're just taking you for a little ride," I assure him. "If you struggle, you'll be lights out. Promise."

My knuckles are already split. One more punch wouldn't kill them.

I glance around the room, and my attention lands on a figurine.

A mermaid.

"This what Caleb asked you to work on? Ironic, since

you're so into tech..." I go over and pick it up. "Is there still information on this?"

He glares at me, then slowly nods.

"Excellent." I pocket it. We'll figure out how to get rid of the incriminating shit later. Like this casual abduction.

Anticipation creeps through me when we exit his room and go back to the one we entered through. Matt's room faces the street. It would be too conspicuous if someone happened to see. The already opened one, however, faces shrubbery.

We make it without incident. Eli waits for us at the window, and his expression is exasperated.

"Took you assholes long enough."

Theo rolls his eyes. We shove Matt's legs through first, which Eli guides to the ground, and then his head. He shoves Matt to the ground while we come out.

None of us are in a particularly gentle mood.

Caleb is pretty much a brother. The four of us? Family. And this asshole masqueraded as a friend, but he *hurt* Caleb and Margo.

We're going to find out why.

"Ready?" I ask.

Eli and Theo heft Matt up. He's starting to put up a resistance again, and I grin.

One promise I can fulfill: time for Matt to go to sleep.

Chapter 23
Caleb

My phone buzzing jars me awake. I fumble for the phone. It's the first night without Margo here, and I tossed and turned for a while. I guess I fell asleep. But I'm groggy, and it takes me a second to accept the call.

"What?"

"Come outside." It's Theo.

I glance at the screen. It's late—like, two in the morning, the rest of the world is sleeping late—and that piques my interest.

That and the urgency in his voice.

"Be there in a minute."

"Backyard," he says, then hangs up.

I wait a beat. I cross to the bathroom and splash water on my face. Get dressed, grab my shoes. Creep up the stairs, through the kitchen and out the back door, then put my shoes on.

Eli and Liam are waiting for me just beyond the brick patio.

"Took him long enough." Liam grins. "Guess Theo didn't spoil the surprise."

I shake my head. "He didn't."

"Right this way." Liam turns and disappears into the darkness.

I glance at Eli. "A surprise? For me?"

He shrugs. "I dunno."

We follow Liam up the hill, to the shed at the back of the Blacks' property. They used to keep lawn equipment in here, but now it just houses a few jet skis on stands. Summer with the Blacks is never a dull moment.

We arrive just as Liam cracks the door, sliding it open wide enough for us to enter.

"We're lucky the snow melted," Eli whispers. "Or else my parents would question why we were up here."

I grunt my agreement and step in ahead of him.

He closes the door behind us, then the overhead light flickers on.

Theo stands in the center of the room, grinning like a fool.

"Best. Christmas. Present. Ever," he says. "Just saying."

I look around. "Yeah? A little early for Christmas."

He steps to the side, revealing...

Ah, hell.

Matt Bonner. He's curled into the fetal position on the floor. His wrists are taped, as well as his ankles. A strip covers his mouth. He jerks when he sees us. *Me.*

"Come now, Matty, you didn't think we *weren't* bringing you to Caleb?" Liam says, approaching and crouching down. He grabs Matt's jaw, tilting his head back. "What do you think, Caleb? Free hall pass."

"How the hell—"

"Matt's sister sure is a pretty one," Liam says. He leans

in close to Bonner's face. "Sure would be a shame if something were to happen to her..."

Matt lunges, knocking Liam back with his bound arms.

Theo quickly hauls Matt away, holding him upright, and Liam laughs from the floor.

He climbs to his feet and shakes his head. "See? He knows not to talk."

Eli shifts. "But don't kill him. Not sure how I'll explain that to my parents."

I take a deep breath. "Remove the tape from his mouth."

Theo rips it off in one motion and shoves him back down to the floor. He falls to his knees hard. He stretches his jaw, his glare burning into me. But this isn't about him or me, or our past friendship. This is about if he's involved with Margo's stalker.

Or if he *is* Margo's stalker.

A prickle of unease slides down my spine. Getting answers seems to suddenly be the most important thing. If it protects Margo... no holds barred.

"Are you going to answer our questions?" I step closer.

He glares up at me. "Fuck you."

I tilt my head. "I thought we were friends."

"We are—"

"*Were*," Eli corrects from my left, his tone dark.

Liam stands behind Matt. Theo to my right. I feel their presence, and it gives me strength. My demons are coming out to play, and no one here will reel them back in.

I think even Margo would be okay with this.

"Did you take her?"

He doesn't reply. His gaze would cut through me if he wasn't such a fucking coward.

"Answer me, Matt. Did. You. Take. Margo?"

His gaze slides away, which is an admission of guilt in and of itself. He's not denying it. He can't look at me.

Sudden clarity hits me. I hate him more than I've hated anyone in my life. Dad, Uncle David, the way I used to feel about Margo... it's all dust compared to the fury welling inside me.

He hurt her.

Took her.

Tied her up and left her to die—

"Just fucking hit me already, Asher," Matt growls. "Because I'm not saying a goddamn thing one way or another."

"We'll see about that," Theo mutters.

"Who owns your loyalty?" I squat in front of him. "Honestly, Bonner. What the hell would make you clam up? You're not denying your involvement—that's a guilty verdict in my eyes."

He shakes his head. "There's someone a lot scarier than you."

I snap my fist out, connecting with his nose. All of my senses come to life, exploding through me. It's like a fight on the ice, the duty of enforcing good behavior during the game. There are no free shots. If it's not a clean hit, you pay the price.

Blood gushes from his nose, and he brings his hands up to his face.

But he doesn't say anything. Hardly protests.

"Cut him loose," I order.

Liam frowns.

"Cut. Him. *Loose.*"

Eli pulls out his knife and cuts through the tape on his ankles, then his wrists. It's painfully similar to how we found Margo.

Matt shakes out his arms and stands quickly, spinning in a circle.

"Eyes on me, Bonner," I growl. "You hit me, you get to walk out of here. Right now."

His eyebrow goes up. "What's the catch?"

"No catch."

Liam steps forward. "What are you—?"

"Hit me, Bonner," I goad. "You took Margo, and I think you did it to get back at me for something. Jealousy?"

"Jealous of you?" he scoffs. "No."

He stands still for a moment, then springs toward me. He stumbles, wincing in pain, and I easily dodge him.

He stumbles to a stop and spins around. "Your whole family is fucking crazy."

I shrug. He's right, there's no point denying it. Although, I'm not sure when he would've formed that opinion.

He charges again, his fist barely missing my cheek as I twist away. I stick out my foot, and he catches on it, sprawling out.

My blood is pumping. Theo was right—best fucking Christmas present ever. Revenge is a dirty thing, like a stink that you can't wash off. But this isn't revenge.

This is justice.

Eli pulls Matt up, slapping his cheek. "You still with us, Bonney?"

He shoves Eli away and spins back toward me. The blood from his nose has stained his front teeth red. I'm itching to hit him again—just like I'm itching for him to hit me.

When he comes back around, I get in two quick punches to his torso, then back away. If I get him flat on his back, I know I won't be able to stop.

Matt yells. It shatters the night.

Liam grabs him from behind and slaps a hand over his mouth. In his other hand is a knife, and he raises it to Matt's neck. "What did we say, huh? You want to die tonight?"

Eli shifts.

Yeah, we didn't sign up for murder.

"You talk or you get a hit in," I tell Matt in an even voice. "That's the only way you're getting out of here on your own two feet."

Theo grins, making a show of looking Matt up and down.

Matt swallows. "I'm dead if I talk, so... there goes that option."

Liam releases him, shoving him toward me.

Margo's face flashes in front of my eyes. What would she think about this? Justice or not, she calms the bloodlust. For sense to trickle in. There's a bit of hopelessness to this situation. Four boys beating up a fifth. Is that what we've reduced ourselves to?

He comes after me, and I stay still long enough for him to get a hit in.

His knuckles glance across my jaw, harder than I would've wanted—but definitely not as bad as it could've been. My head cranks to the side, and my cheek is torn open by my teeth. The metallic taste of blood fills my mouth.

I spit onto the floor.

Silence.

I stare at Matt. He's watching me like he can't believe he actually hit me—and if I'm going to uphold my promise.

"I will get to the bottom of this," I warn him. I'm sure my teeth are stained red like his, and I make sure he sees it. "And until then? You better stay the fuck away from anyone you care about. We'll be watching."

He slowly raises his arm, wiping the blood from his mouth off on the back of his hand.

Eli steps aside to let him pass, and he follows out to watch Matt go.

"You let him off the hook too easy," Theo says.

"Hitting him felt good, but..." I crack my neck. The adrenaline is leeching out of me, reminding me that it's the middle of the night. "He's smart. He wouldn't have done this on his own—and clearly he wasn't going to spill."

Liam grunts. "Maybe."

I tilt my head back, gaze on the rafters. "And... thank you."

Theo chokes. "Yeah?"

"We didn't learn a fucking thing," Eli says.

I shrug. "We learned Matt's afraid of someone."

"He's a pussy." Theo grabs a flashlight from the floor and clicks off the overhead light. "He plays a tough game, but he's afraid of his shadow."

"A lot of people in his life could be threatened," I say. "And honestly? We're in no position to threaten any of them."

"Just his sister," Liam says. We close up the shed and slowly walk toward the house. "Have you seen her? Instagram model, hot as hell. Lips—"

"All right." Eli shakes his head. "I love you crazy fuckers, but I need sleep. You two staying?"

Liam and Theo trade a look.

"I've got to get home," Theo says. "Ma will flip out if I'm not there when she wakes up."

Liam sighs. "Yeah, I've gotta take Colby to school now that my car is functioning. So..."

"Keys are in my room," Eli says. "Come get them."

Theo doesn't enter the house, just disappears around

the corner without a word. I watch Liam and Eli head toward the stairs, and I contemplate an apology. But what for?

I flip my light on in the basement, half expecting Margo to be waiting for me again. But no, she's asleep, safe in her room. Away from my darkness.

She sure does know how to bring out the light in me, but the moment she's gone... she takes the good with her, leaving the broken mess she created.

No, that isn't quite right. I need to stop blaming her.

I rinse the blood away.

I was willing to break Margo so our pieces would fit, but Matt took that away from me. She's more damaged than I am now. Fragile. One wrong move and she'll shatter, and it wasn't *my* decision. Hers, neither.

No matter.

I'll throw myself against the truth until I'm dust. And then nothing will separate us.

Chapter 24
Unknown

There's no calling this one off.

You may take a piece off the chessboard, but I'm still here.

And I'm coming.

Chapter 25
Margo

L enora finds me in the hallway.

On the floor.

She falls to her knees beside me, grabbing at my shoulders. "What's wrong? Are you hurt?"

I point toward my room with a shaky hand. The door has swung almost all the way closed, leaving just a crack visible. It's all I can focus on, although I'd rather close my eyes. Scrub them out and forget I ever came back here.

Home. Someone clearly disagrees.

She stands and forces my door open farther, her hand flying to her mouth.

Robert makes it to the top of the stairs then, coming toward me.

"Robert," Lenora gasps.

He helps me to my feet, and I follow him closer.

My room is a wreck.

Destroyed.

My mattress is off the box spring, ripped to shreds. Bits of foam and feathers from the sliced pillows coat the floor. The box spring is splintered, one leg completely demolished. And my bookshelf... Every book has been thrown off the case, some pages torn out, crumpled.

But the worst part is the red paint, resembling a murder scene. It's splashed across the walls, the floor, the books. My desk. The window.

And on the wall, a message.

Pretty bird, broken wings. Oh, what a glorious fall.

He takes my hand. "Len, call the detective. Let's just close this off..."

He tugs me out of the room.

I gasp for air.

Pretty bird.

Where have I heard that before? Who's called me that?

"Detective Masters, this is Lenora Bryan..." Her voice fades as she goes down the stairs.

"Is this related to who took you?" Robert asks.

That would make sense. We've been digging into my stalker.

Is this a warning?

Unknown calling me out for...

I shake my head. "I don't know."

"Let's go downstairs," he suggests, guiding me away.

I stop short at one of the framed photos. There's a faint spot of red on the glass, like whoever painted the message in my room came out here and took their sweet time leaving.

Robert doesn't notice my distraction.

"I'm going to the bathroom." I quickly withdraw. "I'll meet you downstairs."

He nods. "Take your time."

I duck into the bathroom until I hear him talking to Lenora. Then I back into the hallway and lift the photo from the wall.

Isabella hid a note behind one of these. It could be irrelevant, but...

This particular photo is one of the new ones. It's Caleb, Eli, Riley, and me from the masquerade ball. One of the few where we weren't wearing our masks.

The red spot—a fingerprint, I realize upon closer inspection—is right over my face.

Erasing me completely.

Pretty bird, broken wings. Oh, what a glorious fall.

I tighten my grip on it.

How dare they come in here and threaten me? After everything—

I shake my head, knowing that line of thinking is foolish. They won't just *stop*. Unknown won't stop until they get what they want.

And... what is it that they want, exactly? To run me out of town. To stay away. And more specifically, to stay away from Caleb.

Why?

Because I might ruin his focus at hockey or turn him on a different path for his future? Because I might capture his attention, unlike Unknown?

"Margo?" Lenora calls. "The detective is here."

I race into the hall and rehang the picture. If he notices, he notices. If he doesn't, well...

"Ms. Wolfe," Detective Masters greets me.

I shake his hand. He makes me nervous, even though I've done nothing wrong. Maybe it's the fact that he arrested Caleb without any real cause, then seemed to forget about any other leads. No more follow up.

"Did you find anything from the car that hit Robert and me?" I ask.

His stare is criticizing. "No."

"Have you even been trying to find it?"

"I'm not at liberty to say," the detective answers. "Your room was vandalized? Would you mind showing me?"

I take a deep breath and point to my door. "See for yourself."

Robert wraps his arm around me. "We'd rather not…"

"Understandable, sir." Masters puts on a pair of gloves, then gingerly opens the door. He sucks in a breath. "That sure is something."

We wait in the hall as he takes a closer look. Lenora chews on her lower lip, more stressed out than I've ever seen her.

"I locked the door every time I left," she said. "I just don't understand it. We have an alarm!"

The detective reappears. "What's your alarm hooked up to?"

"The first-floor doors and windows," she says. "We only set it when we're gone. Maybe that's foolish, but—"

"There's some scuffing on the outer edge of the windowsill," he interrupts. "The vandal probably went in and out the window. Is anything else missing?"

"I'll check our room." Lenora slips past us, down the hall.

I try not to panic. Caleb came in and out of there so many times… if the detective finds even his fingerprint out there, he'll automatically assume it was him.

"Why would someone do this?" Robert asks. "Target Margo?"

Masters eyes me. "You piss anyone off?"

"Just a stalker," I say, half joking. And then I realize what I just admitted… I had told the detective about Unknown when I was in the hospital. But, according to him, they couldn't do anything unless they knew who it was. The messages weren't threatening enough to warrant the phone company to release the blocked number either.

I never told Robert, though.

"Excuse me?"

I wince. "I've just been getting some... unsavory texts." *And phone calls. And I was kidnapped. And I've been feeling like I'm being watched all the time.*

No big deal.

"What can we do about this?" Robert demands.

"Margo filed a complaint in the hospital," Masters answers. "So it's on record. But until something—"

"Please do *not* be about to say something worse," Robert snaps. "And what does your office plan to do about this?"

"We'll have a cruiser do some drive-bys for the next week, to make sure you all are safe." Detective Masters glances at me. "Has anything else happened?"

I cross my arms over my chest. What would I admit to, a creepy-crawly feeling occasionally?

"No."

He nods like he expected that answer. "I'm going to take some photos, have a look outside, and we'll go from there."

Lenora reappears.

"Nothing is missing. Not even a hair out of place." She shudders. "After this is over, we're redoing that room. New window with many locks. Whatever furniture or paint you want. Anything—"

"It's okay," I whisper.

Masters goes back into my room, and the Bryans and I go downstairs. I perch on a stool at the breakfast bar while Lenora paces the kitchen. And Robert lowers himself onto the couch, groaning under his breath.

This really isn't fair. Not by a mile.

My phone has been silent. No new messages from Riley or Caleb—nothing from Unknown either.

Detective Masters comes back downstairs. "You don't have any idea who might've done this? Or what the words on the wall meant?"

I shake my head. "I thought it had to be someone from school, since they texted Caleb and warned him that Ian was taking me into the woods. And they were at a party at Ian's house, too. But lately…"

The car belonging to Tobias, who's a known associate of the Ashers, is just too coincidental.

"I don't know," I finish lamely.

"This is probably enough to find out the number that's been texting you," he says. "I'll take some photos outside, then head back to the station and work on that. I'll be in touch."

Lenora nods sharply. "Thank you, Detective."

We sit in silence for a moment.

Police aren't the bad guys in this situation. I've had my fair share of fear when it comes to cops—especially that one time I ran away—and Detective Masters does have a tendency to look down his nose at me, whether because I'm a foster or a teenager, I don't know.

Still. Worth a shot.

I get up and rush after him, outside without even a coat on.

He's under my window in the middle of the lawn. His eyebrows shoot up when he spots me. "Ms. Wolfe?"

"I have a… theory."

He waves for me to continue.

"How does a public defender rise to partner at a big law firm in two years?"

Detective Masters says nothing.

"When I asked Tobias Hutchins that very question—"

He holds up his hand. "When did you meet him?"

"Riley and I went to his office in the city. He defended my dad—badly. If you know anything about that trial—"

"I was a rookie." He seems to contemplate something. His gaze goes to the cloudy sky. "Let's go back inside. You've intrigued me."

Hope flares inside my chest. And hope? It's a dangerous thing. It can lift you up and drop you when you least expect it.

So I shove the hope away and remain cautious. Lenora and Robert both start to ask questions when I walk back in, but they're silenced by the detective's reappearance.

Masters follows me into the dining room. My painting of Caleb is on the floor in the corner, but he makes no comment about it.

"Okay," he says once we've sat. "Let's hear it."

"You know I lived with my parents in the Asher guest house. My mom and his dad were having an affair, which apparently everyone knew except me and..." I shake my head. "I was upstairs in Caleb's room one day—before I found out about the affair—and I heard Mrs. Asher talking to someone."

"Someone. How old were you?"

I wince. "I had just turned ten."

"Okay, so, we're dealing with unreliable memory."

"Yeah... I didn't know who she was talking to, but I remember the guy was upset about what she was asking him to do. She said she was paying him enough. I mentioned it to Caleb, and he told me it was Tobias. That's how, when Caleb and I ran into Tobias in the city in October, Tobias knew Caleb." I pause and suck in a deep breath.

"So you've established a relationship between your dad's lawyer and the Ashers. Go on."

"Why would he have a car in the city? Does he drive it a lot?"

The detective smiles. "You're asking the right questions, at least. And I'm going to humor you." He flips through his notebook. "I talked to Mr. Hutchins myself. He said the car was stored in a garage, and he was planning on a Sunday drive to visit family when he noticed it missing."

I grunt. "It's too neat. He reports it missing mere hours before it's involved in my..."

"Or it's *good* timing, and we avoided a lot of hassle because he did notice."

"You're supposed to be humoring me."

He sighs. "Margo, I'll humor you as far as logic will allow. But reaching for pieces of facts to make them fit your theory is bad detective work."

Like you did with Caleb? I bite my tongue instead of spitting out that accusation.

"Okay, okay." I sigh. "You don't find it fishy that there's a link from Lydia to Tobias?"

His eyes bore into mine. "I agree, there's a connection there. But what of it?"

"Why would Lydia *Asher* have a relationship with my father's lawyer?"

"Is that your whole theory?"

I raise my eyebrow. "Honestly? Yeah. I have no idea who Unknown is, just that they're probably my age. Which means they're someone who knows Lydia and goes to Emery-Rose."

"Matt Bonner went to Emery-Rose," Robert says from the doorway.

I jump.

"He transferred, but I suspect he knows quite a few kids at your school. Still friends, even." Robert frowns. "You mentioned he had some hand helping Caleb with a project, Margo? Sorry, that's unhelpful."

Oh my God.

Matt was the one who led us to the diner. To my mother *and* Lydia Asher. Of course he went to Emery-Rose. It was how he and Caleb became friends.

Which means he probably knows Lydia.

White spots flash in front of my eyes. I blink hard and swallow, trying to get rid of the light-headedness.

"Quite all right," Masters says. "How are you feeling?"

Robert lets out a small chuckle. "Like someone scraped through my insides with a blade. I'll be fine in due time."

"You're welcome to join us." The detective motions to a chair. "You knew Matt?"

"Not personally." Robert lowers himself into the seat next to me. "What are you chatting about? Besides Matt."

"He has to be working with Lydia," I insist.

Masters shakes his head. "Where's the motive? She moved away after the trial and would have no reason to... what, exactly? And the other factor: usually kidnappers call the family with demands. A ransom. That didn't happen."

"Because Caleb and Eli found me."

"A burner phone texted Caleb's phone with coordinates. That's how he found you." Masters pats the table. "I understand that you want to connect Bonner to this, but you're grasping at straws."

"Margo has had a crazy few weeks," Robert says softly.

"You don't think the person who has been texting me and who kidnapped me—apparently without an actual reason—was the one to do that to my room?" I shoot to my feet, except there's nowhere to go. "And you don't believe that Matt Bonner could be that person?"

"I'll dig around the Ashers, see if I can find anything suspicious, okay?"

"Is this the first time?"

His eyebrows scrunch. "The first time for what?"

"That anyone has ever looked into the Ashers?" I shake my head. "Caleb's uncle has been beating him since he was a kid. But I guess it's all too easy for the Asher family to sweep everything under the fucking rug."

"If that's true—"

"*Fuck* your truth," I yell. I storm out and up the stairs, locking myself in the bathroom. I grab my bag on the way, sinking to the floor once I'm alone.

God, I just yelled at a police detective. He was going to help me, but I probably just ruined any chance of that.

I slide my phone out. I stare at it, debating calling Riley.

But wasn't it me who said Caleb and I needed to work together?

That means relying on him sometimes.

ME

You remember anyone calling me a pretty bird?

CALEB

?? No. Why?

Someone wrote it on my wall. It's bugging me.

His contact picture fills my screen, showing the incoming video chat request. I wipe at my face, then answer it.

He frowns at me. His phone is held at a low angle that

shows off his sharp jawline. "Please tell me I read that wrong."

"I wish."

"Have you been crying?" He seems to be home, but now he's climbing the steps out of the basement.

"Do I look it?" I fixate on the tiny picture of me in the corner, wondering if he sees something I don't. My eyes do seem a bit puffy, and my face is pale.

"You're upset. I can tell that much."

I sigh. "Unknown vandalized my room. Destroyed everything."

He loses all expression. "You're joking."

"Why would I be joking? Lenora called Detective Masters. He was just here."

The phone drops, and all I can see is the black fabric of his shirt. "Guys."

When he shifts his phone, he shows me Eli, Liam, and Theo.

"All hands on deck, right?" he says.

"What's going on?" Liam demands. "You okay, Wolfe?"

"My room got vandalized." My damn voice wobbles.

A muscle in Caleb's jaw clenches. "We'll be there in five minutes. You guys shouldn't be alone."

Someone knocks on the bathroom door, and I freeze.

"Margo, it's Detective Masters. I took some pictures of the room and am heading out. Just wanted to let you know that I'm going to look into what we discussed."

"Thanks," I call.

Caleb stares at me. "Can't wait to hear what you *discussed*."

"The police are supposed to be the good guys," I whisper.

He just shakes his head. They're outside now, and

someone is yelling after them. Theo yells back, but the words are snatched away on the wind.

"We'll be there soon, okay?"

I nod, and he hangs up.

My head falls back on the door. I don't know what the hell we're going to do. What *can* we do? We're teenagers. Kids, really.

My eyes fill with tears. The whole situation is hopeless.

See what I said about hope? It can drop you.

Real fast.

Chapter 26
Caleb

"Food," Eli demands. "We can be hospitable and bring food."

Theo rolls his eyes. "How about delivery? That's easy."

"I'm in the mood for sushi," Liam adds, "but only if someone else is buying. Or lobster."

I twist around, looking him up and down. "Your mom isn't doing the soup for every meal thing again, is she?"

He shrugs. "It's all we can afford at the moment. Do you know how cheap it is to make a million different soups? They last us a while."

"You're starting to run more," Eli points out. "Which means you need to carb up..."

"Winter sucks for us," he mutters. "Always has, always will. Doesn't mean we won't get through it."

"So, maybe Chinese?" Theo says. "The Bryans aren't going to like us crashing their house."

I contemplate that. Robert just got out of the hospital. Anyone who knows them would also know she's been sleeping there. It isn't rocket science. They have a solid marriage. Real love between them. I'd have been more shocked if Lenora left his side.

Eli gets us to Margo's house almost too fast. He drives recklessly at times, but right now, there's a growing feeling of dread building up in my chest. It's going to explode if I don't see Margo safe.

I jump out before the truck has fully stopped, jogging up the walkway.

Margo yanks the door open and launches into my arms.

I scoop her up, breathing in her scent, and she locks her legs around my waist.

"Thanks for coming," she whispers in my ear. "I told them you all were on your way. I think Lenora is going to ask if I can stay with you guys again."

I wince. "It's that bad?"

She leans back into my arms, eyebrows raised. "It's..."

I set her down, and we all enter the house.

Robert is on the couch, flipping through television stations, and he waves to us. "Hello, boys. I'd get up, but..."

"Please don't stress," I say, going over to shake his hand. "You look better."

He laughs, and it turns into a cough. "Better than what? Being at death's door?"

I shrug.

"I'll take it."

Eli nods at him, and Theo waves.

Liam's eyes are wide. "I like what you've done with the place." He walks farther in, peering into the kitchen. "This is new."

Margo tilts her head. "Why are you acting like..."

"My family used to live here," he says. "Although there used to be a wall here." He mimes a wall that would've made the kitchen a lot smaller. "And the dining room didn't open up onto this porch."

We follow him as he wanders.

He goes up the stairs, pausing on the picture of Lenora and Robert, then into the bathroom. "That's the same."

He comes out and points to her door. "Your room, Margo?"

She grimaces.

"Caleb and I practiced sneaking out of here quite a bit in our youth." He winks at me. "Dare I say that's helped him out quite a bit in recent months."

"Whoever did this came in through the window, too." She shoves the door open.

My mouth drops, and I step into the room. My friends follow me, while Margo stays in the hall. Honestly, I don't blame her. A tornado of fury went through the room, destroyed every good thing about it. The walls will need several coats of paint to cover the red, and the writing...

Pretty bird, broken wings.

I narrow my eyes. It's chilling, but... wholly unfamiliar.

"What the hell is that?" Liam points to something on the floor.

"It looks like..." Oh God.

I cover my mouth. I've never been one to have a weak stomach, but this...

A white bird sits just below the words.

Dead.

Oh, what a glorious fall.

"Fucking hell," Theo growls. He herds us out of the room, slamming the door closed. "Did you see it?"

"See what? The writing?"

"The fucking dead bird," he says, eyes narrowed at Margo.

She blanches. "Excuse me?"

"It's a threat," I declare. "Calling you a pretty bird, then giving you a dead one?"

She bursts into tears.

Shame flushes through me, and I go to her. Cradle her head against my chest. "I'm sorry. This isn't your fault."

She grabs my shirt, holding me close. "I don't want to die."

"You're not going to." I shake my head. We know the connecting pieces—it's only Unknown who is still a mystery. But who's pulling their strings isn't. "You're coming with me. I'm sure they'll let you."

"You want to bring her home?" Lenora asks, coming up the stairs. "Honestly, that's... not a bad idea."

"You'd let me go?" Margo goes to her foster mom and takes her hands. "I almost don't want to leave, but—"

"This house doesn't quite feel safe, does it?" She sighs. "Not the warm and fuzzy night we had planned. The detective said we're free to start cleaning the room, so I'm going to have a service come in tomorrow. Anything you want to salvage?"

Margo's nose wrinkles. "I don't think I can go in there."

"I will," I say. "I'll see if anything is... untouched."

I slip back into the room, closing myself in. Once the fresh air is sealed off, the dead bird smell fills the air. It's a wonder the whole house doesn't smell like it.

I grab the tipped-over trash bin and dump out the liner, using it as a barrier to scoop the bird into. Poor sucker. It appears to have had a quick, painless death. Hell, maybe Unknown stumbled upon it and just brought it in here.

Sure beats the alternative.

Her clothes look undisturbed in the dresser until I pull them out. Holes have been cut in the fabric of her shirts, her jeans have been cut, but whoever did it folded them back up.

One more *fuck you* toward Margo, apparently.

We aren't just dealing with someone who wanted to mess with Margo.

Somehow, she's made them mad. Worse than mad.

I ball my fists and walk out, giving her a quick shake of my head. "They ruined everything."

She exhales slowly, leaning against the wall.

"I called Dad," Eli says. "He okayed her return once I explained what happened."

"You have the knife, Margo?" Liam asks.

She nods.

"Good."

I roll my eyes. "Let's hope she doesn't have to use it, yeah? Now, let's get the hell out of here."

Downstairs, we wait by the door while Margo says her goodbyes. It's hard to watch. She latches on to Robert and doesn't let go for a long while, and he doesn't force it. In fact, his eyes are closed, and he hugs her just as tightly.

The crash affected them more than physically.

"Margo," Lenora says. "We'll pick you up at eight to go into school. The principal wanted to make sure we were on the same page about your schoolwork."

She nods, biting her lip.

I want to touch her.

Shield her from all this shit.

God, I was an idiot for ever wanting to break this beautiful, strong girl. She stands tall even as her world crumbles around her, while people are out to get her. In the face of tragedy and anger, she's collected.

If I had it my way, I'd take her far, far away. To somewhere no one could hurt her. We'd live a happy life away from literally everyone. Have outrageous sex everywhere, get her pregnant, marry her—maybe not quite in that order.

That dream *pops*.

I don't have my way. I have an inheritance controlled by my uncle for another four months, no power, no control.

No fucking clue.

She walks toward me, and I focus on her dark eyes. They're glazed with unshed tears, but she still smiles at me and holds out her hand.

I take it and pull her close.

"Remember my promise," I say in her ear. "No matter where you go, I'll find you."

It used to be a threat, but now…

It's much more than that.

Norah and Josh give Margo two big hugs when we all walk in, and that seems to shock the hell out of her. She stands frozen for a minute, then relaxes into each of them.

"We're going downstairs," Eli tells them, giving his mom a peck on the cheek. "We ordered food."

She smiles and pats the side of his head. "You all deserve some happiness."

I agree. Especially Margo, who's beginning to resemble a ghost with her paleness.

I haven't released her hand since we left her house. Even in the car, and climbing out, I didn't let go. Her bag is over my shoulder, and I guide her downstairs. She comes willingly, squeezing my hand softly.

The boys appear a second later with drinks, passing out the sodas. We all flop onto the couch.

"Lydia is the connection," she blurts out. "I'm sorry, Caleb. But—"

I wave off my words. "I know."

"Why is she working at that diner?" she demands. "Lenora mentioned something about the will, but—"

I rub my eyes. "Yeah. That."

Eli grunts. "Story time."

"It's not that interesting."

"Sure it isn't," he counters. "Just your mom's entire motivation may rest on that one day. One moment where her life went..." He whistles, miming something falling and exploding.

I grit my teeth. "Fine."

And then... Well, I do what I've been trying to avoid for a long time. I remember.

Past

Mom held me close. She hadn't touched me in three days, but today she was a leech. Sucking my energy out of my body.

That's what I told myself anyway.

It was the day before the funeral, and all we had been wearing was black. My shirt was starched and scratchy under my suit jacket and pants, and the tie strangled me.

I didn't understand why we had to get so dressed up to read Dad's last words. They were just words on a piece of paper.

Uncle David and Aunt Iris came into the room. She ruffled my hair, which Mom immediately finger-combed back into order, and Uncle David knelt in front of me.

"How are you holding up?" he asked.

I shrugged. I just wanted to go home, but home was different now. Colder. Margo was gone, too, and I couldn't figure out why. Her parents were gone. Mom hadn't said a word about it, just locked the door to the guest house and... walked away from it.

She'd tucked the key into her pocket, and I wasn't sure where the Wolfes had hidden their spare. If Mom caught me digging around in the grass, in their planters, she'd yell and cry.

Margo's house was collecting dust, and my soul was, too.

It was dramatic. Ian would say I was being a sissy, but she had pulled a piece of me out when she left, and I was... abandoned to rot.

"Lydia," Uncle David greeted her, straightening up.

"Did you come all the way to Rose Hill for this?" She sniffed.

"Wouldn't miss this for the world." He winked at me.

I didn't know what that meant, but Mom yanked me closer to her.

The lawyer walked into the room and paused beside Mom. "Good to see you again, Lydia. I wish it was on better terms."

She nodded.

"My son is transferring to Emery-Rose next year." He looked down at me, then got on my level. "Would you do me a favor, Caleb? Keep an eye out for Eli Black. I'm sure he'll be needing a friend when he goes to a new school."

I nodded.

"Caleb might not be at Emery-Rose next year," Lydia informed him.

Mr. Black shrugged. "Perhaps not. I guess we'll see."

He crossed to the table and opened his briefcase. There were chairs around the room, but no one was sitting. Relatives I didn't know very well were scattered around, plus Uncle David and Aunt Iris. Mom at my back.

"No matter what happens," Uncle David whispered to Mom, "you have a place with us."

She stiffened. "What is that supposed to mean?"

"Careful, dear," Aunt Iris cooed. "The wolves may come out of the woodwork if you show... weakness."

Mom glared at her. "How dare—"

Mr. Black started talking, silencing the room. It appeared that no one wanted to miss a word of this. "'I, Benjamin Asher, am of sound body and mind...'"

I zoned out. It sounded like gibberish, and my attention was on the window. On the way the light reflected through the prism hanging from the window lock, casting a pale rainbow on the floor.

"'To Lydia Asher,'" Mr. Black read, "'I leave only the dust beneath my shoes. You...'" He cleared his throat. "'You deserve nothing, not even our son.'"

Gasps filled the room.

I looked up at Mom, whose face was... horrified.

"No," she whispered. "That bastard."

"Mom?"

"It'll be okay, honey," she said.

Mr. Black coughed behind his fist. "'To my son, Caleb Asher, I leave in a trust my shares of Prinze Industries, all monies and investments, and physical properties, to be matured when he turns eighteen years old.'"

My mouth dropped open. "What does that mean?"

"He left you... everything," one of the relatives said.

"'And finally, to my brother, David Asher, I leave the stewardship of Caleb's inheritance and the board position, to guide and protect until it is transferred to Caleb's name. This includes potential guardianship of Caleb himself, should David and family remain fit per state standards."

Uncle David turned to Mom and me. "Well, that was... worth the trip, dare I say?"

Mom pushed me behind her. "You had a hand in this," she snarled. "All because—"

"You got into bed with the wrong person," he finished. His attention moved to me. "I'll be seeing you soon, I suspect."

I glared at him, and it just made him laugh.

It was the last thing I heard out of Uncle David's mouth as he walked away.

"Josh," Mom said, shoving through relatives until we were up to the desk. "He can't be serious. When were these changes made?"

Mr. Black shuffled some papers. "July 5, 2008."

She gasped. "He knew."

"About your affair? I suppose he did." He produced a sealed envelope and passed it to her. "He left this for you. And one for you, Caleb."

I took the envelope he handed me carefully. "Can I read it?"

"Whenever you want." Mr. Black raised his head. "Give us the room, please."

People grumbled behind me, but I paid them no mind. Dad had always taught me that lesser people will always make more noise—it's action that mattered.

I took a step away from Mom, who was... well, I wasn't sure if she was *crying*, exactly, but she was definitely in shock.

I half listened to their conversation. "David and Iris aren't fit parents," she said. "But his will made it sound like Caleb..."

"He can't take away your parental rights," Mr. Black said.

"But I have nothing, is that right? Just a savings account in my name that I can..."

I pulled out the letter and unfolded it.

Dear son,

I am writing this in the event of my death. You could be reading this when you're twelve or twenty-two, I don't know. And for that, I apologize in advance. Things between your mother and I are getting more tense, and I'm not sure to what ends she would go.

Be strong. Everything is left to you. If you're not yet eighteen, your Uncle David will take care of everything, including you. He's a good man with a short temper—kind of like your old man—but I trust him to do right by you.

You're holding up the Asher name on your shoulders, and that is no easy task. Your fate in life is uncertain. To sell the shares, move away, become your own person with a healthy bank account? Continue as I was?

Make us proud, son.

With love,

Dad

My memory of him did have dark spots—when his anger boiled over. But overall, he was good. He taught me important lessons without being too harsh, took me to the park when work allowed. He worked for the family.

His whole life was dedicated to building up our name.

And one night ruined it. Dragged it through the mud.

I ran my finger across his signature, folded the letter, and shoved it in my pocket.

When I turned around, Mom was still clutching her unopened one, arguing with the lawyer.

"We're going back to the house," she informed him. "It's Caleb's."

"It's David's to control," he corrected, shrugging. "I can't stop you either way."

She came to me, holding out her hand.

I took it.

"Goodbye, Josh," she said. "Let's hope we never have to do this again."

He just watched us. And when I craned around one last time, he winked.

Present

I relay the story as best I can. I don't tell them the contents of the letter—I did have the thing memorized for a while, when I would read it under my sheets with a flashlight—but the gist of everything.

"Your mom was having an affair?" Margo asked. "With who?"

I shake my head. "It didn't occur to me to question her."

Eli groans. "And your dad wrote you a tragic fucking letter. Of course."

"It was comforting at the time."

We lapse into silence.

Then Margo says, "Norah did say Josh being Dad's lawyer was a conflict of interest. But she had said him and your dad weren't on good terms. Why did he use Josh for his will?"

Eli leans toward her. "She talked about that?"

"I asked," she says, sheepish.

"She's never bothered to answer any of my questions about it. I transferred to Emery-Rose soon after you had left, and Caleb sought me out—evidently because of Dad," he adds with a smile. "But they both clammed up whenever I asked about..."

"Our dads were friends," Margo says.

Surprise ripples around the room. Through me. I had never got that impression from our fathers' interactions.

"Norah said it was the three of them, and mine left... came back with Mom, engaged or whatever. And they had a falling-out."

"That isn't what we should be focusing on," Theo interjects. "Unless Tobias is the one she was having an affair with..."

I snort. "Seriously?"

"How else would you get someone to risk their entire career?"

"Money," Liam says. "So much fucking money. Enough money to swim in. Not that you idiots would understand, since you already have that. But for someone like Tobias? Who started at the bottom? Yeah."

"So, Caleb's dad suspected his own death because Lydia was having an affair? That doesn't make sense." Eli scowls. "Jesus. This is making my head spin."

"Who would've known? Besides the parties involved who might lie?" Margo asks.

"Well, there was your parents and mine," I list, "and whoever Mom was sleeping with. I guess your dad would be the most impartial."

"Besides the whole murder thing," Eli says.

"He didn't do it." Margo glares at him. "And you know what? For the first time in this crazy mess—I actually believe it. Your mom had more motive than he did. Did the police even look into her?"

"I don't know."

She groans, but she leans into me. I hold her close. My chest fills with something light, because we're actually doing this together. A place I didn't think either of us would get to.

"You should talk to him," Eli suggests.

She straightens. "The last time I talked to him, I—"

"We'll go with you. In two cars."

Her attention flips to my face. "What do you think?"

"I..." Fuck, I don't know. Am I ready to see her dad again? To get answers? To judge for myself if he's lying or not? "Yeah, we should."

Liam pulls out his phone. "Visiting hours tomorrow are in the afternoon."

I run my hand over my face. "I've skipped so much damn school. What's another day?"

"I'll be at the school in the morning," Margo says quietly. "To determine when I'm coming back."

"We only have two weeks left until Christmas break," Liam points out. "They should just let you work from home."

"That's a rich kid treatment," she mumbles.

"If that's the sorry excuse they give you, they'll have to deal with Lenora. And then me." I crack a smile. "She's fierce when she needs to be."

Margo laughs.

It brings the whole mood up a few degrees.

"Food's here!" Mrs. Black calls from the top of the stairs. "How much did you guys order? My God."

"We're growing boys, Mom," Eli hollers back. We all stand. To us, he says, "At least we figured some things out, yeah? A game plan."

"Visit Margo's dad," I repeat. "That's... not much of a plan."

Not to mention, the idea of seeing him again—even if he's innocent—makes me feel week inside. After all those years of conditioning by Uncle David, it's hard to shake the disgust. And the blame. But now, along with it, comes guilt.

"Worst comes to worst, you know where to find your mom." Liam shrugs. "And apparently, she's with Margo's mom. Isn't that a bit fishy? Shouldn't those two hate each other?"

"Mom looked semi-decent," Margo says. "Which... was surprising. Like she wasn't using anymore, you know? I haven't seen her clean..."

"She might be clean, but... let's not count on that, okay?" I lead them upstairs.

I think back to meeting my mother outside the diner only a few weeks ago. I asked her where Amber was, and I'm pretty sure she lied right to my face.

Shame, Rose Hill isn't good for that woman.

I curse to myself. We weren't *in* Rose Hill. Lucky's Diner sat proudly just over the town line, in Beacon, which made Mom's answer not *quite* a lie. She knew. Margo's mom was probably inside the diner as we spoke, making me the biggest fool on the face of the planet.

"I'm curious if you saw your life going in this direction from the beginning," I said. "I'm mostly curious about why you let your brother-in-law run the show?"

"Your father wants it that way."

Wants, like he was still around.

But then again, his memory was a pungent one, and the will left no wiggle room.

Could my mother have had something to do with it? She seemed more surprised than anything that the will had been changed. But if it was something that was done because she cheated on him, he wouldn't tell her.

Money is a good motive, Liam said it himself.

Norah is opening containers across the kitchen island when we get up there. The guys move around me, grabbing silverware and plates.

Margo looks up at me, touching my cheek. "You okay?"

"I just realized..." I glance over at Eli's mom. "Mrs. Black, did you know my mother before she married Dad?"

She frowns. "That's an out-of-the-blue question, Caleb."

I wait.

"We both went to Emery-Rose, although she was a year older. I didn't really interact with her until we both started dating the boys." Her gaze slides away. "It's disgraceful how far she's fallen."

Margo flinches.

"They had a falling-out, right? Mr. Black and my dad." I don't wait for her response. "Yet he was the one who read the will."

She nods slowly. "He did. It was Josh's firm that held Ben's will, and neither of them saw the sense in changing it once things got... complicated."

"Complicated is an understatement," Eli whispers.

"So for a while, you were friends. Or friendly."

"Somewhat. She was a hard person to get to know. And then—" She stops abruptly. "Excuse me, I think I hear my phone."

She leaves, and the five of us are left in silence.

"Why do I get the feeling she's hiding something?" Margo finally asks.

Eli shakes his head. "Hopefully your dad will be able to fill in some cracks."

She swallows, then nods firmly. Mind made up, determination coloring her expression. I want to cheer, *that's my girl*. The little lamb seems so far removed, now. Even scared, even traumatized, she's keeping her head up.

"Right. Tomorrow." She looks at me.

My stomach twists, and I nod along slowly.

Visiting my father's murderer.

Alleged murderer?

Time will tell if I can keep my temper—and tongue—in check.

Chapter 27
Margo

Lenora and Robert pick me up shortly after Josh and Norah leave for work.

I slide into the backseat and pull off my hat, grimacing. "When did it get to be winter?"

Overnight, we got at least six inches of snow. While there's been a few snow showers, this just feels excessive. I look at the seat beside me and smile. There's a pair of fur-lined boots with a little Christmas bow on it.

"An early present," Lenora says, winking at me in the rearview mirror. "Don't worry, it's fake fur."

"Thank you so much." I tug off my shoes and slip on the new boots. They're a warm, perfect fit, and I sigh.

"Someone's happy." Robert frowns. "How many winters have you gone through without properly insulated boots?"

The ones I always wear are more hiking-slash-everyday boots, leather, and definitely not *warm*. "Um... A girl I was living with had grown out of hers and gave them to me. I was twelve? They were a bit big, so they lasted two seasons." I smile to myself. "I gave them away when I outgrew them."

They're quiet. Contemplating how different our lives must've been, I'm sure.

"How are you feeling?" Lenora asks.

"Better."

Except my wrists. I woke up this morning dripping blood down my hands. It seems like once I opened up a little wound, I now constantly pick at it. I covered the damage with a bandage and a long-sleeved shirt, but I doubt I'll be able to hide it for long.

"My head doesn't even hurt much anymore."

Robert makes a face. "I wish I could say the same."

I lean forward. "Are you sure you're up for visiting the school?"

"I'm ready to see some familiar faces," he says, glancing back at me. "And besides, I'm not sure what sort of antics they'll try."

"We have a teacher and a corporate mediator," I joke. "Hopefully things will fall on our side. But... what kind of antics?"

"Just that you're not fit to come back to school. They'll probably try to push time off—but that will just hurt you in the long run," Lenora says. "Your case worker agreed that it was up to our discretion. Unless you don't want—"

"I'd like to return to normal. Sitting around, moping and dealing with..." *Trauma,* I don't say. I clear my throat. "Normalcy is what I need."

Robert nods. "Exactly."

We get to the school and walk across the deserted parking lot, up the steps into the school. The secretary gets a little teary when she sees us—more Robert than me, I'll admit—and circles her desk to give him a hug.

And then we're shuffled into the principal's office.

She's a stern lady. Luckily, I haven't had too much interaction with her or the guidance counselor since the beginning of the year, and I *had* planned on keeping it that way. She analyzes me over the top of her reading glasses, which are perched on the end of her nose.

Lenora explains what's been going on at home. Between the craziness, I've managed to catch up on most of the work my classes covered. That appears to be the clincher, and the principal agrees I can come back tomorrow.

The principal sends me out, and I go stand in the hallway.

And... the bell rings.

Figures.

This part of the school isn't too busy unless students are coming to the office, so I don't worry too much about being seen. That is, until Savannah appears. I suppress my sigh.

She hurries in my direction, clearly distracted, and stops dead when she spots me. "You're back?"

"It would appear so."

"Rumor had it that you croaked." She plants her hands on her hips.

"I guess they got that one wrong." I force a laugh.

"Hmm." She looks me up and down. "You might consider bangs."

My eyebrow jumps, and my face flushes. "Why, to cover the barely visible scar? I'm not that petty."

She smiles. "It might help avoid the staring, you know?"

I lean against the wall, crossing one ankle over the other. "I've been meaning to ask, how's life at the top of the pyramid? Still holding Amelie's spot until she gets back?"

Because Amelie is back in France, and Sav is the queen regent. Only holding power until her best friend returns.

She grits her teeth. "I'm not a placeholder. *Freak.*"

She rushes around me, hurrying down the hall.

The office door opening catches my attention. Lenora and Robert walk out, saying their goodbyes.

Lenora grins at me. "Ready?"

"Absolutely."

We head out. I almost expect something to have happened to the car while we were inside—someone keying it or popping the tires—but it seems the same.

I wonder when I should tell them about going to see my dad. If I should even mention it.

We make it all the way back home before Lenora smacks her forehead. "Should I have taken you to the Blacks' house? Would you prefer to be there?"

"No," I say, hopping out. "They're at work." And Caleb is in school.

She nods. "Okay, great. I do have to head into the office for a little while today, otherwise I think I'll be without a job myself. But you two can finally have your movie marathon day."

"We stocked up on popcorn," Robert tells me. "And a cleaning company is coming over this afternoon to take care of your room."

I nod, swallowing. I just won't think about the room or what's written up there. I'm still trying to figure out where I've heard *pretty bird* before...

We go inside. I realize halfway through to the kitchen that I've been holding my breath. I let it out in one shallow exhale, reminding myself to breathe.

Robert is a bit slower on his feet, but we busy ourselves making popcorn and hot chocolate. A weird combination, but he insists that we can have both. And then we each take our separate corners on the couch, blankets on our laps, and settle in for a weird, happy day of movies.

Chapter 28
Caleb

My day starts with a phone call from my mother. The harsh buzzing managed to wake up only me, not the octopus wrapped around me. I hit the button to silence it, then managed to dislodge Margo's arms and untangle her legs from mine.

"Hang on," I say into the phone. I put it on mute while I yank on my jeans. I trot upstairs as quietly as possible, then unmute her. "Good morning, Mother."

"Caleb." She sniffs. "Something bad has happened."

I rub my eyes. "What happened?"

"M-my apartment was broken into."

"Really." I didn't even know she had an apartment. I mean, I should've realized. It's one of those things you don't think about until you have to think about it. Obviously she was staying *somewhere*. I just never spared a thought for whether it was an apartment, a house, a hole in the wall...

"Can you come help me? You're all I have—"

"What about Uncle David?" I can't help but ask. She's leaned on them pretty heavily over the years. I pull the phone away from my ear, checking the time. Not even five o'clock in the morning. The first floor of the house is completely silent.

I cross to the living room window, peering out. The sun is barely starting to rise.

There's a car parked across the street, its headlights glowing, and it drives away fairly quickly. Weird. At least this one didn't go screeching off into the night like the other night...

"Are you listening to me?" Mom asks.

"No."

"I said, I need you to help. I don't have anywhere to go. David is being horribly moody, what with his *house guests*, and I simply cannot fathom who else to ask."

I tilt my head. "Wait, back up. House guests? Who?"

"Oh, never mind that. You know Aunt Iris is always trying to save people." She scoffs. "It'd serve her better at the gates of Heaven if she served her own family—"

"*Mother*," I snap. "Seriously?"

"Everything is gone," she moans. "My jewelry, the money..."

"What, were you stockpiling cash or something?"

She's quiet, and I feel my eyebrows lift almost of their own accord.

"You can't be serious."

"What? You can't expect me to live like this forever. Like—"

Like someone who works. Who earns their paycheck instead of just sitting behind a desk and letting the money pile into their bank account.

With sudden clarity, I realize that I don't want to follow in my father's footsteps. I don't want to sit behind a desk and order people around, or push paper, or—

"You've tuned out your poor mother again."

I shake my head. "Listen, Mom. I'm seventeen. I can't drive because of the concussion Uncle David gave me a week and a half ago. I don't really know what you expect me to do before I have to be at school."

"Forget it."

Gladly.

"If you find my body tucked behind a dumpster, or beaten to death, or dismembered, or—"

"Why the hell are you talking like someone is going to murder you?"

"Because," she whispers, "someone is *after our family*, Caleb. Someone will always try to take what we have. And, oh, I'm afraid we've made some terrible mistakes in our lives."

My stomach twists.

"Mom...?"

"Margo found out about Amber, Caleb. She came into the diner, and I tried to get Amber to leave, but she knew it was Margo out there. She—" She sucks in a ragged breath. "God, what am I doing?"

"Calm down," I order. "Do you live with Amber?"

"Yes, she came into town looking for a fix, and I couldn't let that happen. It's my fault she's in this mess—my fault. I just wanted to get her clean." Her voice cracks, and then her sobbing fills my ear.

I hate it.

Hate her.

And yet, I pity her.

"Mom... just breathe. What do you mean, it's your fault?"

"She never should've got involved with my husband," she says in a low voice, suddenly crystal clear.

"You're obviously not in the right state, yourself," I snap. "Stay put, okay? I'll come get you."

She tells me where she is, and I hang up.

Fuck.

No wonder she wouldn't tell me where Amber was when I asked. For a while, I was no better than her supplier. Giving her money was the easiest way to get her out of town. If I didn't, she'd wash up closer to Rose Hill, each and every time. And eventually, closer to Margo.

I only found out Amber knew where her daughter was when we were fourteen. Margo refused to give her anything —the brave, beautiful girl managed to stand up to her own mother. That was when I decided I had to be easy on her.

Move Margo one last time and make sure Amber wouldn't be able to find her. Give her enough to send her away—either out of town or on a nice, happy overdose.

Of course Mom has her.

Cleaned her up.

There's some sort of leverage there, I just can't see it yet.

I groan. I need a clean shirt, to brush my teeth, shoes. And to wake Eli up.

I wake him up first, calling him from where I stand.

"You know it's not time for school, dickhead."

"We have to run an errand," I inform him. "Be ready to leave in fifteen."

"Fuck."

I hang up on him and go back downstairs. Margo has curled into a ball in the middle of my bed. I crawl across it and hover over her, leaning down to nuzzle her neck.

She makes the sweetest noise, reaching up and sliding her hand into my hair.

I don't usually tell her, but I love when her nails scratch

my scalp. I press a kiss to her neck, moving up to her jaw, then just under her ear.

She turns her face, catching my lips with hers, and smiles. "That's one way to say good morning," she whispers. Her hand leaves my hair, trailing down... "Caleb, why are you already wearing jeans?"

I steal another kiss. "Because I have to go."

"How much longer do I have?" she whispers.

"To sleep?" I glance at the clock. "Another few hours. Two."

"Good," she murmurs, rolling over and giving me her back.

I shake my head, grinning, and sweep the hair off her neck. I nip the shell of her ear, then whisper, "Dream of me."

It's hard to leave her, but I do it. She's breathing heavily by the time I grab my boots and jacket and climb the stairs.

I have to work hard to ignore the ball in the pit of my stomach.

"Where are we going?" Eli asks.

He's got a black beanie over his blond hair, black jacket, black jeans. He could be ready to rob a bank or pose for a freaking fashion magazine, and that irritates me.

"Mommy dearest called." I open the door. "Said some nonsense about her apartment being broken into and losing everything."

"So we're running to her rescue?"

"She also said she's been living with Margo's mom, getting her clean."

Eli's eyes widen. "Ah."

"*And*, apparently it's her fault Amber got addicted in the first place? I'm eager to hear that story."

We climb into his car.

"Where's she staying? Maybe we can be back before my parents notice we're gone."

"Beacon," I say, giving him the address.

He groans. "Or not."

"I'll buy breakfast."

He perks up. "Sold!"

It takes us about thirty minutes to get there. Mom is standing out on the sidewalk when we pull up, and she tears the sunglasses off her face.

"Sunglasses at six o'clock in the morning?" Eli asks.

I just shake my head, hopping out. She launches herself at me, wrapping her arms around my shoulders.

"Thank you, thank you," she cries.

I take a deep breath... of whiskey.

I draw back sharply, holding her by her shoulders. It's no wonder she was wearing sunglasses. Her eyes are red and puffy—from crying or a hangover, I can't be sure which is the dominant cause—and her skin is dull.

"Mom?"

"What?" She wrinkles her nose. "Why are you looking at me like that?"

"Because... are you drunk?"

She lets out a shrill laugh. "Goodness, no. Hungover, maybe."

"Mrs. Asher," Eli greets her. "How are you?"

Mom releases me and stumbles toward him. She pats his cheek. "You must be Josh's son. You look quite a bit like him, I must say."

"Right, er, thanks. Can we... help you?"

She straightens. "Yes! My home was broken into. This way."

We follow her down the street, into an alley. Eli and I

exchange a glance before stepping into it. Something about this screams... *fishy.*

She unlocks a metal grated door, then another one inset in the brick building. She's surprisingly agile on the stairs, around the landing, and up another flight. Then she stops dead in her tracks.

"In there," she says.

I glance between the door and her. "This is where you've been living? This whole time?"

"Goodness, no. Just temporary."

"Is Margo's mother in there?" Eli asks.

"No!" Mom shouts. "She's at Lucky's already."

I push open the door. There's broken glass across the floor, a shattered vase, flowers, and water. Picture frames that've been knocked off the wall, overturned furniture.

"Where were you both when this happened?" Eli asks, picking his way through the small room.

It seems strange that they might've been in here when it happened—unless whoever did it...

I turn toward Mom and grab her wrist.

She cries out.

"You were here." I stare down at the bruises on her arm. "You know who did this."

"I do," she moans. "But I didn't think he would go crazy like this. H-he took Amber."

Eli's head jerks up. "I'm sorry, you're just telling us that your, I don't know, *roommate* was abducted?"

Mom is full-on crying now. She falls to the floor, starting to gather larger pieces of glass in her hand. To herself, she mumbles, "This isn't safe. You might cut yourself."

"Dude," Eli says, pulling me away from her. "She..."

"Yeah. Hey, Mom? Any reason you called me instead of the police?"

She lurches toward me, but this time Eli intercepts. He shoves her against the apartment wall, holding her there with one hand on her collarbone. She stares at him with wide eyes.

"Cut the shit," he tells her.

And... she does. The stupid, sad expression slips off her face, replaced only by the mother I used to know. She tugs at her sleeves, putting them back in place, and glances up at me.

"Honestly, Caleb. This is a family matter."

"Amber Wolfe isn't part of the family, Mom."

Her attention goes to my wrist. The damn bracelet that is—and has always been—a symbol of how much I care for Margo.

Her gaze flicks back to my face. "Dare I say she will be?"

"We're out of here," Eli snaps. "Jesus, you people are fucking mental."

He pushes on her chest and points in her face. "Stay."

She laughs. "Am I a dog?"

"May as well be—"

"Okay," I say. "Let's go."

She follows us downstairs, back into the alley. My skin crawls at the filth she's been living in, and I pick up speed. I only take a deep breath once we're back on the sidewalk.

"Caleb—"

"Stop." I pause. My headache has come back full force, pounding behind my eyes. I blink a few times, trying to just see clearly enough to focus on her. "This is fucked up. You should call the police to help you."

She lifts her chin. "Right."

I shake my head. "Yeah, right. Okay. Bye, Mother."

Eli's already in the truck by the time I get there. Warm

air blasts out of the vents, which just goes to show how long we were inside—the truck hadn't even had time to get cold.

"That's messed up," Eli says. He catches me rubbing my eyes again. "Concussion headache?"

He would know. Last year, he and another hockey player collided wrong. Knocked him out cold, which was an automatic ambulance ride. He was dizzy for a week.

"Yeah, or a tension one." I force a laugh, dropping my hands into my lap. "School is going to be fun."

"We're leaving early, right? I love skipping last period. It's just a freaking study hall."

"I miss driving my own car," I grumble. "But, yes. We're going to see Margo's dad."

Eli hums. "Bet he'll be interested to know that someone took his wife."

"Ex-wife?" I glance at him. "They got divorced, I think."

"Oh. You don't seem overly concerned that she's gone."

"I'm not." I sigh. "I should've blamed her from the beginning. You know, because it's really her fault that everything happened. Instead, my uncle twisted my view on the subject."

His *lessons* involved making me hate my best friend.

We get home in time for me to slip back downstairs and steal another kiss from Margo, make sure she's awake, and then head to school. My stomach churns the entire day. Eli must say something to Liam and Theo, because they don't ask. If anything, they double their efforts to keep people away from me.

Savannah comes up to me at lunch. Well, she tries to.

"Your girlfriend is fucking crazy," she spits.

Theo chuckles, and she takes a step back. She's a dog with a lot of bark but no bite.

Easy to rule her out as Unknown.

That, and she's not Theo's biggest fan. Never has been, probably never will be. Thanks to Amelie's sister...

Still, I perk up. "What did she do?"

"She *threatened* me!" She tries to push past Eli, but he won't budge. "What? I can't have a conversation with him?"

"You're an evil bitch," Eli retorts. "So... no."

"Wonder how fast Amelie would come back if we called her up and told her the whole school had forgotten about her little... incident?" Theo asks. "We could call her and find out—"

"Ugh!" Savannah shrieks.

I smile, and she storms away.

"Two peas in a freaking nuthouse," Theo says, shaking his head. "Not sure which is worse—Amelie or Savannah."

"Where did Amelie go, by the way?" Liam nudges Theo and grins.

Theo just glowers at him. "Away, I've heard."

"The pretty little princess couldn't handle the rumors." Eli laughs. He grabs his lunch tray. "She's finishing the semester in France."

I squint down at the table. The headache hasn't gone away, and the fluorescent lights aren't helping.

"Amelie knew where Amber was," I muse. "How?"

Eli shakes his head. "You're just thinking about this now?"

"Been a bit preoccupied, if you haven't noticed." I cover my eyes with my hand.

"What's Amelie's relationship with Amber? Or, better yet, your mother?" Liam asks.

I shrug. "No clue."

"She was fucking Ian," Theo says suddenly.

I drop my hand and narrow my eyes. "Thanks for the reminder."

"I'm just saying, Ian's mom and your aunt are cousins. There's your connection. We all know those old bats gossip more than schoolgirls." Theo looks around, eyeing the cheerleader table. "Honestly, it's not such a stretch to think Amelie overheard something she shouldn't have."

"So, what, Amelie and Matt?" I groan. "Impossible. She was already... wherever she went. France or something."

"Yeah, but she might've been tempted to do whatever it took to get you back," Liam points out. "Psycho, remember?"

Fair point.

"The car that struck Margo and Robert, driven by someone we don't know, which belonged to Tobias, was either stolen or loaned out. Tobias and Lydia have history." Eli exhales. "Lydia also has history with a lot of Emery-Rose students because she was, for a little while, very involved in Caleb's life."

"We've been over this eight thousand times," Liam grumbles.

"But we're nowhere closer to solving this puzzle, now are we?"

"What are they hiding?" I ask. "Mom's apartment was broken into, and she now claims Amber was taken. But she refused to call the police. Why?"

"Because..." Liam shrugs.

Eli and Theo both shake their heads.

Because, because...

"Because Margo saw Amber at the diner. What if that's related to everything?" I stand. "Whoever took Amber very well might be targeting Margo, too. They just couldn't get to her because she's been with someone this whole time."

They stand, too, quickly grabbing their things.

"We'll cover for you," Theo says. "Take my car."

Eli catches the keys he tosses, and then we're gone. Through the athletic hallway, into the locker room. Someone has already propped open the emergency exit with a pencil, barely keeping it from closing, and we slip through it.

"You don't think Margo's in danger, do you?"

"She's at home, and normally I'd say there would be no way, but..."

Eli nods. "Happy to assist, man. Let's just get out as quietly as possible."

It has been rather quiet, now that he mentions it.

And that's never a good thing.

Chapter 29
Margo

Caleb glances at me. He ended up skipping school and coming to get me in Theo's car. He said something about getting that chat over with, and my stomach swooped. I knew exactly what he meant.

So here we sit in the prison's visitor parking lot, staring at the entrance.

It's just as nerve-racking the second time.

"Do you think they told him what happened?" I ask.

He lifts one shoulder. "I don't know."

"He hasn't called or anything."

"I don't—"

"Know, yeah. Got it."

He reaches over and laces his fingers with mine. "Nervous?"

"How'd you guess?"

"Because you're not really breathing. And you're snapping." He smiles reassuringly, but it doesn't do much to calm the buzzing in my veins.

I force myself to take a deep breath. "Right. Okay, let's go."

We walk into the prison shoulder to shoulder, and he visibly shudders once we pass through the gates. I take his hand and squeeze. It's hard to believe Detective Masters wanted Caleb to end up somewhere like this.

The paperwork with the guard is faster this time, and after we hand over our IDs, we go to a corner of the room and sit.

"You're not going to interrogate him, right?" My leg bounces.

"Interrogate him? No. I have some questions—"

"Some *nice* questions, since he doesn't have to tell us anything—"

"Relax," he says, putting his hand on my knee.

I stop jigging.

"I'll be on my best behavior," he promises. "We just need to find out about Tobias..."

"Imagine telling him his lawyer was a filthy rotten—"

A buzzing sound cuts me off. *Here we go*, I tell myself.

We stand with the few other people in the waiting room. Mid-week, it isn't busy. The woman I met at the first visit isn't here. Not that I expected her to be, but it would've been nice to see a friendly face.

Caleb walks a step behind me, letting me lead. Down the hall, to the door a guard is holding open. We pick a bigger table in the back corner, as far from the others as we can manage.

This time, we don't have to wait long for another buzz, and then, "Inmates entering."

Dad appears in the doorway. His head swings around until he finds us, and then he frowns.

For an instant, I wonder if he'll turn around and go back to his cell without seeing us. Without talking to me.

But that fear dissipates when he moves toward us.

I rise, stepping past Caleb, and throw my arms around my dad. Dad's arms come around me tightly, crushing me into him. One hand cups the back of my head, and I'm ashamed that the action reminds me of Robert.

"My girl," he whispers in my ear. "I'm so glad you're okay. God, I've never felt so helpless in my life."

So they did tell him.

We separate, and Dad regards Caleb.

Dad extends his hand, an odd look on his face.

And Caleb... he's white as a ghost.

I squint at him, but he seems like he's in a trance. Finally, he blinks and reaches out, clasping Dad's hand. The two stare at each other for a moment, the handshake suspended between them.

Maybe this is how Dad would've reacted to all of my boyfriends, if we had managed to stay a family long enough for me to get there. Maybe I never would've had a boyfriend —just Caleb.

That thought warms my cheeks, and I quickly push it away. No use pondering what might've been.

"You taking care of my daughter, Caleb?"

Caleb winces. "I'm trying to now, Mr. Wolfe."

Dad releases his hand and barks out a laugh. "'Mr. Wolfe?'" he repeats. "Jesus. You never called me that."

"Well, we never figured on being here, so..."

Okay, this is awkward. I motion to the table. "Can we sit?"

Around us, everyone else has settled down. We're the only ones still standing, and the guards are eyeing us.

Dad dips his chin. Once we've settled around the table, he leans in. "Margo, a detective came to see me after you left. Said—"

I take a deep breath. "We have some... explaining to do. In that regard."

He motions for me to continue, and I tell him what happened. The quick version anyway: car accident, abduction, Caleb finding me and taking me to the hospital, his interrogation.

Dad is gripping the edge of the table by the end of it. His gaze goes to the scar on my forehead. "Is that...?"

"Glass from the accident, I think," I say. "And I still get headaches from the concussion..."

Caleb grunts. "Same."

Dad raises his eyebrows.

"Caleb's uncle hit him in the back of the head for standing up to him," I tell him. "I found him in a room... which actually brings us to our visit. We've been uncovering some strange things."

He rubs at his face. He's sporting a bit more scruff than I remember, and while the hair on top of his head is still dark, the beard is peppered with gray. "Say what you will about your father, he never fucking hit a child."

I press my lips together.

"They don't have any leads?" he asks through his hands.

"*They* don't," Caleb answers.

Dad drops his arms and glares at him. "What the fuck does that mean?" His gaze goes to me. "Tell me you haven't been pulling any cowboy shit."

I shift. "Well..."

"We have." Caleb pats my leg under the table. "And we found something which led us here."

Dad's eyebrow goes up. "I'm almost tempted to walk away, just because you put my daughter in danger—"

"Caleb saved me, Dad." I reach out, taking his hand. "He found me."

Dad touches the bracelet on my wrist. "I didn't recognize this the last time you were here, but this is the one you made, isn't it? One for each..."

Caleb shows him the bracelet on his own wrist.

"Inevitable," Dad murmurs.

"You think so?" Caleb slides his sleeve back down.

I check Caleb's expression. He's thoughtful, and not... not as judgmental as I would've expected.

"What happened between you and my dad?" he asks.

And there goes that 'not as judgmental' thought.

"Norah told us that you used to be friends," I blurt out.

Dad's eyes widen, then he chuckles. "So, you've been playing detective?"

I shrug. "Had to figure out the truth somehow."

"Okay, Margo," he says. "Ben, Josh Black, Phil Mardzen, and I were best friends in high school."

"Wait," Caleb interrupts. "You were best friends with *Coach Mardzen?*"

Dad smiles. "Is he coaching now?"

Caleb crosses his arms over his chest.

After a second, Dad shakes his head. "I moved away to go to college in Massachusetts, which is where I met your mother. When we moved back to Rose Hill, I was... significantly different. Unfortunately, I wasn't the only one. Ben and Josh had split from Phil just after graduation. He wasn't even in Rose Hill when I moved back. Ben and Lydia were dating, and things were pretty serious. Norah and Josh had gotten together, too. Everyone was shocked when I brought Amber home, newly engaged."

I tilt my head to the side. "What about you being disowned?"

A laugh bursts out of Dad's mouth. "Yes, that's true. My mother was not happy with my pick of a wife." He sobers quickly. "She died a few months after our wedding. I only found out about it after I was put in here."

I sober, too. "I would've liked to have met her."

He smiles sadly. "The last letter I sent her that she would've received was the one in which I told her Amber was pregnant with you. I sent more after that, pictures and stories, but... The letters were never returned to me, so I assumed she read them."

"How was my parents' relationship?" Caleb asks.

Dad levels him with a look. "The adult perspective?"

"They argued a lot," Caleb says, attention fastened to the table, "late at night, when they thought I couldn't hear them."

"They had some trouble," Dad allowed. "Obviously, Margo's mother didn't help the situation any."

"You say it with such ease," Caleb says, finally raising his head. He leans forward. "You say that your wife was cheating on you like it doesn't even bother you, when in reality, you're in here for *murder*."

"Let it out, son." Dad motions for Caleb to give him more.

"How do you live with it? I found Dad in his room—" Caleb sucks in a ragged breath. "When I look at you, all I can see is my father's blood."

My heart hurts for Caleb. That he was the one to find his father dead. That he's had to live with it all this time, *alone*. His family warped his perception. My dad was the closest thing to a saving grace for us when we lived on Caleb's family property. And his uncle and mother made sure those memories were forever tainted.

"We were friends," Dad continues. "I never laid a hand on him, and I certainly didn't kill him."

It's about as serious of an admission as... well, as admitting to murder. He's already in prison. He doesn't have anything to lose.

Caleb stares at the ceiling, blinking rapidly.

I hate that he's so bothered by this.

"Dad, when did you first meet Tobias?"

"After I was arrested. Amber had just..." He shakes his head.

"Mom had just *what*?"

"We received a suspiciously large deposit in our shared bank account, so the police froze it. I had nothing after I was arrested. I met Hutchins after they read me the charges and I asked for a lawyer."

"You hadn't seen him... at the house?"

Dad squints at me. "What are you saying?"

"We're definitely not accusing Lydia of paying him off, convincing you to get a shitty plea deal, *right*?" I lift my chin. "And we'd never insinuate that the person who hit me and Robert—and then abducted me—borrowed the vehicle from Tobias."

Dad closes his eyes. "You cannot talk about this."

"Why not?"

"Margo," he warns.

"Five minutes," the guard by the door calls.

Breath hisses past my teeth. "You can't tell us to drop this. I have a stalker, and every *fucking* piece of it is connected."

"The Ashers—" Dad stops and glances at Caleb.

Caleb's jaw muscle jumps, but he doesn't say anything.

"Ben lost his wife the minute he invited mine into his bedroom," Dad murmurs. "And everything that resulted from it is on his shoulders."

Caleb locks up next to me. "Mom knew?"

Dad gives Caleb an odd look. "Have you forgotten? She knew… everything."

Well, then.

Chapter 30
Caleb

Past

Iwas supposed to be sleeping, but there was a weird noise coming from downstairs. It was like...

Laughter.

There was never laughter around here anymore, not unless it was coming from Margo.

I crept to the first floor, inching down the hallway. It was completely dark except for a light coming from the kitchen.

Giggling.

I twitched, but curiosity drove me all the way to the threshold.

Dad and Margo's mom were on either side of the counter. She was cutting strawberries. And Dad... he had his sleeves rolled up, stirring something in a bowl. There was white powder caught in his beard.

Mom appeared silently beside me, raising her finger to her lips. When she held out her hand to me, I took it.

She guided me down the hall, into the library.

"You should be in bed," she said, kneeling in front of me. "Why are you awake?"

"I heard..." I glanced toward the door.

She frowned. "Never you mind them."

"Why is he happy around her and not us?"

"Because she's something new." She rose to her feet. "And because she's not his. Not yet anyway."

Present

The memory of witnessing Amber and my father, then what my mother said about it, snaps to the forefront of my mind.

Not yet anyway. What did that mean?

"Caleb?" Margo touches my arm. "You okay?"

I wince. It's too bright in here, and my eyes sting.

"I do remember," I say to Margo's dad. It's hard to look at him, but I force myself to meet his gaze. "I had just... forgotten."

"You remember Lydia knowing?" Margo asks.

"I went downstairs because I heard a noise, and Mom pulled me away. She said he laughed around her because..." I pause. I'm an asshole, but not a big enough one to wave Keith's wife's infidelity in his face.

Keith clenches his jaw. "Go on and say it, son. You won't hurt my feelings."

I let out a sigh. "Because she was new and not his. Not yet."

He nods. "Your father always did like to have the best toys."

"She said that? Not yet?" Margo asks, latching on to the important part.

I knew she would. She's whip-smart when she wants to be.

"Right. Implying..."

"That Lydia knew exactly who her husband was," her dad finishes sourly. "Shocker. I knew the bastard, too."

"Dad!"

He presses his lips together. "I'm sorry. I know what you believe and how long you've believed it. But I did not kill your father."

He sounds sincere.

That's the most dangerous part. He could be telling the truth or he could just be a fantastic liar.

"If you didn't, who did?"

He drops his head into his hands. "I swore I wouldn't speak of this, *especially* not to—"

Margo leans forward and yanks his hands away, trying to get him to look at her. "Dad. Please."

"Okay." He lets out a ragged breath. "Caleb... your mother orchestrated the whole thing."

My stomach drops into my shoes. I misheard him, I think. The words jumble in my head, and I shake it to clear them out. What he's saying is ridiculous. She orchestrated the whole thing meaning what? Dad's death? Or... more?

I let out a laugh. "She's not capable of that."

"Time's up!" the guard yells.

Around us, people rise and say their goodbyes. Margo and her dad do, too. She hugs him while I sit there dumbly.

She knew.

She orchestrated the whole thing.

Not outside the realm of possibilities.

"Caleb," Keith says, his hand on my shoulder.

I rise automatically and flinch when he hugs me. When's the last time I was hugged by a man? Certainly not Uncle David.

My eyes burn.

"It's okay, son," he whispers. I'm barely taller than him. "And I'm so, so sorry."

He pulls away, cups my jaw like a father might, and then...

Well, he just walks away. Toward the guard, through the doorway.

I shake off the chills.

Margo takes my hand. "Well, now we both have allegedly murderous parents."

"That only counts if they commit two separate murders, I think."

My girl leads me out, to our locker to retrieve our things and then into the cold. I take a deep breath in, the sharpness of the air waking me up a bit. I needed this like a slap in the face.

Wake up.

"I never asked... how did he die?" Margo asks.

I blink. "What?"

She stamps her foot into the snow-dusted road, pausing by the back bumper of Theo's car. "I didn't even know he was dead. What was I supposed to ask Dad—'How did you kill him?' No thanks."

"I..." I shake off the memories. Battle them away. In as monotone a voice as possible, I say, "He was stabbed."

She reaches for me.

"I can't, Margo," I say quietly. I step away from her.

She sets her jaw and comes for me anyway.

I never thought I'd be the one running, but here I am. Backing away from her like she's fire and I'm ice.

My shoulder hits the car's side mirror, and she pushes me against the door.

"No running." Her eyes narrow.

I start to shake my head, but she presses her finger to my lips.

"You can't run from me—and you definitely can't run from whatever you're trying not to remember."

A snowflake lands on her head, and more follow. I follow them with my eyes, contemplating. Her finger is still on my lips.

I talk through it. "If my mom did it, then what does that mean? She helped put an innocent man in prison. Did Uncle David know? And does that explain the conversation I overheard between Tobias and her *before* my dad's death? If she was planning it, truly, then she looped in a lawyer. She found a fall guy. And everything I know is a fucking lie."

"Yeah." She drops her hand and blows out a breath. "But you know what that means? This is bigger than either of us."

My head is killing me. "We should get back."

Robert and Lenora weren't exactly approving of me whisking Margo off, but they softened when she said where we were going. And they don't know the half of it... but they're doing their best.

When I arrived to take Margo to the prison, a cleaning team was dealing with her room. She and Robert were both dozing on the couch in similar poses. It was kind of adorable. But now, all I can think about is getting her back safely. Protecting her.

With all the revelations about our family history, there's still someone stalking her.

She steps away from me. I immediately miss her body

heat. She must, too, because she comes rushing right back. Her arms wrap around my neck. She stands on her tiptoes to reach my lips, but her kiss is forceful. Aggressive and... short-lived.

She pulls away, and there's blood on her lips. "That's for trying to run."

She watches my mouth.

I lick my lips, surprised to taste it, too. The pain makes sense.

"You bit me," I marvel.

She just grins.

"Little wolf." I smile.

She just lifts one shoulder. Her smile falls pretty fast once we're in the car. She stares straight ahead, and I take a moment to realize...

"Oh fuck. Is it because it's snowing?"

She nods.

"We'll be okay," I promise her.

"You shouldn't even be driving." She closes her eyes. "God, they could've followed us here—"

"It's like lightning striking the same spot twice." I reach over and take her hand. "Improbable."

"You didn't say impossible," she whispers. She clutches my fingers like I'm a lifeline. "Okay, okay. Let's just go before it gets worse."

We're the last car out of the parking lot, and the road is deserted.

"I have excellent reflexes," I tell her.

Even so, I drive more carefully than I've ever driven in my life. I check each intersection three times, barely make the speed limit. The entire way, Margo just holds on to my hand. Her eyes are closed, and she's pale.

My tongue touches my lower lip again. I'm still shocked

that she bit me and I didn't even feel it until after. It might be bruised.

Bruised like my mind was after I relived walking in to find my dad's body. And here I go again, about to replay it in my mind for the thousandth time—although this time, maybe I'll remember something new.

Something to exonerate Margo's dad.

Past

Mom and I walked into a silent house.

She muttered something and dropped her purse on the side table, striding away from me.

Dad should've been home. There was always a hustle and bustle in our home—whether it be Amber in the kitchen or Dad in his study, on the phone, or playing music to cover up the sounds of Amber's...

We heard that exactly once before Mom put an end to it.

I checked the kitchen, but it was empty. Mom appeared in the doorway of Dad's study, shaking her head. So he wasn't in there either.

"Did he go out?" she asked herself. She met my gaze. "Honey, go upstairs."

"But Margo—"

"Keith's car is gone," she said. "And so is Amber's. I doubt she's home."

I nodded and went to the stairs. I should've gone to my room, but I didn't.

My parents' door was open, and a lamp was on.

A lamp in the middle of the day.

It drew my eye, and I went toward it like a moth drawn to a flame. Couldn't help it.

"Dad?" I called.

Nothing.

Up here, I couldn't even hear Mom moving around downstairs.

I steeled myself and pushed the door open.

It was stupid. He was going to be coming out of the bathroom or dozing in the chair they kept in the corner of the room for reading. A chair neither of them used for anything except not-clean-not-dirty clothes.

But my imagination told me that he'd be in that chair, and there he was.

Except his eyes were open, fixed on the ceiling, and...

"Dad?"

Silence.

So much silence, it reverberated in my ears.

I stared and stared, trying to make sense of what I was seeing.

He was covered in blood, but it wasn't bright red like in the movies. It didn't pump out of the hole in his neck or abdomen, between his fingers that were over his stomach.

It was dark. Still. Like it had flowed and then stopped when his heart finally gave up.

I couldn't blink. Couldn't move from the single step I had taken into the bedroom.

"Honey, did you find—" Mom grabbed me, pulling me backward. "Oh my God."

She covered my eyes, holding me to her chest.

My body was already wooden.

Dad was dead, or it was a trick. An awful trick.

I tried to get away from her, but I had lost my chance to

check him. To shout, *Joke's on you, Dad! I'm not falling for it.* She held me fast.

It was ketchup smeared across his face, that had run in rivers down the chair. It was soaked into the carpet, even, around his feet.

So much blood.

A whole body's worth, spilled out of him.

"Don't look," Mom whispered into the top of my head.

My eyes were burning, but I couldn't *not.*

"I'm sorry, Caleb."

A groan worked its way out of my chest. The first noise, but certainly not the last.

She picked me up, grunting with the effort, and carried me downstairs. I was starting to come back alive then, the puppet cutting his strings and becoming a real boy.

My eyes were on fire, but I didn't cry. I just sat at the breakfast bar, turned toward Margo's house, and wished on every stupid thing I could think of that she'd be home soon.

She would understand, even if she didn't go through this kind of thing. She hadn't lost a parent, but she would know what to say to make it better.

"We have a chef," Mom told a detective behind me. "She and her family live in our guest house. Her husband and her have always had some marital problems, but we tried to offer support as best we could..."

I glared at Mom. She was forgetting the part where Dad's version of *support* was his—

"Caleb," Mom warned, like she could read my thoughts.

Maybe the ugly truth was written across my face.

"Can you wait outside, please, honey?" She turned to the detective. "I just don't want him to hear..."

"Understandable, ma'am." He was an older man with a

full head of gray hair and a mustache to match. "My partner can go sit with him outside, if that's all right?"

His partner was young, bald, and probably as freaked out as I was. He looked pale, and sweat dotted his brow.

"We could both use the fresh air." The bald guy motioned for me to hop down, and I led the way to the patio furniture outside. "You know the Wolfes well, son?"

I flinched. "I'm not your son."

He raised his hands in surrender, settling across the table from me. "I meant no offense."

I thought about it. "Keith is nice. Margo's my best friend." I grinned, forgetting the horrors of the house now that we were in the sunshine. "I'm going to marry her."

He smiled at me. "And Margo's mom?"

I paused. I wasn't sure if I was supposed to keep the secret that she and Dad were... more than friends. So I decided on, "She and Dad were close."

He nodded like he knew what I was saying.

"Where is Margo?"

The older detective slid open the door. "Come on, Masters. We've got work to do."

Mom came outside and knelt beside me. "We're going to go on a little trip, okay? Just while they figure out what happened to Daddy."

I hadn't called him Daddy since I was six, but I kept my mouth shut.

She took my hand and led me around the side of the house, putting me in the car. I hadn't realized the older detective had followed us, but he stopped Mom in front of the car.

I cranked my window down an inch.

"Caleb mentioned Amber Wolfe and your husband being close," he said.

"Close? They do talk often." She blinks. It seemed she was coming apart at the seams at a faster rate than before. "But what does that have to do with anything?"

"Ma'am—"

"My husband wouldn't cheat on me," Mom swore. She covered her mouth just before she burst into tears. "He was just *murdered*—"

The detective shuffled backward. He handed her a handkerchief, and she took it, sparing him a smile. I watched in utter disbelief as she dabbed at her eyes, then offered it to him.

He shook his head. "Keep it. Don't leave town, all right? We'll be in touch."

He extended her a business card, and she shoved it into her purse.

She nodded, standing in front of the car until he turned and went back into our house. Then she got in the car and met my eyes in the rearview mirror. "You told them they were *close*?"

I shrugged.

To my surprise, she smiled. "Good. That will set them on the right path."

Chapter 31
Margo

Caleb is pale by the time we get back to my house.

I reach over and stroke his cheek, frowning. It does the trick. He shakes his head and comes out of whatever trance he was in.

"Are you okay?" I ask.

He frowns. "I was just remembering..."

Ah. If he had to relive finding his dad, that's on me. I'm the one who brought it up. I put my hand on his arm. "I'm sorry."

He meets my gaze. "It's not your fault. And besides... I realized a few things."

I lift my eyebrow. "Yeah?"

"Masters was the detective's partner on my dad's case," he says.

I jerk back. "What?"

"It only just occurred to me." He grimaces. "Masters knew Theo's mom. I wonder if he went to school with our dads."

Our dads. It's so weird to hear him say it like that. Up

until this year, we had no idea they were anything beyond acquaintances. Two men burned by Amber.

"The police made the arrest quickly, right? Within the day?"

"An open-and-shut case," he answers. "So they thought."

"I just wish I could remember what happened after." I grind my teeth. "There's still the blank wall that I can't get through. I go back home and then what? My memories skip to being at the park."

His expression borders on sympathetic. "I don't think your memory alone will free your dad. We need proof."

My stomach twists. "What would the implication be if he *did* go to school with them?"

"He wasn't in charge, so I don't know how much he could've swayed. And it would depend on their relationship, you know? People didn't really like my dad. He was known as the developer."

Real estate. Insurance. His dad did it all, and happily—until he sold his company to the highest bidder.

Caleb snaps his fingers. "Yearbook!"

"What?"

"I know Mom kept her old yearbook from high school. And your dad might've kept his from their year. Maybe we can go back to your house—"

I grab his hand before he can put the car in reverse. "It's no use, Caleb. Everything is gone."

He pauses. "Huh?"

Oh shit. Did I not tell him?

"My house. It was completely cleared out except for my parents' bedroom." A giggle bubbles out of me. "All this time, I thought you did it just to keep it away from me. That you had everything in a storage room somewhere—I put it out of my mind because I didn't want you to see it got to me."

"Margo, no," Caleb murmurs. His hand slides around my neck, into my hair. "I had no idea."

His hand is grounding.

"It's your house," I remind him. "Who else would do that?"

"I have a few guesses." He puts the car in park, killing the engine. "Unfortunately, none of them will be forthcoming unless we're sneakier about it. Let's go inside."

I zip my jacket tighter and follow him to my front door. Robert and Lenora are both on the couch, curled up together, when we come in.

"How was your visit?" Lenora asks. There's unveiled concern shining in her eyes.

"We had a good conversation," Caleb says.

I nod.

I loop my arm in his, pulling him toward the stairs. My room is clean, albeit stark. There is now a new bed frame and mattress, and a white dresser, but everything else is in limbo. We plan on painting and going shopping for new decorations once the weekend hits. The two coats of primer cover the red almost to the point of invisibility.

Pretty bird, broken wings. I shudder to think about it.

"Who do you think did it?" I whisper on the stairs.

Caleb pauses next to the picture of me and him. The detective never did notice the red fingerprint, but he homes in on it. "Was this—?"

"Yes."

"It's right over your face," he says in a low voice. "You didn't think to mention this?"

"It isn't like it's a threat."

He gives me an exasperated look. "It *could* be, since everything Unknown does seems to have hidden meaning."

I don't have a response to that. Because, yeah, he's totally right. It could be a threat, as subtle as it may seem.

"They wrote on my wall," I point out. "Isn't that a bit more..."

"Precise?" He scowls.

"I think I'm going to paint the room light blue," I tell him, walking into my room. My things—what were salvaged anyway—are neatly stacked on top of the dresser. The primer is a creamy white color. It's not awful, but it isn't my first choice.

"Is that, 'Oh, what a glorious fall' from something?" Caleb asks. He plops down on my bed, smoothing the blanket. "Or do you think they made it up?"

I sit next to him. "I've been stewing over that myself," I admit. "And at the same time, it infuriates me that I'm even wasting the brain power on it."

"Fair."

"Pretty bird, though... it reminds me of something just out of reach."

He lifts a lock of my hair, twirling it. "It'll come to you. Is that the painting?"

My attention goes to the canvas in the corner of the room, leaning against the wall. Small mercies that it wasn't in the room when it got destroyed.

I still need to finish it, now that my view of Caleb has changed once again.

"It's due soon," he reminds me. "And my eyes are blank."

My cheeks heat. "Yeah, I haven't really had much time..."

"You're right. Me neither. Luckily, I finished mine weeks ago."

I stare at him. "Seriously? And you didn't show me?"

He leans forward, kissing my forehead. It's way too sweet for… him.

He's not sweet.

Or kind.

Or *nice.*

But… he has been. Unfailingly sweet and supportive and gentle.

What on earth is wrong with me?

"Is this the new us?" I blurt out. "You being nice?"

He smirks. "Is this not what you want?"

Is it? Not if it isn't real.

He seems to realize the seriousness of my question, because he leans back and drops the piece of hair he was still twirling. "Margo. I think our situations in the past few weeks have called for niceness. Would you prefer…?"

"Caleb the jerk?" I look away.

His thumb brushes my cheek, catching a tear I didn't even realize was falling.

"I just want stability, you know?" I whisper.

"I'm starting to think you never deserved anything I did to you," he admits. "It was so black and white, and then you just… changed everything in a matter of months."

I nod. "Your uncle?"

His jaw sets.

"It's okay. We'll undo whatever he did."

I kiss him softly. Honestly, I meant it as a peck. But his hand cups the back of my head, trapping me there, and he deepens it. His tongue slides into my mouth.

I groan and fist his shirt in my grip.

"Margo, you have visitors!" Lenora calls from downstairs. "I'll send them up."

We break apart, and he grins at me.

It's a little devious—a hint of the old him.

I shake my head, straightening my clothes. Caleb just leans back, doing nothing to fix his shirt or the way his hair sticks up in every which way. Did I do that?

My door flies open, and Hanna bursts inside. She takes a minute to gape at the room, then shoots into my arms.

"Ah, hi, Hanna," I laugh, hugging her to me.

She squeezes tight enough to steal my breath away.

Claire follows, but she doesn't come all the way into the room. Her attention goes to Caleb. "Sorry, are we interrupting something?"

I glance at him, but he says nothing.

"No," I manage. "No, it's great to see you."

Hanna releases me. "Claire drove us! Our foster parents finally said she was good enough to drive me."

Caleb squints. "Did they, now?"

"She drives fast," Hanna tells him. "But she lets me sit in the front seat, and I like to stick my hand out the window."

Maybe he's remembering that I don't know how to drive, because he says nothing. He barely even looks at Claire, and her stare is hot enough to melt plastic.

"So, to what do we owe this visit?" I ask her, slightly moving so I break her line of sight.

She's always been boy obsessed, but she can't be obsessed with *this* one. I shift slightly, blocking her view of him.

She blinks, like she was dozing, and grins at me. "Well, we were out for ice cream and decided to check in on you. Hanna got an A on her final project in math." She makes a show of checking out the room. "I'd say I like what you've done with the place, but..."

"It was time for a change," I lie. "This is just the beginning stages of me making this place feel like home."

"Oh?" She ventures farther in, touching a little clay pot Hanna had made me last year. It holds a few beads, an earring—lost things.

Forgotten things.

So they wouldn't be misplaced anymore.

I almost cried when she gave it to me, because I know she meant *me*. I was the lost and forgotten thing. And so was she. And so was Claire.

We're not lost anymore, I almost say. It's on the tip of my tongue.

"I'm thinking of painting it blue."

She picks up the canvas. "You've been working on this forever. Are you going to finish it?"

"You should paint the walls orange!" Hanna says, throwing herself onto the bed next to Caleb. She scoots all the way back, until she can lean against the wall. "Orange is my favorite color."

"Silly girl," Claire murmurs. "An orange room would practically glow when the sun rose."

"Exactly."

"Is your room decorated in orange?" I ask Hanna.

"Yeah, orange and pink. The best combination!" She kicks her feet. "It's nice when the rest of the house is creepy."

"It's not creepy," Claire says. "It's just old and big."

I ruffle Hanna's hair. "I'm sure it'll feel like home soon enough."

"Do you go back to school before the holiday?" Claire asks me. "If I were you, I'd push for all the time off I could."

Caleb tilts his head. "Because of the accident?"

She ignores him. "Did you know we found out about your *kidnapping* on the news? The freaking news, Margo!"

I wince. "I'm sorry. It was..."

"Traumatic," Caleb finishes. "And she shouldn't have to tell everyone about it."

She flinches, then rushes to my side. "I'm sorry." She picks up my hands and squeezes. "God, I didn't mean it like that. It was just surprise... and worry."

"You could've called," Caleb said. "Instead of..." Barging in here and interrupting our kiss? That's where it sounds like he's taking this conversation.

I shake my head. "I should've reached out."

Claire pats my cheek. "I forgive you."

Caleb stands and moves toward us. His gait is slow, lazy almost. It's just a few feet to cross the room. But somehow, he makes it feel predatory.

His gaze locks on Claire. He circles around her, then stops beside me.

"Let me get this straight. You forgive Margo, who was in a car accident and then abducted, and in the hospital for three days, for not calling you?"

Claire's face turns red. She presses her lips together, staring up at him.

"He's right," Hanna pipes up from the bed. "A bit rude."

I snicker. Leave it to the twelve-year-old to call it how things are.

"You're right," Claire says, barely able to look at Caleb. Her whole body trembles. "I'm sorry, Margo. That was insensitive. I was worried, and it came out wrong."

She hugs me, burying her face in my neck.

I pat her back awkwardly.

Hanna jumps off the bed and throws her arms around both of us.

"Together again!" she yells into my arm.

Claire and Hanna leave soon after that. It would appear that they just wanted to check on me. Caleb and I eat dinner with Robert and Lenora, and then he, too, leaves.

The three of us settle on the couch. I go back to school tomorrow, so we're soaking up the last night of no home-work. Robert puts on a movie, and Lenora makes popcorn in the kitchen. I drag a blanket over my lap in the armchair, bringing my knees up to my chest.

When Lenora comes with two bowls of popcorn—one for me and one for them—Robert pauses the preview.

"We want to talk to you now that your friends are gone," Robert says.

Worry immediately knots my stomach. *A talk* is never a good thing.

"You seem panicked." Lenora reaches out and offers her hand.

I take it and suck in a deep breath. "Maybe a bit."

"Lenora and I have been discussing adoption." Robert smiles at me. "Our main concern is whether you'd be open to such a thing."

"We want you to be part of our family permanently," Lenora adds, squeezing my hand.

My mouth drops open. Yes, they'd said as much before the accident, but...

My heart tears itself in half.

It happens between beats. One minute it's whole, and the next, it's broken and I'm being pulled in two different directions.

Dad is innocent, and we just need to prove it to get him out.

And Robert and Lenora... they want to make things official. A home with two stable parents who love each other, who don't fight. Who would've thought they'd pick me?

I don't know how to stitch myself back together again. How to make my heart halves beat in sync.

My eyes burn, but I don't cry. There's a weight on my shoulders; it lands heavier than I would've thought I could handle.

"Thank you," I say over the lump in my throat.

Any minute, I'm going to lose it.

"It's a lot to process," Lenora says. "And this is your decision."

I push the blanket off and stand, wrapping my arms around Lenora. She gives much better hugs than my mother ever did.

An image of Mom standing in the diner flashes through my mind, but I shove it away. She left me alone, to fend for myself. And when I did see her? It was only about money to feed her habit.

Lenora rubs my back. "You're shaking."

"Just trying to forget about my mother." I lean back and wipe at my face.

All I've done lately is cry. I hope I run out of tears soon.

"Should we watch the movie?" Robert asks.

I smile. "Yeah."

As good a distraction as any.

My chest hurts. I wrap the blanket around me, sinking into the armchair. It's nice to zone out at the screen for a while.

Adoption means my dad would have to give up his rights. I'd have a family, but I would lose him.

How the hell am I supposed to choose?

Chapter 32
Caleb

"Why aren't we going inside?" Eli asks me.

"You can go," I say. "I'm waiting for Margo."

He glares at me. "Margo, who's arriving with Riley."

They haven't talked. *Still.* And while I'm curious, there have been other pressing concerns stealing my attention.

I exhale, watching my breath make little clouds.

"Okay, fine," he snaps. "I'm going in."

I flip him off.

He salutes me with his middle finger back, then saunters toward the building.

No sooner is he gone than Robert's car arrives, and Margo climbs out. She grins when she sees me, and I pull her in for a kiss. Foster dad be damned.

She smiles when I linger.

"Let's go in," she says. "It's freezing."

"I thought you were getting a ride in with Riley?"

She shrugs. "She said she was running late. Not sure what she has planned."

I roll my eyes. "Did she say she was planning something?"

"No, but she's never late—"

"Ms. Wolfe," the guidance counselor calls. "Could you join me?"

I reluctantly release her. "I'll see you in homeroom."

She gives me a brave smile, then disappears into the office.

Savannah walks past, her fur coat held tightly closed in her hand. She has such a thick layer of makeup caked on her face, it's like she's wearing a mask.

She doesn't acknowledge my presence, and my eyebrow jumps.

"Hey, man," Liam calls.

We slap hands, and he yanks off his hat. His blond hair goes everywhere. He runs a hand through it, messing it up further, and I shake my head. Girls love that untamed look.

"Margo's back?" he asks.

"They called her in." I hook my thumb toward the office.

He grimaces. "She's an old coot. You're waiting?"

"Figured I would."

He nods, stuffing his hands into his pockets. "Kid gloves."

I narrow my eyes. "What?"

"You're treating her with kid gloves." He shrugs, smiling innocently. "It's okay. I'm sure Margo appreciates you not leaving her alone…"

I shake my head. "You're just…"

Jealous?

No.

If anything, Liam's attitude is more of a brotherly nature —to me *and* Margo. I try not to think about the time I walked in on them at the party. She was across the room from him, but still.

"It's going to be a long week," I say.

He laughs. "Yeah. See you in homeroom."

Margo appears just as the bell rings. She sticks out her tongue. "So much for meeting you there, huh?"

I put my arm around her shoulders. As we walk, people part for us. They do it more for me than her, but judging from the glances she gets, I would say they're curious about her. Word must've traveled quick.

"You know what's interesting?" she asks under her breath. Without waiting for my answer, she continues, "Since you found me, I haven't heard from our mystery stalker. Besides the writing on the walls—literally."

I sigh. "Unknown called me right before the police came. Everything they're doing is escalating."

She shivers. "What's next?"

More dead birds in her room?

My mood plummets. "I'm not going to let anything happen to you."

That's a fucking promise.

The rest of the day passes quietly and quickly. Between the four of us, we keep tabs on Margo. Riley showed up after second period, seeming a bit worse for the wear, and she silently joins the team.

It isn't like I think something is going to happen to her. I don't. I just... am worried that I might be wrong.

I come up behind Margo and loop my arms around her waist, pulling her back against my front. She gasps, stiffening for a moment. Once she realizes it's me, she relaxes.

My lips touch the tip of her ear. "Did I startle you?"

"No," she lies.

I let her get away with it.

"It's Robert's first day back," she says. "I wonder how he's doing."

"Well, we won't have long to wait." I close her locker, and together we walk to the art wing. Everyone has been more subdued, and I'm blaming it on my friends. God only knows who they threatened to make the entire school act... normal.

We slip into Robert's classroom, and he shoots us a smile.

"Hey, guys," he says. His desk is a wreck. Papers everywhere, folders, various tubes of paint and brushes. "How's your day?"

"Peachy," Margo answers. "You okay?"

"Oh, the substitute teacher probably wishes she had another week to get things more organized." He rolls his shoulders back. "I'm just still trying to get everything sorted. Plus it's the end of the year, and final projects are due. God, every year I think I should stagger the classes—"

"Mr. Bryan!" one of his students squeals. They come in with a few others. "You're back!"

"Yes, hello." He motions for them to take their seats. "You, too, please."

I take Margo's hand and pull her toward the back of the room.

"He seems frazzled," Margo whispers.

"I would be, too, if my desk looked like that."

She hides her laugh behind her hand.

"We're getting to the end of the semester." Robert closes the door. "And I would like to take this opportunity to remind you that your final project, the portraits, are due at the beginning of next week. Can I see a show of hands to who's already completed theirs?"

Half the hands in the room go up, including mine.

I was done a while ago. And in fact, Robert already graded it.

I didn't breathe a word of that to Margo. I was already mostly done by the time I tried to hurt her relationship with the Bryans. It was only after, when she started standing up to me, that I revisited it. I changed a few things—the feeling behind it, but not necessarily anything physical.

For my first oil painting, I was impressed with myself. And I got an A on it, of course.

Margo frowns at my raised hand.

"What?" I mouth, holding back a smile.

I saw my eyeless self immortalized on the canvas yesterday, and I can imagine how conflicted she is. To paint me with a scowl? A dead look in my eye? It's how most of the world sees me nowadays. But she's always been able to see deeper.

And that's where her struggle comes in.

Robert gives us an assignment, a bowl of fruit set up on a table in the center of our circle, and goes back to his desk.

It occurs to me that the end of the semester brings something else besides holidays and a weeklong break: college application deadlines.

I lean over to her as she's putting paint on her palette. "Did you apply yet?"

"Did I apply for what?" She glances at me and pushes hair out of her face.

"School."

"When would I have had time to do that?"

I roll my eyes. "You were out for over a week."

"Because I had a head injury." She readjusts her stool. "Seriously."

"Don't you want to go to NYU? There are other schools if you didn't like that one—"

"Listen. If I could have whatever I wanted, there's another school I'd love to go to. It's farther away, though. Even if I could afford tuition, *maybe* the Bryans would let me commute from here. That's why NYU sounds like a good idea." She shakes her head. "Haven't we been over this? I can't afford it, and I can't ask the Bryans—"

I narrow my eyes. "We're going to talk about this dream school later. Because they'd give it to you. Anything you wanted."

I mirror her earlier movements, putting little dabs of paint on my palette. It's rough wood on the underside, old dried paint smoothing the top. A lot of other students took the plastic ones, but I prefer this. It doesn't let me forget I'm holding it as it scrapes against my hand.

"I'd give it to you, too," I add.

"You would not."

I watch her until she spins her entire body toward me. She's rigid, and her eyes are wide.

She's cute when she's alarmed.

"Caleb. You can't waste money like that."

"Do you know how much I'm inheriting?"

She pauses. "Why would I know that?"

"I'll be a multimillionaire at eighteen, and I didn't earn a penny of it. So if I want to pay for your education so you don't have to graduate with debt, I'm going to." I set my jaw.

She stares at me, and I realize... maybe she *didn't* have any idea what I'm going to be receiving on my eighteenth birthday.

Four months to go, a voice in the back of my head whispers.

"Did I just scare you?" I ask.

She forces a laugh. "Me? No. No, I totally... expected it. You know, with the crazy uncle controlling your money and the house left empty and your mom not getting a penny. That makes perfect sense."

"Mom did something," I say. "Something that made Dad hold a grudge."

"And I doubt she'd actually tell you, right?"

"Right."

She shakes her head and turns back to the canvas. "If we both don't even get our brushes dirty, Robert will ground me and send you..."

"To detention?" I smirk.

She grins. "Maybe."

We lapse into silence, and I put my best effort into the bowl of apples and oranges. It passes the time quickly, and it feels like minutes later Robert is clapping, giving us the five-minute warning.

We pack away our things.

"Are you bringing me home?" she asks.

"We're back to conditioning for hockey," I say. "A five-mile run is in my future."

She nods.

I snag her hand. "Maybe today would be a good day to go over my uncle's house?"

Her eyes widen. "Really."

"They're out of town." I grab my phone and pull up a photo my aunt posted on Facebook. The picture is of her and Uncle David on a beach somewhere. He's moody—a remnant of his drowning modeling career—and she's beaming.

"How can she look so... happy with him?"

I shrug. "I'm pretty sure she's acting."

She frowns.

I lean in close, until my nose touches hers. "As long as you never put on an act like she does, we'll be okay."

She sucks in a breath, and my heart skips. I could listen to her little reactions for the rest of my life and be happy.

Her dark eyes meet mine. "As long as you don't put on your mask, we'll be okay."

"You just want me vulnerable."

"Yep." She pops the p, then winks.

The bell rings, and she flinches.

Students flood out into the hall, but we remain where we are. She takes a step back and crosses her arms. She's trying to hide again, but I know she's afraid to go into my aunt and uncle's house.

"They're gone. The house will be empty," I reason. "And since I have practice…"

"God," she moans. "I hate you."

Robert clears his throat. "Are you waiting on me, kiddo?"

She spins around. "Oh, um, no. Riley is going to give me a ride. I think we're going to do homework at her house."

He smiles. "Okay. Just let Lenora know, okay?"

"Will do."

I follow her down the hall and tug her to a stop outside of the athletic wing. "I've gotta go."

"Right."

"I'm just going to get changed. We'll discuss this in a few minutes."

She nods curtly, and I leave her standing there. She'll need to be brave—but I have a feeling Riley will be able to help with that.

Besides, we need answers.

I get changed quickly, meeting up with Theo. Eli and Liam are in the far corner.

"Eli said he wasn't in the mood for whatever bullshit I had in mind," Theo says. "So, you're with me."

Lucky me.

"What suicide run are we doing today?" I ask, lacing my sneakers.

He just grins.

Coach walks into the locker room, pounding on one of the metal doors to get our attention. "Remember: do not run alone. I want five miles, and you log what time you come back on this sheet. Got it?"

"Yes, Coach," we all call.

"Great. Now get out of here."

I flip off Eli as they leave. He returns the gesture, laughing.

"We need to make a pit stop," I tell Theo.

His eyebrows go up, but he says nothing. We shove the door open and head around the building. It's easy to spot Margo and Riley by her car.

Margo clutches her jacket tighter around her, frowning at me. "It's freezing out here."

I shrug. "We need to get in shape."

Coach's voice in the distance drifts closer on the wind. I would've thought he'd stay inside, but I guess he wants to make sure we actually run. Theo and I need to get moving before he spots us chatting—otherwise we'll end up with another two miles on our plate.

I tilt her face toward me and steal a kiss. She rises on her toes, trying to deepen it, and I grin against her lips. "I have to go."

She huffs. "Fine. I'll see you later."

I stuff a folded envelope in her hand. It has the key to my aunt and uncle's house, as well as the code to their alarm system.

"Tonight," I promise. I'm going to take her on an actual date—nice clothes, flowers. The whole thing. I'll pick her up and take her to the fancy restaurant, and we'll drink fizzy cider and pretend its champagne. It's a surprise I've been holding on to for a few days now, and I'm proud of myself for not ruining it.

After all, we deserve a spot of happiness in our senior year.

"Come on," Theo groans.

I touch her cheek, smiling to myself, and turn away. That kiss will keep me warm.

Theo and I head off, quickly finding a pace that both of us can sustain.

"I'm thinking the old mill road," he says.

It's a dirt road, winding and long, with a giant hill in the middle.

Kind of perfect... kind of awful. At least it's cold enough that we won't sweat to death. The snow is gone from the roads, but there are still thick patches of it coating the grass. My breath puffs out in front of my face.

This is the worst. I'd rather be bag skating—hockey's version of torturous sprinting on repeat—than this. But here we are.

I grunt, then catch his grin out of the corner of my eye. *Bastard.*

Coach's one rule is that we have to stay together. It's why I don't generally run with Liam—he likes to go slow, then sprint toward the end. Eli and I run best together, but Theo... when I need a push, he's my guy.

Even now, he speeds up a bit.

I lengthen my stride to match his long one. "I'm gonna be in pain by the time this is over."

"That's why I like this route," he tells me. "Once we get over the hill, it's all downhill. The first half is just a bitch."

"Speaking of bitches..."

He rolls his eyes. "Nice segue."

"Have you heard anything about Amelie?" I ask. "I never thought to ask her how she knew about Margo's mom."

He nods. "Right. She knew where Amber was staying."

"Kind of a weird thing for her to know..." I roll my shoulders back.

We turn onto the dirt road. It takes us a few strides to adjust to the new texture under our feet, and both of us slow a fraction.

"What are you thinking?" he asks.

"Matt knew people from Emery-Rose," I reason. "So it wouldn't be crazy to think Unknown goes to our school."

"But..."

"But my top suspect was Amelie, since she has her sticky fingers in everything. It wouldn't have been a stretch for her to tell Savannah to send the picture of Ian and Margo to me. She's since left the freaking country."

"What are you and Margo going to focus on once this is over?"

I glance at him. "You and your love life, of course."

He bursts out laughing. "Fuck you, man."

"Come on. You don't think you and—"

He elbows me. "Other people need more immediate help. Like Eli. Or Liam."

"Truth."

Liam has a quiet fixation on his neighbor. He never talks about her, though. I think she broke his heart when they were younger. So he's hopeless. And I don't know what's going on with Eli and Riley. They're just fucking around, I think.

And Theo is miserably obsessed with Amelie's social outcast sister.

It would be funny if it wasn't so sad.

We quit talking and focus on running. We've reached the hill, and it's taken us almost thirty minutes to get here.

I check my watch, which tracks distance, and groan when I see we've already run four miles. I'm going to kill him for almost doubling our running distance—but it's too late to turn back now.

Both of us are breathing hard by the time we make it to the top a few minutes later, and I motion to stop. I bend over, elbows on my thighs, and suck in air.

"That was like a mile-long hill," I gasp. "Fucking hell."

There's a reason I don't come this way. It's also the reason Theo's in better shape than I am—he runs this route a *lot*. Eli and I prefer flatter roads.

"You gonna live?" Theo asks.

I shake my head, tempted to flop over. "Maybe not."

He slaps my back. "Walk it off."

And then he takes off, continuing down the road. At a walk, at least. But still.

I catch up to him easily enough, sucking in deep breaths. "Okay. Let's get this over with."

"That's the spirit."

And off we go.

We're near the bottom of the hill when a car comes up behind us. We scoot to the side, Theo jogging directly in front of me.

I move farther over when the car behind me doesn't pass us. There's a whole stretch of road to our left, but... some drivers are weird. Overly cautious.

The vehicle comes up next to us, keeping pace until I glance over at them.

Margo's foster sister.

She waves at me, frantic, until Theo and I stop. The car

shoots ahead of us, then the taillights illuminate. The car rocks to a stop.

"The fuck?" Theo says.

I walk up to the passenger window, my brow furrowing. "Claire?"

"Caleb, I've been trying to find you! Margo was in an accident. Lenora asked me to come find you. You weren't answering your phone..." She covers her mouth with her hand and shakes her head. "I'm sorry."

My stomach drops into my feet. My phone is safely tucked in my gym bag in the locker room. And I *just* left Margo not too long ago.

"Is she okay?"

"I don't know." Her eyes fill with tears. "They wouldn't tell us anything."

I glance up and down the street, but it's quiet. The need to get to her is insane, spiking adrenaline through my system. I could run back to school, but we're almost two miles out.

"Go," Theo says, reading my mind.

I yank her door open and slide inside.

She gasps. "What are you doing?"

"They took her to the hospital?"

"Y-yes."

"Take me there," I urge. "Please."

She hits the gas, and I'm thrown back against the seat. I pull my seat belt on and turn toward her, ignoring the guilt I feel at leaving Theo alone. It's against the rules, but this trumps Coach's stupid rules.

"Claire. The hospital?"

She blinks, wiping the tears off her cheeks. "She never saw it coming."

"You didn't say what happened. Or how." The car is

picking up speed. My stomach is in knots.

The hospital is ten minutes away from here, fifteen at the most.

Where did Margo get hurt? It must've been closer to the hospital than here.

When Claire doesn't answer, I look around the car. It's clean to the point of newness. Not a speck of dust on the dash or the floor. The fabric mats are free of dirt—except what's come off from my shoes.

I almost feel bad leaning on her leather seats. Sweat rolls down my chest under my sweatshirt, and my back is soaked.

Who runs in the middle of winter? I can hear Margo's voice in my head.

"Was it Riley's car?" I ask. "Did she get in a car accident—"

Two in one month? What would the odds be on that?

Or maybe it was Unknown. They could've taken her. Something more violent, like with a gun—

Claire glances at me, then away. "You care about her so much. How? She told me how you hated her when she started school."

I shake my head. "Hate is temporary. Love..."

We pause at the stop sign, and her grip on the wheel flexes.

"Love," she repeats. Sighs. "That is just... the sweetest thing I've ever heard."

There's a moment when I think she might be up to something. Left is the hospital, and right... the road to the right goes out of town. Away from Rose Hill and toward the freeway.

"You love her, too."

When did I become a person who discussed *love*? It's

easy to see the way Claire cares. She came all the way out here to find me, after all. Why do that if not for Margo's sake?

She shakes her head. "A foster sibling's relationship is complicated. Sometimes I think she hates me. But, as you said—hate is temporary."

She turns left.

"Lenora and Robert—did they get to the hospital already?" I probe. "How did you find out?"

"I was there for bloodwork." She pushes the sleeve of her sweater up, showing me the rolled gauze taped to the inside of her elbow. "Happened to see them all rush in, and Lenora and I had met before. They didn't want to leave her."

"Right."

She lets out a ragged breath. "I just hope she's okay."

"Me, too," I murmur. I look out the window and will Claire to drive faster. I could be nice and ask her about herself—when she'd learned to drive when Margo still hadn't, where her sister is, how she found me on a random side road miles from school...

But instead, I keep my mouth shut and just hope that whatever happened to Margo, she's still fighting.

I'm coming for you, Margo.

Chapter 33
Margo

I watch Caleb jog off with Theo. The sky is clear, ice-blue, and the wind has died down. As he pointed out before he left, *Now's as good a time as any.*

I tuck the envelope into my jacket pocket.

"They have to stay in shape," Riley repeats. "Dumb boys."

I shrug. "Did you want to talk about your thing with Eli?"

I follow her line of sight to where she's picked Eli out of the trio of hockey players running down a different road.

She snorts. "No."

"He's bound to be planning something. Like, a way to get you back." In fact, I had heard as much. Eli swore me to secrecy, but he isn't my best friend—Riley is. So I add, "There's nothing he can do to fix... whatever it is that happened?"

"Fat chance." She shakes her head. "Where are we going? My place or yours?"

"Actually..."

She gives me a look. The one that says, *You're about to drag me into some shit, aren't you?*

"Caleb's aunt and uncle are out of town," I blurt out. "And we think there might be something in that house that can help us with everything."

"Something that can help with *everything*? What is everything? Do you actually know what you're searching for, or are you grasping at straws?" She sighs. "You two have got yourselves so wrapped up in this mystery—"

"Riley," I interrupt. "We didn't choose this. It's been haunting us, and with everything happening with Unknown..."

She pulls me into a hug. "I'm sorry. I didn't mean how it sounded. I'm just worried about you." After a second, she leans back and visibly steels herself. "Okay. So, Caleb's aunt and uncle's house."

"I have the address in my phone."

It takes us almost twenty minutes to get there. The last time we were there... I shudder, remembering the state I found Caleb.

"What are we looking for?" Riley asks.

I fish out the set of keys Caleb gave me, and we hurry to the side entrance. I cross the entrance to the alarm panel, but it's already been deactivated.

"Weird," she whispers. "Maybe they only put it on when they're home?"

I squint at her. "Why on earth would they do that?"

She shrugs. "He really wanted you to get in here, huh? The key, the code..."

"He's busy, and this couldn't really wait." I glance around. "Should we split up?"

"No."

I raise my eyebrows.

"You still haven't told me anything about what we're looking for."

I nod. "Right. Sorry. We need to find anything Lydia might've kept—an old yearbook, preferably, or pictures from high school."

"Lydia, Caleb's mom?"

"Right."

She shakes her head. "Isn't most of her stuff still at their old house? Why—"

"Caleb suggested to start here," I interrupt. We're still speaking as quietly as possible, and I clear my throat.

She hums. "Okay, fine. May as well start in the bedrooms, right? Upstairs?"

I nod, then hesitate. "Or his uncle's study…"

"After," she says.

We go to the stairs, jogging up them with light footsteps. I don't know why we're moving like we're thieves in the night—no one is here.

At the top of the stairs, there are two immediate doors: one to the left and one to the right. Farther down, there are more doors.

"Start at the back and work forward?" Riley points to the end of the hall.

We creep along and pass four closed doors before we get to the last one. I push it open, almost expecting Caleb's uncle to be sitting there, waiting for us.

It *is* the primary bedroom, although it's empty.

Riley goes to the nightstands while I hurry across to the bookshelves built into the wall. They frame a huge flat-screen television and an armoire below it.

I run my finger across the book titles, but nothing with Emery-Rose's gold-and-black colors or its sigil jumps out at me.

"Nada," Riley calls. "Just some lube, and I could've happily gone my entire life without knowing that was there."

I stick out my tongue. "Gross."

I take the next room down on the left, and Riley opens the door on the right.

"Bathroom." She appears in the doorway. "What's in here?"

It must be a guest room. Everything is in shades of white and gray. The drawers in the dresser are empty, the bed made neater than a pin.

"Moving on." I ignore the discouraging feeling twisting my stomach. It isn't just foreboding—that we're intruding on a dangerous family's home—but also... like something bad is going to happen.

This is a *literal* gut feeling.

I grab Riley's hand, pulling her to a stop. "Maybe you should be lookout."

There's a narrow walkway next to the stairs that goes to a window. From there, she'll be able to see to the driveway and the front door. She sighs, then goes to the window. We parked across the street, which will hopefully not tip anyone off that anything is amiss.

I crack the second to last door and pause.

I was expecting something more masculine, a room Caleb would've stayed in as a kid. Instead, it's feminine. The walls are a blush color, and the comforter on the bed is pink and orange flowers.

Slowly, I leave the doorway and walk farther in.

It's not as neat as the monotone room we just left. This one is... lived-in. Papers on the desk, a pile of dirty clothes in a hamper in the corner. One of the dresser drawers is cracked open, denim sticking out.

Spooked, I back out into the hallway.

"What is it?" Riley asks.

I shake my head and go to the last bedroom, shoving the door open.

Blues and purples. An unmade bed. More clothes.

"Do they have a kid?"

I go to the desk. It's white, not inexpensive, with a blue chair on wheels tucked in. A laptop sits on top, plugged into a power strip.

Fuzzy pens in a cup.

A mouse pad with the picture of a dog.

The desk itself is pushed up against a window. To the left of it is a bulletin board. I stand in front of it, putting my finger on the one of the pins.

Newspaper clippings.

Cut-out articles.

Fatal Two-Car Accident on Elm Street and *Drunk Driver Kills Teenage Boy* and *Rose Hill Child Fatally Struck.*

"What is this?" Riley asks, just behind me.

I can't breathe.

The board is filled with them. So many car accidents, dating back at least four years, all over Hillshire County.

"Margo," Riley snaps. She grabs my shoulder and drags me around. "You look like you're going to be sick."

Because my stomach is a roiling mess.

"I didn't know they were—"

The front door slams, and both of us duck.

"Shit," Riley whispers. She runs to the door and closes it most of the way.

"I'm home!" a familiar voice yells. "Matt gave me a ride since you were sick."

Hanna.

"We're standing in Claire's room," I say in a low voice.

Riley slowly pivots back to me. "Excuse me?"

"I didn't know this was where they—"

Footsteps on the stairs interrupt me.

"Claire?" Hanna calls.

Sweet, beautiful Hanna.

I only pray her sister left her *out* of this mess.

"Closet," Riley whispers, hauling me across the room.

We slip into it, and I take a moment to be thankful for the size. She closes the closet with the tiniest *snick*. We both back away. I spin around. The closet is deep and narrow, with Claire's clothes on both long sides. In the back are a few rows of shelves, sparse except for the boxes at the top.

Claire's bedroom door flies open. "Claire, I asked—"

My heart cracks. Wherever Claire is, Hanna expected her to be here. And now the twelve-year-old is alone in the *big, creepy house*, as she called it. I take a step toward the door, ready to reveal myself.

Riley grabs me from behind, covering my mouth with her hand.

"Please, be quiet," she whispers in my ear.

My lungs stop working.

I'm so sorry.

Flashes of being in the same position—both as a child and just recently, yanked from the wrecked car—fill my mind. I can *smell* the smoke. *Feel* the bite of glass in my skin. I thrash and claw at her arms.

She holds on tightly. "Stop, stop," she whispers in my ear.

"Claire," Hanna sings, her voice farther away. "Are you downstairs?"

Riley releases me, and I fall out of the closet.

I land on my hands and knees, gasping for air. I wasn't here in a closet. I was there. It was so fucking real.

She crouches beside me. "Margo, I'm so sorry. I'm an idiot, I just... we can't be caught. You said Claire lives here—did you know? Did she mention it?"

It takes a minute for me to regain my breath, but then I grab Riley's offered hand and stand. Ignoring her other questions, I say, "She's obsessed with car accidents."

Riley nods slowly.

I go to Claire's desk, yanking out the chair and taking a seat. Her computer is bound to be password protected—but at least it's more proof that she has a laptop. *Portable computer.*

"It can't be her," I mumble.

I open the drawers and riffle through loose paper. At the bottom of the last drawer, there's a wooden box.

I pause. Whatever is in this box was worth her hiding it —or it's nothing.

If I don't open it, the contents can't hurt me. Claire remains innocent.

"What?" Riley takes the box from my hands and flips it open. Inside is a folded picture of me and Caleb. She pulls it out and flattens it.

I gasp. I can't help it.

She's...

"That bitch scratched your face off." Riley's tone is appalled.

I shudder.

"We need to get out of here. Fast." She looks over her shoulder. "I hate to say Hanna's right, but I'm getting creeped out."

"We still need the yearbook. What if Masters is in on it?"

"Can't we just trust the police for once?" Riley retorts.

I shake my head, then snap a picture of the photo with my phone.

She puts the picture back in the box, dropping it in the drawer. "Come on."

I start to follow her, then freeze. "Riley! The boxes."

Her eyes narrow. "What?"

I slip back into the closet, standing on my toes to reach the boxes on the top shelf. Riley is suddenly beside me, taking the one I hand her so I can grab the second.

We bring them out and set them on the carpet, ripping the lids off.

Sure enough...

A box of jewelry with the initials L.A. engraved in the velvet, a few different baubles, a...

"Is that a mermaid?"

I pick up the glass figure. It looks remarkably similar to the one Caleb found in my room. There's another one made of porcelain, and a third...

"She collected them," I say slowly. "And Claire must've just needed something to use."

Riley grunts. "I always had a bad feeling about that girl. But this seems bigger than just her."

"L.A." I shake my head. "Lydia Asher?"

"Fucking weirdo."

I nod my agreement, and we focus on the second box.

Against one of the sides is a black-and-gold hardcover book.

The yearbook.

I choke on my laugh. "Holy shit, we found it."

"Great," Riley says. "Now we need to get out of here before we're discovered by a twelve-year-old."

"Right."

She puts the lid back on, but a notebook catches my eye. I stop her, removing it. I quickly take pictures of the box and then nod. We tuck everything into place, take a look around the room, and creep into the hallway.

The notebook and yearbook are under my arm. We make it almost all the way down the stairs before Riley hits a creaking step.

"Shit," she whispers. "Go, go."

We bolt.

Out the door—I close it as quietly as possible behind me —and off the porch. We cut across the grass, sprinting to her car.

"Fuck, fuck," she yells.

"Riley, go," I snap.

I dial Caleb's number.

Straight to voicemail.

I call again, just to be sure.

"Wait, wait," I say, just as we get to the end of the road.

She pulls over, turning toward me. "He's probably still running."

"Yeah." Still, that bad feeling I had? It only gets worse.

Maybe I'm panicking over nothing.

I call Theo.

"Wolfe," Theo answers on the first ring. "You okay?"

"I... me? I'm fine." I shake my head. "I was looking for Caleb."

"Um... Like, you're fine, as in, they're releasing you from the hospital?"

I jerk back. I put the call on speaker, because maybe Riley will be able to make sense of what he's saying. "Theo, I'm not at the hospital."

"Oh. Girl must've been overreacting. She was crying like you were on the verge of death."

In as calm a voice as I can manage, I say, "Theo. Where is Caleb?"

"We were on the run, and Claire came by. Said you had been in an accident—I'm glad you're okay, by the way. She was taking Caleb to the hospital."

I close my eyes. "I wasn't in an accident."

He's quiet.

"Riley and I went to Caleb's uncle's house searching for something. And..." *Just spit it out, Margo.* "Claire is the one who's been harassing me."

"Fuck." Something crashes in the background. "You're telling me I let him get in the car with a psycho bitch?"

"I'm sure he made the choice himself," Riley mutters. "Bullheaded boys."

"I *heard* that, Applebottom," Theo snaps.

"Okay, enough." I glare at the phone. "We'll find them."

"Keep me posted," he says.

The line goes dead. The fear working its way up my throat is going to bubble over at any moment.

"We can find him," she says. "You know your foster sister—"

"Clearly *not*." I drop my head into my hands. "How long has she had him? Twenty minutes? An hour? Is she going to hurt him? Kill him?"

Riley pinches my arm, hard enough that I flinch away from her.

"Stop it." She pats the same place she pinched, a silent apology. "We just need to think."

"I may not know her as well as I should," I say slowly. "But..."

"Hanna," Riley and I say at the same time.

She makes a U-turn and pulls into the driveway. "You want me to come in?"

I frown. "No. I'll talk to her."

I go back into the house that has started to feel much more terrible than I originally thought. It holds too many secrets and too many grudges.

I follow the sounds of the television to the living room set toward the back of the house. It's one of the more lived-in rooms. I stop in the doorway.

Hanna is on the couch, a blanket across her lap, and a bowl of ice cream hugged to her chest.

It makes me smile.

"This is what you do when you're home alone?" I ask.

She jumps. "Oh my God, Margo!"

She puts down the bowl and races toward me, colliding into me.

I wrap my arms around her and push down the panic. The need to immediately question her. Hanna is a sensitive soul. The first to cry when someone yells or start at a loud noise. The foster system hasn't been kind to her—but she's still good.

I try to hold on to that.

"Hanna, I need to ask you an important question."

She releases me, bouncing on the balls of her feet.

"Do you know where Claire is?"

A frown flits across her expression, there one minute and gone the next. "Did you just come to see her?"

I take a deep breath. "No, hon. I'm sorry." I guide her to the couch and sit next to her. "But I think she knows where my friend is."

Hanna perks up. "Caleb? He's all she ever talks about. She said she was going to date him when you were gone."

I exhale. "When I'm gone?"

She shrugs, leaning over to grab her ice cream. "I dunno.

She seemed pretty convinced that he was going to fall in love with her."

Bitch.

I shove away my anger and fear, and instead put my hands on her shoulders. "Can you do me a favor, Han?"

She looks at me with wide eyes.

"I just need to know if there's somewhere special Claire might've gone after school."

"Well..." Hanna glances around. "She does like to go visit her boyfriend."

I pause. "She has a boyfriend?"

"Matt! We had to play a silly game and act like strangers at the football game. Isn't that weird? They said it was like role-playing."

I blink a few times as more pieces of the puzzle click into place.

Of course. Who else would lie—or was it even a lie? She said she was with him, and for all I know... she could've been behind my abduction.

"She has a boyfriend but she thinks Caleb is going to fall in love with her?" I make my tone light. "That's kind of greedy."

She giggles.

"Come on, Hanna. She wouldn't take Caleb to Matt's house, right?"

Hanna's smile drops off. "She took Caleb?"

"I don't know." I shake her shoulders lightly. "Think. Where would they go?"

"I don't—stop!" She bursts into tears.

Shocked, I release her.

Oh God.

I'm no better than my mother, shaking a child.

I jump to my feet, ready to bolt.

"T-the diner," she says through her tears. "She's always talking about hanging out with her future mom."

Lydia.

The diner.

My mother.

I take a step forward—to hug her, to thank her—but she flinches away from me. It stops me dead in my tracks.

"I'm so sorry," I whisper. "But Caleb..."

"Yeah." She swipes at her face. "You and her are the same. Only focused on him."

Only focused on him. How did I miss that about her?

I run out of the house, down the steps, and straight into Riley's car. "You remember how to get to Lucky's Diner?"

Chapter 34
Caleb

Time is a tricky thing. Sometimes it moves slowly, like when I realized Margo had overheard my conversation with the Bryans, or walking into my parents' room and finding Dad covered in blood. It inched along every second Margo was missing.

Other times, it moves too quickly: racing like the clock can't withhold it anymore.

Time.

The only thing that could possibly save me is working against me.

I count down the seconds, eyes glued to the dash, and too soon, handfuls of minutes have passed.

Claire asked if I remembered her, and I didn't have an answer. But the truth?

Yes. I did, and I wished I didn't.

Past

Margo had just left for school. It had been a while since I was here. I had been trying for almost a year to scrub her from my brain. Since I'd been living with the Blacks, my mindset changed the slightest bit.

She wasn't the boogieman I had to fear, like my uncle always pushed on me.

She was just a disease to be eradicated.

I watched her disappear down the sidewalk, into the mist. There was a bus stop around the corner. At the beginning of the year, I checked the Stone Ridge paper to see where she might take it. What time. I wondered at the commute length, if students on the bus would pick on her or leave her alone.

I climbed out of my car and crossed the street.

The door flew open before I could ring the bell, and a young girl stared up at me. Her mouth dropped open.

Another girl appeared. She was closer to Margo's age.

I silently cursed myself for not waiting just another moment.

"Caleb," the older girl blurted out. "Right?"

My lip curled. How did she know my name?

Their foster mother appeared behind them. "Girls? What—oh, hello. Can I help you with something?"

"I just wanted to speak to you," I said.

Foster siblings.

Interesting.

How attached did she get to them?

Cindy, the foster mom, huffed at me. She was in a certain state of distress: her hair still had curlers in it, her makeup seemed mostly finished, but she still wore pajama pants.

"Come in, then," she said.

She called to her husband, and suddenly the three of us were in the kitchen.

I looked down at the table we had gathered around. There were dirty bowls—only two of them, one was by the sink—and a half-drunk glass of milk. The husband was a bit frazzled, too, with his hair sticking up straight and his tie loose.

"I must commend you both on taking on such a problem foster," I said to them.

"Problem foster?" Cindy asked. She turned to her husband, raising her eyebrows. "Claire?"

My eyebrow ticked up.

"You don't mean Margo," the husband, Jeff, said. "She's been a saint."

"She's a good actress," I lied.

I told this family that I knew her. That I could see right into her soul and know the truth. Even though it was a lie—I had known her in the past, but not anymore. We grew up apart. It was just my need to keep uprooting her that forced me to hunt her.

The foster parents were worried. I saw it in the lines creasing between their brows and the way they glanced at each other.

"She gets jealous easily," I said.

Cindy's hand was resting on her stomach, and I went with my hunch.

"She can dissolve into fits of rage. I saw it happen a time or two. I can't imagine what she would do if there was a baby in the house stealing all the attention."

Jeff shook his head. "How do you know that?"

"We used to be friends." I shook my head. "But she caused my father's death and broke apart her whole family.

She's destructive. Dangerous. Even if..." My lips twisted. "Even if she acts like a saint."

"Two years," Cindy said faintly. "Two years we've had these children, and Margo..."

I watched her. It only took an ounce of doubt to infect her viewpoint. She was already classed as a runaway—what next?

"Thank you for letting us know," Jeff said. "But why now?"

I glanced away. Part of the act. Shame, guilt. "I lost track of her, and honestly? I thought she might get better. But then I saw her the other day, and she was acting just the same as she used to."

I never saw her. Today was first time I'd even glimpsed her in a year, and it was the back of her head.

It wasn't enough.

But soon, she'd be back. Time was running out, and a certain foster home had opened up in Rose Hill.

Did I have a hand in it? No.

Did my uncle? Well, he never denied it.

It was my time to leave. Cindy and Jeff didn't strike me as particularly trusting people, and they were starting to eye me. It may not be an immediate decision to make Margo move on, but as I said—an ounce of doubt was all they needed.

Just out the door, and Margo's foster sister—the older one—was waiting for me.

"You are Caleb, aren't you?" she asked.

I raised my eyebrow.

She grinned at me, eyes wide. "You're more handsome than she said."

"She shouldn't be talking about me." I let my gaze run

up and down her body. "And you shouldn't be talking to me."

"I've never been one to follow the rules." She winked. "Nice meeting you, Caleb. I'll see you around."

Chapter 35
Margo

The diner is forever away. While Riley drives, I flip through the yearbook. There's nothing connecting Masters to the Ashers. In fact, it would appear that he ran in an entirely different circle. Until I get to the last page, which appears to have student-submitted photographs.

"Holy shit," I whisper.

It's Jim Masters, and his arm is hooked around my dad's neck. They're surrounded by other students in some sort of academic competition. There're wearing the school uniform from back then, and one of the girls in front holds a trophy.

"What?" Riley asks.

"He knew my dad."

"This is all sorts of messed up," she mutters. "I skimmed the journal while you were inside. The most recent entry was from a few days ago, and it's seriously twisted."

I close the yearbook and reach for the notebook, skimming through until I get to the last page with writing on it.

Why is she so obsessed with him? She hasn't

done anything to deserve his attention. She doesn't deserve <u>him</u>.

The last line is underlined three times, and it seems like she wrote over each sentence three times.

"Lydia wrote this?"

Riley shrugs. "It sounds weird, right?"

I go back to the beginning, turning the pages slower.

"Wait..." The car slows as we come up to a red light, and I show her the page. "Does this handwriting look different?"

"What do the earlier ones sound like?"

I open to a page dated mid-2010 and read, "'Ben was not happy with my admission. Unfortunately for him, he doesn't have a choice over my body and what I choose to do with it. I fear our marriage won't overcome this.'" I squint at the page. "She moves on to talking about some art project Caleb brought home from school."

"So, they didn't have the happiest of marriages."

I scan the pages, finally finding one from July. "Okay. Oh God."

"Read it!"

I clear my throat. "'It had to happen. My poor baby. It was easy enough to hide from the kids, but Ben... I fear he's never going to look at me the same. I know he's taken a lover to get back at me. The betrayal stings. I thought he would be better than this.'"

"Shit," Riley says.

We're both quiet for a moment.

Then she asks, "What do you think she means by that? What had to happen?"

"Something she hid from me and Caleb," I guess. "Which could be anything."

"We're almost there."

I grab her arm. "Park around the corner. Just in case."

"Roger that." She glances at me. "Should we call someone?"

"Like the police?"

"Well... *yeah.*"

I bite my lip. She parks near the diner, and we both hop out. I draw my jacket closer around me. The wind is fierce downtown, funneled between taller buildings.

"We don't know if anything is wrong," I eventually say. "Unknown—*Claire*—has been targeting me this whole time. Why suddenly take Caleb?"

"Classic villain move," she murmurs. "He's the bait."

We get to the first window of the diner, and I hold her back. Carefully, I push up on my tiptoes and peek inside.

I don't see Caleb, but Claire is pacing up and down the main aisle. I crane even farther. Maybe he's sitting in the short row of booths, just out of my sight.

Claire turns toward the window, and I duck.

"Did she see you?" Riley hisses.

"I don't think so. I couldn't see Caleb either." I steer Riley back around the corner, to safety. "There's always a back entrance, right? For safety?"

She stares at me. "You're not seriously—"

"She has Caleb." I'm firm but also shaking. My hands tremble. "And if she does anything to him... Yeah, absolutely not. I can't just sit out here."

"Fine." She pulls out her phone. "I'll call them."

"Good idea. May as well tell Eli's dad, too. I have a feeling at least one of us is going to need a lawyer."

She groans, but I ignore it. I jog around to the alley and

slip into it. The street is deserted, which is the weirdest part. Not a single car has passed us. Then again, this area of town is run-down. Old and tired. The corner of the brick building is chipped and crumbling, and the alley is gross.

I stop in front of a large metal door. Someone put a *Lucky's* sticker on it. A big leprechaun with a green hat, the name of the diner in thick yellow script, and it's skewed to the left.

The door very well may be locked.

Claire could have Caleb at knifepoint or something.

Taking a deep breath, I twist the door handle. It opens easily, and I pause.

Listen.

I can't hear anything.

Here goes nothing.

I slip in through the back door, careful to shut it soundlessly behind me. I creep through the kitchen and realize that everything in me has gone quiet. My hands aren't shaking, my heart has slowed.

The sound of sirens is faint, but it raises goosebumps along my arms.

I duck down next to the fridge when Claire appears in the window.

"Get over here," she snaps. "Who the hell called the police?"

"Oh, maybe anyone who walked by and saw you waving a gun around," Caleb answers. "Not your brightest move."

Holy shit. Grateful for that piece of information, but also—where the fuck did Claire get a gun? I wouldn't know the first place to look for one, or how to use it.

She pivots. "What *was* my brightest move?"

"Hmm... probably using my mother the way you did. I can only assume you pushed her into this."

"Me?" She laughs. "I was *elated* when I discovered whose house we were going to. David and Iris Asher. They have pictures of the family on the wall, you know. David caught me staring at your photo one day and asked if I knew you. The whole story just poured out—"

"Whole story? What, that you saw me once, a few weeks prior?"

My heart goes into my throat.

What am I doing, just crouching here? I came in to make a difference. To save Caleb from the evil bitch I thought was my foster sister.

"Claire," I call, rising. I shove through the swinging doors. "Don't shoot me."

She's behind the counter, just where I thought. And Caleb, between us, is on the floor. He leans against the wall, his wrists duct taped.

His eyebrows go up, but other than that, his face stays blank.

I hate that she's made him put the mask back up.

"Well, well, well." She sounds like she's quoting a bad movie. "Look what the cat dragged in."

"Apt analogy, since apparently you like to think of me as a bird."

She grins. "I knew you'd understand."

"You wrote about it," I continue. "Where you thought we wouldn't find it."

Her expression drops. "You went in my room?"

Always so possessive.

Any feeling of sisterly love I was holding on to drains away. Claire will kill us all if she's allowed to continue.

"I did. Found your newspaper shrine, the picture..."

Am I purposefully instigating her?

Yep. Anything to get her away from Caleb.

She stalks toward me, shoving the gun into my chest. "Sit down."

Cold fear pulses through me for the first time. There's a gleam in her eyes that I haven't seen before. It makes me think she's been dreaming about this moment for a long time.

I start to sit next to Caleb, and she screams, lashing out. She shoves me away, still shrieking.

"You don't get it! He's not yours anymore!"

I raise my hands in surrender. "Okay, okay."

Her head lifts. The sirens are getting louder—not just coincidence anymore. They're screaming toward us.

Her eyes fill with tears, and she squats next to Caleb. "Did you call the cops on me, Margo? Afraid I might hurt your precious boyfriend?"

"I didn't call the police."

She clicks her tongue. "Change of plan. Up. Into the kitchen."

I rise from my half-crouch, risking a glance at Caleb. His eyes are on me.

Claire shoves me into the kitchen, seeming unconcerned about Caleb behind her. She presses the gun into my spine, and I leap forward, getting away from her.

"What started this?" I look back at her.

She just scoffs. "*You* started this."

"How on earth?"

"Come along, Caleb, or I'll shoot Margo in the spine. Probably won't kill her, but she'll sure as hell never walk again."

He growls behind us. "This isn't the way to do things."

"Just get in here," she snaps. She grabs my shoulder and yanks me back against her.

I grit my teeth, seriously regretting my decision.

"Sit down next to the stove," she orders him.

He slips past us and lowers himself to the floor. He'd probably do anything to protect me—including listening to whatever she said. *Fuck.* Maybe he has this handled.

Maybe Claire is going to kill us both.

"This wasn't all you," I try. "Right? You had help."

She sighs. Her breath hits the back of my neck. "Six months ago, I was just a girl with a crush on someone I'd never even met. The way you talked about him when you were kids..."

She leaves me standing in the middle of the galley and crouches next to Caleb. He doesn't move as she runs the tip of the gun down his temple.

"Stop touching him," I snap.

Caleb's jaw tics.

"You're not in charge here," she says. She trades the gun for her finger, sliding it down his jaw. "Is she, Caleb? Tell her she's not in charge. *I*'m the one with the power."

"Power. Is that what you think Caleb is going to give you?" I shake my head, balling my hands into fists.

I could just charge at her. But then she'd probably shoot me, or maybe Caleb.

I run my hands up and down my thighs, and freeze when my palm hits the clip on the knife Liam gave me.

Shit.

We're lucky she didn't see it. Didn't pat me down and freak out.

Slowly, I pull it out and slip it into my jacket pocket.

And meanwhile, Caleb's eyes are tracking my every movement. Claire... her nose is in his hair.

She stands and laughs. "Power, you said? Hmm, what an interesting idea."

"What, then?"

The gun is loose in her grip, and she waves it around as she looks between Caleb and me. "I was a girl with a crush, and then he became someone real. He came to our house to destroy us—but he only destroyed *me*. Look at you. You're fine. A rich family that gives a shit—"

"And how did he destroy you?"

"Bet he didn't expect Cindy and Jeff to kick *all* of us out. Hanna and you got good deals. Families. And me..."

"You live with Caleb's aunt and uncle," I blurt out. "With your sister. How—"

"She is *not my sister*!" Claire shrieks. "She belongs with them."

I tilt my head. "You read Lydia's journals? That's why you started writing in them. Because you'd read about—"

My poor baby.

Twelve years ago, Lydia did something so awful, Ben wrote her out of his will. Something awful that she hid from us. And in revenge...

"Is Hanna Caleb's half sister?"

Claire's lips twist. So she came to the same conclusion I did, but she has no relation to the Ashers. Not through Ben. And that's not how custody works anyway. You don't drop off a kid with her mother's deceased husband's brother.

"David and Lydia?"

"What?" Caleb chokes out.

Claire laughs. Tips her head back and lets it pour out of her. "Isn't it ironic that you got Caleb's dad killed for sleeping with your mom, and meanwhile, Caleb's mom was fucking his *brother*?"

"More like fucked up," I whisper.

Caleb shakes his head, faster to process than me. "Where do you come into play, Claire?"

"My parents adopted Hanna," she says quietly, hopping up onto one of the counters. "Apparently my birth caused some complications in the form of a full hysterectomy, and Mom wasn't ready to be done. Hanna never knew. One minute we were a family, and the next, they were carrying in a newborn."

"Does she know now?" I ask.

"I'm sure." She laughs. "We went to a group home, and some man came in to meet us. They DNA tested her. Came back soon after, said she was coming with him."

"She made them take you, too." Caleb scoffs. "Of course. She's nice and you're..."

"Not," Claire finishes. She grins. "We complete each other's sentences."

I bite my tongue so I don't say something I'll regret.

The phone on the wall rings, and all three of us jump.

She stares at it. "They're closed. Why is it ringing?"

"It's probably for you," Caleb points out. "You know, to negotiate."

Her eyes light up. "Margo, answer it."

I approach it slowly, like it's going to attack me. "Hello?"

"Claire Evans, this is the Beacon Police Department. My name is—"

"Um, this is Margo." I lick my lips. "She made me answer the phone."

"Margo—"

"Ms. Wolfe," Detective Masters says, seemingly taking over the phone call. "You weren't supposed to go in there."

"She needed someone to talk to." I glance at Claire.

She waves the gun at me. "What do they want?"

"Can you tell us if anyone is hurt?" Masters asks.

"No. Caleb and I are okay."

"We just want to resolve this peacefully."

"What is he *saying*?" Claire snaps.

My temper is fraying. "If you wanted to know, you should've answered the damn phone."

She comes over and snatches it, shoving me away. In the years we lived together, she never laid a hand on me. Now it's twice.

I go to Caleb, immediately ripping at the tape on his wrists. It's useless. She wound it around so thick, I'd need scissors to break through it.

"You okay?" He leans his forehead to mine. "You shouldn't have come in here."

"Don't." I glare at him. "If something happened to you—"

His taped hands come up and grab the front of my shirt, hauling me to him.

He slams his lips against mine, fast and furious.

When he pulls away a second later, I narrow my eyes. "That better not have been your way of saying—"

"Margo," Claire says.

Caleb's grip slips from my shirt, and I straighten.

I raise my eyebrow. The phone is back on the wall, and she saunters toward us. My attention goes to the gun, which she's slowly raising in my direction.

"Step away from Caleb," she orders. "He isn't yours anymore."

"Like hell," I mutter.

She slaps me.

My head whips to the side, pain exploding across my cheek and jaw. She just *hit* me.

"You're lucky I didn't shoot you," she says. "Maybe I just should and get it over with."

She cocks the safety, and my heart stops.

And then Caleb is between us. His closeness forces me to step back, and we keep going until my hip hits one of the counters.

"Always the freaking knight in shining armor," Claire says. "Saving her again?"

"Saving you," he answers. "How do you expect to walk out of here if you shoot either of us?"

Her eyes round.

"Besides, we were having a conversation. Remember?" He rolls his shoulders. "How did they know Hanna was my mom's kid?"

Claire purses her lips. "I don't know."

He takes a step forward. "You're smarter than most. You didn't figure it out?"

She lifts her chin. "Lydia had kept papers of the adoption contract. Once the Ashers discovered them... It was just a matter of time before they took her back."

Dirty little sneak.

"And then I found her diary, and it was painfully obvious what had happened." She hops back up on the counter. "She documented all of it."

Caleb glances back at me, raising his eyebrow.

He's asking, *Did you find that?*

I barely lower my chin. The most silent *yes* I can manage.

"Then what, Claire?"

I admit, I want to know, too. I try not to show it—leaning backward and crossing my arms instead of leaning in. His hands are still bound in front of him, but somehow he portrays *sincere* so much better than me.

My wrists itch just thinking about the duct tape residue, and I dig my nails into my palms.

"Then..." She shrugs, smiling.

I've seen that face before. Devious, cunning Claire, who used to lie through her teeth when it suited her. How many times had Hanna and I covered for her when she snuck out? She'd serenely tell our foster parents that she was just in the bathroom when they checked, then laugh behind their backs.

My stomach twists.

"Did you blackmail her?" I ask.

Her gaze hardens. "Blackmail? I just told her what I knew. It was *her* idea to break you apart. After the scheme your mom and her tried went wrong—" Her lips press together. "Oops, I wasn't supposed to tell you that."

"Our moms were planning something?" Caleb takes another step toward Claire.

She lifts one shoulder. "I don't remember."

Slowly, I pull the journal out of my pocket. "Would this help you remember?"

She pushes off one of the counters. "Give that to me."

The phone on the wall rings.

"Shut up!" she screams at it. "I just need some freaking quiet!"

I shrink away from her, snatching at the back of Caleb's shirt. He shouldn't stand so close to a lunatic. I tug, but he doesn't budge.

"Have Margo answer it," Caleb suggests.

"What are you doing?" I whisper.

"Trust me," he replies through his teeth.

I do. There was once a time when I would've said I didn't, but that seems far in the past.

Claire grabs at her hair. The gun is abandoned on the counter behind her, and it's all I can focus on.

"Margo, do it," she snaps.

I slip past Caleb. I could go around Claire, down a different aisle—and put the kitchen's center countertop between us—or... I walk toward her. My heart hammers, and I keep my eyes wide.

Looking fearful—of Claire, and also what I'm about to do—isn't an act.

She moves to the side.

The phone keeps ringing and ringing.

Two feet away, then one. She groans, her hands releasing her hair and sliding down her face.

This is your moment, a voice in my head whispers.

It's a combination of Dad and Caleb. Liam and Riley and Robert and Lenora.

I throw myself sideways, into Claire. We topple, but I grasp the counter to keep from going down.

She shrieks as she falls, her fingers losing traction against the smooth material of my jacket. She locks on to my wrist and yanks me down with her.

Forget the gun.

I fall on top of her. My elbow digs into her stomach, and she lets out an *oof*.

But that can't just be the end of it. She's a fighter.

She grips my hair, yanking my head back, and we flip. My scalp stings at the pressure.

I flail. My elbow vibrates all the way down to my fingers when I make contact with bone—shoulder or head, I can't tell. She punches me, her fist skating across my jaw. My cheek cuts into my teeth, and blood fills my mouth.

I scramble to my knees and dive for her, pinning her

arms above her head. Once I've straddled her, I lean to one side and spit out blood.

"Let go of me, you freak!" She thrashes. "You're ruining everything! You're dead, you hear me?"

"I've had enough of your bullshit," I answer. I cock my fist back and let it fly. I'm readier for the pain that skitters across my knuckles.

Her head snaps to the side.

We never fought when we lived together, but she sure did know how to get on my nerves.

This was a long time coming.

Caleb grabs me under the arms, hauling me up and away. "That was hot."

I glance at him. His arms are free. He pulls the rest of the tape off, his eyes on me. I turn to Claire, who is slowly climbing to her feet.

"You're going to pay for that." She wipes blood off her mouth with the back of her hand, then looks around.

I find the gun at the same time she does, and we both go for it.

Her fingers graze the barrel, but I'm faster.

I yank it away and swing around. She stops dead when I level it at her chest. My thumb flicks the safety off.

"Just try me," I warn. "You've been harassing me for months. You put a dead bird in my room. Where did that even come from? Pretty bird?"

She stares at me. It would appear that she's unafraid of the gun. "You don't remember?"

I stay silent.

She tips her head back and laughs. "Oh, the irony. The answer is in your *hand*. In your past, too. And I couldn't resist—it was so much fun ruffling your feathers."

Caleb grimaces. "You weren't at Emery-Rose. How did you get that inside knowledge?"

Claire grins. "Amelie was more than happy to assist."

"I doubt that," I say.

"You're right," she answers. "She was more than happy to assist *after* I blackmailed her."

"With what?" I glance from Claire to Caleb, hoping to unspin the mysteries. My head is starting to hurt with all the new information, but... adrenaline keeps my focus on the present.

Claire shrugs. "I can't give away *all* my secrets. What's to stop them from bursting in here?" She rubs at her eyes. "You're the one with the gun in your hand. Are you going to shoot me, Margo?"

"I might," I whisper. "You'd deserve it."

"I'll go away for whatever crimes they can pin on me, but I didn't do anything bad."

"You *kidnapped* me!" Left me for dead in an abandoned barn.

I could do it.

I could shoot her.

All I would have to do is pull the trigger.

My vision tunnels onto Claire. She appears innocent, but she's not. She's going to walk out of the interrogation room and hurt someone.

"You don't feel anything, do you?" I ask her.

"Wouldn't you like to know?" She pinches at her skin of her arm, twisting it. "Do you think I feel pain? You could find out. Watch me scream. Come on, Margo, it's easy. I know you're thinking about it."

I readjust my grip on the gun. I've never hurt anyone, but she's under my skin. Dragging me down with her.

It's easy to let her manipulate the situation. To get drunk on control. *I'm* the one with the power.

"Am I still in a cage, Claire?"

Caleb touches my arm. He's such a presence at my side, my body hums with awareness.

"Come back to me," he whispers.

I shudder. My eyes are fastened on Claire, but she's slowly backing away. Her face is pale, and she... she looks young.

So much younger than she did a moment ago, when our lives were in her hands.

He slides between us, taking the gun out of my hands and setting it on the counter. I let him. It slips out of my fingers easily, and I exhale once I'm free of it.

He tips my chin up, inspecting my face.

Claire isn't a threat anymore. Somehow the tide shifted when we fought, and she's retreating.

I stare up into Caleb's light-blue eyes, wondering when I'll come back to myself.

The back door flies open. It crashes into the wall.

He wraps his arms around me, pulling me down.

Someone screams, and the police flood in. We stay crouched together as they sweep the area.

They're a river of dark-blue jackets and weapons.

"Mr. Asher and Ms. Wolfe," a familiar voice says.

I meet Detective Masters' eyes.

"You're safe." He offers his hand.

I let him help me up. Caleb rises with me, keeping one hand on my hip.

The detective's attention goes to Caleb's wrists. He points out the obvious: "Duct tape."

"Claire bound me," Caleb says. "It's a long story."

"No doubt. Josh is waiting for you both outside, as are

your foster parents, Margo." He lifts his chin toward the door into the main diner. "Let's go out the front."

"That's it?" I ask. I can't help it. "It's over?"

"Claire tried to run. She's in custody. We have some questions for her, and then… we'll figure out where she goes from there."

"She said she didn't act alone," I blurt out. The journal is back in my pocket, safely tucked away. What kind of evidence will it actually be? Anyone could've written in it.

I can see Robert and Lenora huddled together by an ambulance, and my stomach twists.

I continue, "There are things you don't know. Big-picture things."

Masters nods. "There's a time to figure all that out, okay? Right now, I'd like to see a happy reunion. Don't want to keep them waiting, right?"

Caleb laces his fingers with mine, squeezing my hand.

Masters walks out the front door, holding it open for us, but Caleb keeps me back.

"Whatever dark hole you crawl down," he presses a kiss to my temple, "I'll drag you out of it."

Tears fill my eyes.

That's exactly what he did.

And he'll have to do it again, because I'm still there. Drowning in the past that's suddenly right in front of my eyes.

Chapter 36
Caleb

I wrap my arm around Margo's shoulders. She's shaking like a leaf, but I don't think she even realizes. Her expression doesn't change from the worried scowl when we go outside, crossing the street to where the ambulances have parked.

Robert and Lenora rush toward us. They surprise me by not waiting until we're separated. They throw their arms around both of us, so it's like a weird, crying huddle.

I pat Robert's back, but my gaze is on Margo.

There's something in her expression that has me on edge.

The concern, more than anything, is the driving force pushing away my anger. She went into the diner when she *knew* Claire was dangerous. I could've handled it, but Margo played right into Claire's hands. Of course Claire wanted the three of us in the same room, with herself in control.

The EMTs check out Margo and me as soon as Robert and Lenora release us. We sit on the back step. Margo's hand is loose in mine.

She's still not here.

"Caleb," Mr. Black calls. He puts his hand on my shoulder once he gets to us. "Thank God you're all right."

"We made it out in one piece," I say.

Margo shakes her head. "Did we?"

"I think Uncle David has Amber," I tell him. "Can you tell Detective Masters?"

Mr. Black's eyebrow raises. "What makes you think that?"

"Mom called this morning. Eli and I went over, and her apartment had been ransacked. She didn't say as much, but..."

"Got it." He crouches next to Margo. "You okay?"

"Fine, Mr. Black, thank you," she says.

"That's a good girl."

She looks up at the EMT hovering nearby. "When can we go home?"

"I just need a statement," Masters answers. He approaches with Eli's dad close behind.

"A statement," Margo repeats.

"Can this wait, Detective? They just went through a traumatic experience—"

"Which means we should go over it while it's fresh," Masters finishes.

I really hate that man.

"Can we do it now?" I ask.

Masters scans my body, taking inventory of my bumps and bruises. "Okay. Come with me."

We both stand, but he waves at Margo. "No, just one at a time. That's how this works—I get you to tell me what happened, then Margo's version. Then Claire's."

I grunt, slowly releasing her hand. "I'll be right back."

She doesn't react. Her attention is fixed on her hands.

He leads me to his car. "Get in."

"The back?"

He chuckles. "No, front's fine."

I slide into the passenger seat, and he cranks the heat.

"So. What happened?"

I recount the events. Claire showing up on my running route, telling me about an accident. She pulled out the gun when I questioned her about a wrong turn, and... everything went downhill.

"Did you think about getting the gun away from her?"

I shrug. "I don't know anything about firearms, sir."

"Sir." He chuckles. "Haven't heard that out of an Asher's mouth in a while."

Time for some honesty. "Can I ask you something?"

"Sure."

"You went to Emery-Rose, right? Did you know my dad?" I have a feeling that's the reason behind the weird anger he directed at me. Caleb Asher, son of the infamous Benjamin Asher. The expression, *like father, like son* exists for a reason, doesn't it?

He sighs. "Yeah, I knew of him. I was friends with Keith."

I sit up straight. "Keith Wolfe."

"Fresh out of the academy, and my first case was your dad's death. The lead detective followed the lines right to Keith." He shakes his head. "I'm sorry you saw your dad like that. I knew they were friends, even though Ben was always a bully in school."

"A bully," I repeat. "To you?"

"No. Not to me. Other guys in school. The random girl." He shifts. "Keith was good. At least, I thought..."

"He's innocent," I blurt out.

When did I start believing that?

Probably around the same time you fell in love with Margo.

I shove *that* thought neatly to the back of my mind.

"Do you have evidence to back that up?"

"I don't. But Claire admitted that Amber and my mom were scheming. And Hanna—"

"Evans? Claire's sister?"

"Right. She's actually my mom's daughter. I'm sure you can verify that through adoption records. And maybe a DNA test." I'm making a plea. Practically begging the detective to listen to me. I'm holding his attention, but it might not last. "I don't know what Margo's mom and mine had planned, but I think they wanted to get back at my dad."

His expression turns thoughtful. "The case was very cut-and-dry. Fingerprints on the knife he used..."

"A knife that anyone in the house had access to?" I twist toward him. "Tobias Hutchins, his lawyer, screwed him over."

"Proof, Caleb. If your goal is to exonerate Keith, I need more."

I run my hand over my face. "I just... we know he's innocent. He got caught up in a shitstorm."

He exhales. "Okay. We'll talk to Amber and Lydia, see if anything comes of it. They're involved in this, one way or another."

"Right."

"So," he prompts, "Claire drove you here. Then what?"

"She was ranting." I close my eyes. "She duct taped my wrists, and all I could think about was how worried Margo was going to be when I didn't come back."

"Claire has been living with the Ashers," Detective

Masters says. "We did a background check on her. She has a full and colorful file, to say the least."

"And my uncle is an abusive asshole," I grumble. I can't believe I just said that out loud. "What happens if he's arrested for... literally anything?"

"Happens with what?"

"He presides over my inheritance," I say. "But I'm pretty sure the clause in there says only if he remains in good standing with the law."

Wait.

Maybe Dad knew what kind of devil his brother was. So why entrust the money to him?

I fling the door open. "Sorry, I've got to talk to Mr. Black."

I rush toward where Mr. Black is waiting with Margo and blurt out, "You presided over my dad's will."

He squints at me. "Are you okay?"

"You presided over my dad's will. You know what it says—your firm has the papers."

"Yes, that's correct."

"I need to see it."

Margo reaches out and hooks her index finger with mine.

She's with me.

Mr. Black shrugs. "Okay. Let me just tell the detective that he can get Margo's statement at the station tomorrow. I also informed the police that Amber's whereabouts are unknown. They're going to look for her. Wait right here, I'll be back in a flash."

Robert and Lenora press closer. They'd been silent up until now, blending into the background.

"Margo?" Lenora asks. "You okay, honey?"

She shrugs. "Just..."

She's shutting down before our very eyes, but her finger is still gripping mine.

"Is it okay if Margo comes with me and Mr. Black?" I ask them. "I'll have her home before eight."

Margo sucks in a breath, but she doesn't say anything.

Lenora strokes Margo's hair. "Is that what you want?"

"I'd like to stay with Caleb," she answers.

Mr. Black comes back. "We're good to go."

Margo rises, letting Robert and Lenora hug her again. She withdraws rather quickly, looping her arm through mine. She hugs my arm tightly, fingers digging into my biceps.

Worry tugs at me.

In the car, we both sit in the back seat. Eli's dad gives me a look, but after a second of watching Margo in the rearview mirror, he nods.

I trace patterns on her leg.

"We're going to the city?" she asks, lifting her head.

"Yes, my office is downtown," he says. "I grabbed you a water bottle, Margo."

I take the bottle he holds over his shoulder, and she takes a few sips.

"What's going on in that head of yours?" I whisper.

She shifts, pulling the small journal out of her pocket. "Claire never did get her hands on this."

She flips it open, seemingly searching for something.

And then she exhales, handing it over to me.

Amber was singing today. She never mentioned having a voice, but it's surprisingly good. I stayed out of the kitchen and closed my eyes, trying to remember the last time the house was full of happiness.

Well before I destroyed it, that's for sure.

I asked myself if she was singing to Ben, and it almost killed me not knowing. I crept through the house and finally gave in, peeking around the corner. I felt like Caleb on one of his spy missions.

It wasn't Ben—it was Margo. Amber had her daughter on the counter while she worked bread dough beside her.

She was singing 'Blackbird' by The Beatles.

Telling her daughter to escape this house, maybe?

"Take your broken wings and learn to fly." The line Margo was later repeating to herself in the yard.

She looked at me and asked why her wings were broken, and I hated to say it was because of us. What Amber and I were doing to our families.

What I had already done.

What did I say? Something like, "You're a pretty little bird, Margo. Our wings let us fly, but they're also fragile. Protect your wings."

She seemed to like that.

I shake my head. "She *was* scheming."

"Pretty little bird," Margo says. "From Lydia. From my mother."

"Claire read it. The whole thing, probably. Whatever happened between our parents... I don't think it was your dad's fault. Or yours."

"You're right."

I meet her eyes. "I... am?"

She sighs, tipping her head back. "Yeah. Let me tell you what really happened."

Chapter 37
Margo

Past

I fidgeted by the sink. Dad was at the kitchen table, reading a newspaper, but he kept glancing at me. It was rare that he wasn't working in the middle of the afternoon. Nice, too. I crept back home. The door to Mr. Asher's office was closed when I passed it, and Mom's car was gone.

"You seem off, kiddo," Dad said. "Everything okay?"

After Mom left me in Caleb's room, Mr. Asher had rounded on me and demanded to know what I saw. I tentatively told him all of it.

And Caleb hadn't been surprised. That was the worst part. He had a dead look in his eye while I spoke, and after...

He had come alive, grabbing my shoulders the same way Mom had. *Please don't say anything. It'll ruin everything.*

I shook my head, and then I remembered Mom's plea.

"All good," I managed.

He set down the paper and twisted toward me. "The truth, now?"

The gate opening drew my attention. Mom nudged it closed with her foot, her arms full of brown paper bags. Any minute now, she was going to walk in and see my expression.

The look that was one hundred percent guilt.

Dad saw it. A flash of fear.

"You saw them?" he asked in a low voice.

I jerked toward him. "I d-didn't mean to."

Mom came in and stopped short. Her gaze went from my face to Dad's. "Margo, what did you do?"

Dad stood. "Amber."

The bags fell from Mom's hands in slow motion, but the way she moved wasn't slow at all. She was suddenly in front of me, her hand on my chin. She forced my head up, until I met her eyes.

"Tell me what you said."

Tears filled my eyes, but I kept my mouth shut. I didn't say anything. I was going to keep her secret.

"Margo!" she screamed. Her fingers dug into my shoulders, and she shook me. Violently. My head snapped back. She yanked me toward her and away, movements brutal and jerky. "What did you do?"

For a second, everything was still and quiet. Her voice rang in my ears.

And then Dad was there, prying her away from me.

I fell backward. My head hit the edge of the table, and white spots exploded like fireworks in front of my vision. My head throbbed, pain radiating over my skull. I could barely keep my eyes open, but I saw Mom looming above me.

Dad shoved her—the first act of violence I'd ever seen

from him—and lifted me into his arms. He carried me down the hall, into my room, and set me on the bed.

In the other room, Mom was screaming. She must've been throwing things, because the sound of breaking glass came through the doorway.

"Stay here," he ordered. "Please, Margo."

I touched the back of my head. My fingers came away wet with blood, and I burst into tears.

There was so much yelling.

I ran to my door—to escape, to take the blame—but the knob wouldn't turn.

"*You ruined everything!*" Mom screamed.

I flinched away from the door.

"I ruined everything?" Dad yelled back. "You cannot seriously be pinning this on me, Amber."

"Like hell I can't. I had a plan! A way out of this godforsaken *home*!"

Crash. Then... silence.

"Daddy!" I screamed, beating at the door.

No one came for me. I beat and scratched at the door, kicked it, slammed my body against it. It didn't budge.

I backed away, then looked down at my hands. They were covered in blood. Then the pain came, edging through the numbness.

I had kept her secret, but Dad *knew*. He knew, and she blamed me.

"Mom," I moaned and sank to my knees. "I didn't tell."

Ages later, the door swung open. Dad came in and knelt in front of me, picking up my hands. He inspected the damage.

His whole face was eons of sadness.

"Want to go somewhere happy?" He scooped me up. "Let's clean your hands off."

He carried me into the bathroom and gently cleaned my hands, wincing for me at the shredded nails. They stung under the warm, soapy water, but I didn't say anything.

I didn't ask where Mom was.

Or where they both had been.

"Up you go," he said.

I was in his arms again, hugging him like an octopus. He carried me to the car, and then we went to the park. I didn't see Mom, or anyone else. Not until the detective and social worker showed up.

Present

"I didn't do it," I finish lamely. I'm back to inspecting my nails, like I'd be able to see a trace of the past in them.

He's been staring at me while I relayed what I remember, but now...

"God," he chokes out.

This is where he says it was only revenge, and now that the need for it is suddenly gone...

I lick my lips, imagining I can still taste his goodbye kiss on my lips. We could've died. *He* could've died. That was where things were heading. After all, Claire was disintegrating before our eyes.

How long would it have taken for Caleb to bleed out if she'd shot him?

"Stop," he orders.

I blink at him.

"Your thoughts are turning bleak, baby."

Josh has been listening in silence, but now he says, "We're coming up on it now."

I lean toward the window. "This feels... familiar."

Caleb smirks. "Because we came here when we got our masks."

"You left me in the lobby."

His smirk widens into a grin. "Yep."

Josh shakes his head.

We park in a garage, circling down until we get to an empty row of spaces. One of the spots has a placard engraved with, *Josh Black, Esq.*

"Fancy," I say.

"Beats hunting for a spot," he answers.

We all pile out and into the elevator.

"What did you come here for before?" I ask.

"Any time David wants to make big changes, Caleb signs off on them," Josh answers. "While it first appeared that David had full control over Caleb's assets, there were strict rules implemented to keep everyone honest. It requires continual upkeep."

"Until now," Caleb mutters.

His firm is a lot like Tobias's. On a high floor, with huge windows letting light stream into offices and the bullpen. No one is around at this time of evening. The sun has set, casting everything in a twilight-blue hue.

He flips on the light, and we head to his office.

I sit on the couch, pulling my legs up so I can wrap my arms around them. Josh goes to his filing system, locating a thick envelope. Caleb and him go to the desk, and they both pore over it.

Finally, Caleb taps a paragraph. "I knew it!"

I sit up straighter. "What?"

He grins at me. "If Uncle is arrested, all assets immediately revert back to me."

I bolt to my feet. "You—"

Josh shakes his head. "I'm sorry I didn't notice this sooner, or even remember—"

"Caleb!"

They both jerk toward me.

"Your dad had to know that David was Hanna's father, *and* that he was a monster. You..." My features soften. "You could've taken power back from your uncle all along."

His face falls, and his gaze goes back to the will. At the bottom of the page is his dad's signature, the looping *B* and spiked *A*.

He makes a call.

Josh and I trade a confused glance.

"Detective," Caleb says.

My eyebrows hike up.

He's willingly calling Detective Masters?

"I'll do whatever has to be done."

Ah, hell. I sink back onto the couch, dropping my head in my hands. Caleb's slowly turning into the good guy, willing to do anything to set things right. Why does that make me think our troubles aren't over?

Chapter 38
Caleb

Detective Masters arrives in Josh's office in under an hour, accompanied by a woman who he introduces as Detective Carver with the NYPD. She carries a small soft-shell case.

"Brought her in because this is a jurisdictional nightmare," he tells us. "Claire started talking. She mentioned you had a notebook of hers?"

Margo blushes. "Yeah. It was Lydia's, and then Claire started writing in it."

He grunts. "Can I see it?"

She rises, pulling it out of her coat. He takes it carefully, flipping through it.

"We'll get this back to you," he tells her. "But I need to take this as evidence."

"I don't want it back," she says faintly. "If it helps..."

He nods, then turns to me. "Ready?"

"Can I...?" I motion for the journal. "Maybe Mom wrote about Tobias."

I skim through it. She *had* to have written about him.

Margo reads over my shoulder, and her hand shoots out. "There. T.H."

"He's still at work," Carver says, reading something off her phone. "We should go now. Ready?"

On the phone with Masters, I did something a little stupid. I volunteered to go talk to Tobias while wearing a wire.

I don't know how long it usually takes to obtain a warrant, but apparently there's enough evidence for them all to want to move with haste.

Carver reveals the thin piece of cord and medical tape, motioning to me.

I take a deep breath and remove my shirt. They work quickly, taping the microphone to my chest. I carefully pull my shirt back on, and Carver disappears into the hallway, her phone pressed to her ear.

"Testing?" I joke.

"You need to get him to admit to taking a bribe," Detective Masters says. "And whatever else he tells you will be icing on the cake. Okay?"

My smile fades. "Got it."

"Am I going?" Margo asks.

"Yes," I say.

"No," Masters says at the same time.

We glare at each other.

"She's coming with me." I'm not letting her out of my sight.

He sighs. "Fine. If anything goes south, you just say something about the weather—like, 'I hear we're going to have a hot summer.' Some shit like that. Got it?"

"Yep."

"What if he brings up the weather?" Margo asks.

Detective Masters groans. "Get creative."

Josh frowns. "I don't have a good feeling about this. What do you think will come of this?"

The detective's gaze bounces around the three of us, then finally settles on Margo. "Claire told us that your mother's affair with Ben Asher was planned between Amber and Lydia."

I squint.

"Because of Hanna," Margo says. Her voice is so low, we almost miss it. "This whole thing started because Lydia couldn't keep her legs shut?"

I hide my smile behind my hand. My little wolf is coming back to herself.

"Ah—"

"Don't answer that, Detective," Josh says. "Let's get this show on the road. I'd like nothing more than for this day to be over."

We make the short trek to Tobias's law firm. It's just two blocks away, but Josh and the detective insist on driving. Carver nods at us from an unmarked car parked on the street. The van just ahead of her is probably filled with police officers. Or maybe it's just one lonely tech listening to my breathing.

"You're on your own from here," Masters says. "Remember—"

"Weather means help," I say. "Got it."

"Good luck," Josh says.

I take Margo's hand as we walk into the building. "I can't believe you came here without me."

"What was I supposed to do? Ask you to accompany me while I ask him about my dad?" She shakes her head. "You didn't believe me."

"I do now," I say. "Ever since I talked to him. Maybe even before that."

She glances up at me. "Really?"

"Yes. I want your dad out of prison. I swear it."

She smiles. "Thank you."

I call the elevator, and the doors slide open immediately. I hit the button for the law firm's level, and the doors close. Silence descends. I'm too aware of the tape on my skin. The way Margo keeps sucking her lower lip into her mouth. If she wasn't holding my hand, she'd be scratching her wrist. And... the silence is getting to me. Maybe my nerves are frayed from the day we've had, because a strange feeling is bubbling up inside me.

"I'm in love with you," I blurt out. It's about time I told her.

She freezes. "Huh?"

The elevator chimes, and the doors open.

Way to ruin it.

The floor is basically empty. We go past the receptionist's abandoned desk. There are a few lawyers in the bullpen, at their cubicles with their heads bent. Some people never stop working. They're itching to get ahead, so focused on the future that they forget to have lives.

They don't notice us gliding past them.

I'm determined not to be like them. Not to shutter my gaze away from what's happening around me.

Margo takes the lead. She's been here before, and she seems to remember where she's going. Around the cubicles, to one of the offices against the far wall.

Without knocking, Margo turns the knob and bursts inside.

Tobias Hutchins makes a choking noise in surprise. "Ms. Wolfe? What are you doing here?"

"She's with me," I say, stepping into the room.

He's been afraid of me for a while. Since Mom once

slipped that she knew him as *more than a friend* as she shuffled him out of Uncle David's house. At the time, I thought they'd met at Keith's trial. It was the natural connection.

But... I know the truth now.

"Ah, Mr. Asher," Tobias says. "What brings you... here?"

Margo pulls out the journal. "Do you recognize this?"

He says nothing—which is an answer in and of itself.

I take it from Margo's hand and stride closer. "She's quite a detail-oriented woman, my mother."

His eyes widen.

"She took note of every meeting, every chance encounter with our family. When everything goes sideways, who do you think will take the blame?"

"This is ridiculous—"

"You botched my father's trial," Margo snaps.

"It wasn't my idea." Tobias loosens his tie. "You think I ever wanted this for myself? That I thought I'd be sitting on..."

"On what? Guilt?"

"Blood money."

I lift my chin. "Who actually told you to do it?"

"Your mother was conniving." He goes to the window, yanking his tie completely off. "She said no one would know. No one would find out. The knife had his fingerprints on it."

Margo takes a step closer to me.

I tilt my head to the side. Rage has always felt strangely comforting to me. Like a security blanket I could wrap around my shoulders. I try to draw upon it now, but all I can muster is confusion.

Margo inches forward, until she's half blocking me from Tobias.

"Lydia pinned the whole thing on you."

I wonder when she learned to lie so well.

"Are you saying that isn't true?" She crosses her arms. "We just came for the truth. If you can't give us that... I guess we'll see you at your court date." She shrugs and pivots on her heel. "Come on, Caleb. We were just trying to help. But apparently he thought of everything."

I follow her to the door. Doubt creeps up the farther we get, but I'm just about to step out when he calls, "Stop!"

We reenter the room.

"Sit. Please." He gestures to the chairs in front of his desk, then slumps into his own seat. Once we're comfortable, he gives me a look. "You know I had no choice."

"Do I?"

"Your uncle is a monster. He threatened to take away *everything* if I didn't comply."

I scowl. "How did he get to you?"

Tobias shifts. "I didn't use legal methods to get through law school. I was a defender on a case his business partner was involved in, and he..." He clears his throat. "He got to me then. When this case came up, he and Lydia suggested I volunteer."

"That's my dad's *life* you threw away," Margo says. "Like it was nothing but saving your own ass."

"And a payout, I'd imagine." I lean my elbow on the arm of the chair.

He glares at us. "Aren't you listening? I didn't have a *choice*."

Margo opens the journal, practically tearing the pages with her force. "Two days before Caleb's dad died, you were there. Lydia writes, 'Tobias stopped by. He was nervous for what needed to be done. For our children's sake, we've decided that I'm going to take them out.' The next day: 'Keith nearly ruined everything, but in the end, it worked out better than we ever could've imagined.'"

She lifts her head. "You killed Benjamin Asher."

He hangs his head. "I wish I had never gotten roped into this. David and Lydia forced my hand."

I jump to my feet. Screw the fucking wire, and the police listening in—he just admitted to *murder*. "You stabbed him and left him for me to find."

"Lydia was supposed to find him," he says quietly.

"Caleb," Margo says behind me. "Easy."

"It was your car that was used to hit Margo and her foster parent. You gave him the keys because of David—or was it my mother? Sweet talking her way into your—"

"Fine! Yes, it was your mother." He grabs at his hair. "She didn't tell me—"

"Bullshit," Margo mumbles. "We need to leave."

Get in and get out. Last-minute instructions from Masters before patting my back and sending us in here.

"You're fucking twisted," I tell him. "And you're going to prison."

"How's that, Caleb?" Tobias straightens the papers on his desk. "Do you have more proof than just a notebook that could be filled with lies? No one is going to know that I was the one to kill Ben and get paid for it in more than just cash. No one will know that your mom and uncle were the orchestrators of the whole thing—including the so-called affair. Well, no, actually..." He winks at Margo. "The affair was just a plot between your mothers to bring down an angry, rich man. See how well that worked out?"

I pull up my shirt, exposing the wire. "Looks like the sun's going to come out tomorrow. Unfortunately... I don't think you'll be around to see it."

Tobias is calm for a moment, his eyes on my chest. And then he yells, lunging around the desk for me.

I yank Margo behind me, bracing for Tobias's charge.

He stops short when Detective Masters bursts into the room, the door cracking against the wall.

Masters sneers. "Game over, Hutchins."

He nods to me, and I guide Margo out of the room. She's not reacting the way I expected her to—*again*. It means something dark has taken root in her mind.

This was too much for her.

We pass by the police who are filtering in from the elevator, and I opt for the stairs. We get down three levels before I tug her to a stop.

"Look at me," I say.

She doesn't see me. Her gaze goes to my face, but she's not here.

I walk her backward, until she hits the wall.

She blinks up at me, squinting. "What are you doing?"

"Searching for you." My lips touch the corner of her mouth.

She lets out a little breath but doesn't move.

I move to her jaw, peppering kisses down the column of her throat. She's immobile, letting me do whatever I want.

Until my teeth graze her skin, followed by my tongue. She tastes sweet.

I bite harder than I should.

Wake up.

She pushes against my chest. I soothe the tender spot with my tongue, and her pushing becomes pulling. Her hands fist in my shirt, dragging me closer.

I drift away from her neck, going for her lips. She's ready, arching up. Her hands slip under the hem of my shirt, sliding—

"Are they still listening?" she whispers.

Shit.

I rip the tape off and lean down, until I'm almost touching the microphone. "I'm unplugging this so you can't hear me kiss my girl."

She huffs.

A small smile flickers across her face when I yank the mic apart and stuff it into my pocket.

"Better?" I wink.

I lift her hand. Her knuckles are bruised, and she winces when I prod them.

"Where'd you go?"

She looks away. "All of this could've been avoided if I had just *remembered...*"

"Or if I had paid closer attention." I place my finger under her chin and turn her head back toward me. "We can't blame ourselves for our parents' actions."

She shudders. "How do you stop blaming yourself? I feel physically nauseated."

I consider her question. A lot of it is my fault—she didn't realize anything was so vitally impaired until I brought it to her attention. A worm of guilt cuts through me, but I push it away.

"What would your therapist say?"

She makes a face. "She'd probably say some bullshit about forgiveness."

"I forgive you," I say automatically. "Do you forgive me?"

"I didn't hold it against y—"

"Do you forgive me?" I ask again, slower. Darker. I run my finger along the top edge of her jeans, grazing her stomach.

She responds well to my darkness. It makes me think

that maybe I succeeded in my mission to make our edges align.

"I do."

I smirk, dragging my finger lower. I dip into her jeans, past the hem of her panties.

"See what it feels like?" I ask.

She bites her lip, staring at me. She puts her weight on the railing and lets her legs fall open.

Fuck me.

A door above us bangs open, and she leaps up, smacking her forehead.

"Ow."

I chuckle, grabbing her hand and tugging her down the stairs. "You forget you were in a fight earlier today?"

"Easy to forget," she mumbles. She trips over her feet, nearly bringing both of us down.

"That's it." I scoop her into my arms and push through the door onto whatever the hell floor we made it to. I hit the button for the elevator with my elbow.

"Kiss me," she says.

I inspect her face. She seems better. But maybe I should just check...

She grins, reading my mind, and pulls my face toward hers. And the rest, as they say, is history.

Chapter 39
Margo

The last two days have been a whirlwind. I've been kept at home with the Bryans, and Caleb hasn't left my side.

Claire is going to juvie.

Masters and Carver worked together and found a property in Aunt Iris's name. It was a condo in an older part of Brooklyn. Inside, they found my mother. She was surrounded by her past. A near-identical replica to the house I grew up in.

She admitted to conspiring with Lydia, who first got her addicted to drugs and then used that power against her. Drugs were the reason she cheated on Dad, and the reason Lydia then felt a responsibility toward her.

This is all secondhand information from Detective Masters, who called me down to deliver my statement and sign it.

There's a certain sense of shame that comes with finding that out. Knowing Lydia was desperate to avenge the daughter she was forced to give up...

I set the pen down and meet the detective's gaze. "So, what now?"

"Our team is serving warrants as we speak. I expect an arrest to happen any day now."

I swallow. *Good.*

"And my dad? Tobias admitted to killing Benjamin Asher."

That's another thing. The Bryans know, unequivocally, that my dad is innocent. It wasn't just me saying it anymore —it was the police admitting it. The state. The county.

The district attorney, even.

While I wanted a family to want me... I think I'm getting something a little different.

"The judge has set a hearing for tomorrow," Masters says gently. "Is there anything else you want to talk about?"

I lean back in my chair. "Actually, yes. You were never able to pin anything on Matt Bonner, right?"

He leans forward in his chair. "Claire was his alibi, as I'm sure you're aware by now. It means we're going to reopen an investigation into him."

"I have some evidence that may prove useful." I pull out the mermaid figurine that had been planted at my house. Liam gave it back to me after they had a *conversation* with Matt. It feels like weeks ago. But Liam said all the improper stuff had been scrubbed off of it, leaving only Claire and Matt testing it, then Claire planting it.

I place the cord that connects to his computer next to it.

"This disguised a camera that was planted in my room. There are encrypted files on his hard drive, but I also emailed them to myself." I tap it on the table. Her little tail makes a satisfying ticking noise.

He motions for me to hand it to him, and I do. After

inspecting it, he sets it carefully on the table. "I'm not going to ask how you got into encrypted files."

I grimace.

"I don't need anything else from you at the moment. Stay in town, though." He opens the door for me. "Your mother is going into a rehabilitation facility in lieu of serving time. Her drug test came back positive for opiates."

I shake my head.

Part of me wants to hate her for what she did.

An officer is escorting Lydia into the building as we come out of a side hall. I stop short, backing into the detective.

She doesn't so much as look in my direction. I doubt she sees me, because she's arguing with the officer. She's hand-cuffed—another thing I never thought I'd see.

"Lydia," someone calls.

I jerk to my left, where Mom has emerged from another interview room.

Mom's gaze stays on Lydia, who scowls at her former friend. And then...

My mother's attention skips to me, drawn like magnets.

"Do you want to speak with her?" Masters asks.

I sigh. "Yes and no."

She heads in our direction, trailed by another officer. She seems weak, but better than any of the times she's showed up outside my foster homes asking for money. And she seems more relaxed than she did in the middle of the diner.

She stops just out of my reach. "I'm so sorry, honey."

"You put yourself over literally everything else." I shrug, looking away. "I've had seven years to cope with you being a shitty mother."

She winces, then recovers. "I'm willing to try and make things right. I'm going to get clean, and—"

"And nothing." I shake my head. "I have a foster mom who loves me. I don't need..." *Whatever this is.* You.

I glance at Detective Masters, then make a beeline for the exit. I know who's waiting for me on the other side, and it spurs my movements faster.

Past the officer at the reception desk, down the hall. Out the doors into the sunshine. I pause for a fraction of a second as warmth sinks into my skin.

And then I smile at my foster parents and run into their arms.

"All set?" Robert asks into my hair.

"Yeah."

My phone buzzes in my pocket, and I grin.

"What's that smile for?" Lenora asks.

"I just... don't feel any dread when my phone goes off." I didn't realize it until just this moment, but it's true: Claire is gone. A weight has lifted.

CALEB

Can I come over?

I relay the question to my foster parents, and they nod.

ME

Is that even a question?

Robert frowns. "I feel like an awful parent for not realizing what you were going through."

We walk slowly toward the car.

"I hid it well," I admit. "And you've only known me for a few months. I got a text from Claire—Unknown, as I referred to her—the night before I went back to school."

Lenora loops her arm with mine. "Didn't Angela say she needed your number?"

I pause and tilt my head. "She did… But I think that was just something Claire said to cover her tracks. My number didn't change between homes. Claire might've had it memorized or written down."

"How do you feel?" Robert asks.

"I don't know." It's the only answer I can give. I suck my lower lip into my mouth, biting down hard. Sometimes I feel myself slipping back into the darkness that wanted to hurt people: Matt, Claire. I didn't use the knife Liam gave me, but… I *punched* them. I held a gun to Claire's chest and seriously contemplated pulling the trigger.

Who *am* I?

In the car, heading home, I contemplate the situation at hand. My whole body trembles with the words bouncing around in my head.

Just say it, Margo.

"You guys can't go through with the adoption," I blurt out.

Lenora, at the wheel, snaps her eyes to the rearview mirror to see my face.

Robert nods, looking back at me. "Because your dad is innocent?"

I lift one shoulder. There's a lump in my throat. "Because even if he wasn't, I still wouldn't have been able to give that up. I love you both…"

Robert reaches back, snagging my hand. "We love you, too. Adoption just makes things official. And, truth be told, we talked about this last night. You're welcome in our house for as long as you want. And when your father gets out of prison, we'll do what we can to help him, too."

The burning in my eyes gets worse. "Really?"

"Yes," Lenora says firmly. "No question."

"Wow. How'd I get so lucky?"

Robert grins. "All it takes is a spark of luck to connect the right people."

"Or the wrong ones," I say.

He nods. "That, too."

The rest of the trip passes quickly. My mind jumps from what's going to happen to David and Lydia, to my mother's words, to Dad in prison. He's going to get out and have to start over, but he's not alone.

Caleb's car is idling out front when we arrive home.

I grin, meeting him on the walkway. The grass is covered in two feet of snow we got in a sudden snowstorm, and Caleb... I scan him as he comes closer. It's no wonder he gets all the girls fawning over him. With his black beanie, black jacket, and black jeans—he could be a fashion model or a bank robber.

"Hi." He leans down and pressing a kiss to my lips.

"Hi."

He said that he's in love with me. I think about it often: the way his eyes widened a moment before he said it, like it was an unstoppable force.

"What are you thinking about?" He tucks a strand of hair behind my ear.

"You." My cheeks get hot.

And maybe I misspoke earlier. He hasn't been by my side the *entire* time. Today, for example, he left a few hours before we went to the station. He had a meeting, but he wouldn't say what it was.

"I have a surprise for you," he says. "And I'm pretty sure you're going to be pissed."

I snort, then burst out laughing.

"You're happy." He smiles, too.

"Everyone is getting justice."

"Except Hanna. She's…"

The smile slides off my face faster than I can blink.

Shit. How could I forget about her? She slipped through the cracks. Her one advocate—her sister—is a psycho. But me?

"I'm an awful person," I mumble.

"Not… quite."

He motions behind him, and the back door of his car swings open.

Out emerges Hanna.

I squint at her. "What are you doing here?"

She runs toward me, locking her arms around my waist. Even if I'm horrible, she's happy to see me.

I let out a breath and hug her back. She's not wearing a coat. Was she the neglected child in the Asher house once Claire started playing her games? Was she excluded?

Or maybe worse: she was included.

"Iris is the only one left," she says, looking up at me. "We've been eating pizza and watching funny movies every night. She said the only way to get over what happened is to move on."

I nod slowly. "She lost her husband and you…"

Her face drops. "Claire was mean to you."

"She did some bad things." I cup her cheek. "But I'm happy to see you. And I'm sorry how I last spoke to you."

"It's okay," she says. "I get it. Claire took Caleb."

Lenora sticks her head out. "Ah, Hanna! Want to come join us inside?"

Hanna glances at Caleb, who nods.

Once she's gone, Caleb meets my gaze. "I told Aunt Iris I just wanted to get her some fresh air."

"She really didn't have anything to do with it? Your aunt, I mean?"

He shrugs. "She's denying it, and no one's implicated her. She's nice enough. Probably only stuck around the marriage for Uncle David's money, though."

I nod. "Is that the surprise I'm not going to like?"

"No." A mischievous expression comes over him. "That was the balm before I tell you that I got us an apartment in the city."

My mouth drops open. "Why would you do that?"

"Because we're both going to school. You're going to apply to your dream school and get in. And I'll be right there with you."

I look up at the house I've been calling *home* for the past few months. "So, what, we're going to finish high school and just... pack up and leave?"

"It's only an hour away," he says in a low voice. "Leaving doesn't mean forever."

"You said you were in love with me."

He watches me. "I did."

"You haven't said it since," I point out.

He wraps his hands around my waist, yanking me closer. One hand slides up my back, into my hair. It's loose today, cascading in waves over my shoulders. Slowly, he lowers his mouth to mine, stealing a quick kiss before his lips move to my ear. His tongue flicks out, and I shudder.

"I'm so in love with you, Margo Wolfe. The person you were and the person you've become. You're the only one I want for the rest of my life."

I can't stop the sudden tremble running through me.

I turn my head, catching his lips and leaning into it. This kiss is slow and hungry. It's soul-demolishing. His tongue slides against mine, eliciting a groan from deep inside me.

When we break away, we're both breathing heavy. I tip forward, resting my forehead against his.

"I've been in love with you forever," I whisper. "And I'm so totally in love with you right now, I might just float away."

"Forever," he repeats.

I laugh and wave my wrist. The bracelet shines in the sunlight. "It was my idea to get married."

His eyes darken. "When we get married for real, you're getting something better than a braided bracelet."

"*When*, huh?"

He pulls me closer, then guides me toward the front door.

"Yes, when," he says. "There's no escaping us."

I rest my head on his shoulder. "I can live with that."

Chapter 40
Liam

I climb in through Sky's window with ease.

Years of practicing escaping from my window at the house in Rose Hill, and then even more of sneaking *in* this way, has made the journey muscle memory. I could probably do it blindfolded.

Lightning flashes behind me, illuminating the room. The empty bed with its covers thrown back.

And Skylar, curled in a ball in the corner.

"Hey, hey, it's okay." I rush to her and drop to my knees. "Sky, look at me."

She lifts her head just as thunder booms so loud it shakes the house, and her eyes squeeze tight.

I can't hate her for her fear.

Even if I want to.

She's clearly not moving. Another flash of lighting confirms it.

With a grimace, I pick her up. She stays rigid, even when I drop her on the bed. I toe off my shoes and shed my wet sweatshirt and jeans. I climb in behind her, then pull the blankets up over us. I wrap myself around her, sighing noisily so she can focus on some other sound besides the relentless rain and rumbling thunder.

I rub her arm briskly, trying to get some warmth back into her chilled skin. Who knows how long she's been on the floor?

"You don't have to be here," she finally says on a shaky exhale.

"I know."

"I hate this so much."

We haven't done *this* in a long time. Not since her parents warned me to stay away. When I was deemed the problem by her therapist and everyone else in her life.

But we haven't had a storm this bad, either.

I know that's not what she's referring to. It's her bone-deep fear that freezes her muscles and her brain. She hates it more than I do, and I *loathe* it.

"What am I going to do when I'm alone in a dorm room next year?" she whispers. "Or when I'm an adult trying to live my life? I can't—"

Her chest heaves. She covers her mouth with her palm, smothering the sound of her sob.

I push her hair out of the way and kiss the shell of her ear. She smells like sugar, and I fight not to take another, deeper inhale.

"As soon as you're out of Stone Ridge, it'll be better."

As soon as she can leave these wretched, haunted memories behind, *she'll* be better. The trauma sticks with her because she's still here. Living in the same house. Going to the same school, with the same friends.

Change will be good for her. And I want to know where she's going, but I can't.

Won't.

She doesn't answer me. She rolls in my arms and buries

her face in my chest. The thunder makes her flinch, and I hold onto her as if I can keep her head above water.

This is it.

This is all I can take from her.

And all she can get from me.

Outside of this room, I'm useless. My future will be mundane. *If* I can get a full-ride scholarship, I have a chance at college. But if not, I'll be joining my parents in the work-force, doing some stupid job I hate.

And while Skylar moves on, I'll be stuck in the mud.

So I just lie here and soak up her body heat, making the occasional shushing noise when her trembling gets too bad. She eventually relaxes into me, her lips parting as she falls asleep. The rain beats down on her window. I wish it was a soothing sound for her, not a scary one.

I close my eyes, too. I don't let myself fall asleep. It's selfish of me to want to hold onto as much of this as I can. Tonight is an indulgence, pure and simple.

The storm stops before dawn. I slowly extract myself. I brush her hair back and kiss her forehead. The furrows between her brows are gone, her expression free of stress or fear.

Outside of these four walls, we're strangers.

We were once best friends, and now I'm not supposed to know her at all. It's her parents' wish, after all.

I climb out her window and land in the soft, wet grass, where her father waits. He's got salt-and-pepper hair, a weathered look to his tanned skin, and eyes the same shade of blue as Skylar. His hands are in his pockets, and a familiar scowl twists his face.

"Thought you kicked this habit," he says. "Didn't we warn you against it?"

I lift my chin. I will not feel the same guilt they made

me feel before. Guilt for being her *person*. The one she cried out for in the middle of the night when her parents were right there. It probably made them feel like shit, knowing they weren't the ones she wanted.

"I knew she'd need me last night. It's about her, not me." I stare him down, then raise my hands in surrender. "Won't happen again, Mr. Buckley."

He nods and exhales. His breath creates a cloud in front of his face. "Well, she'll be gone soon enough. And you…"

Will still be here.

Right.

Destined to be abso-fucking-lutely nothing.

Epilogue
Five months later

CALEB

I unlock the door and stride inside. The apartment has been furnished to my specifications, but it looks better than expected. I run my finger along the kitchen island, which is the only thing separating the kitchen from the rest of the open space.

It's small, but it'll do.

Keith Wolfe walks in, eyeing me like I'm crazy.

"This is mine?" he asks.

"Free and clear." I bought this small apartment complex back in January and spent the next month bringing it up to code—and fashion. Well, my contractor spent the next month renovating it. Margo picked wall colors and flooring, but she didn't know the half of it.

There are six apartments in this building, tucked in a cozy neighborhood in Brooklyn. It's two blocks from the *other* building I bought.

Real estate mogul at eighteen. Who would've thought I'd end up following in my dad's footsteps after all?

Josh helped me. Once David was arrested, my inheritance was given to me without restrictions. Still, seventeen was a *bit* young to be buying property. I waited until April rolled around, eyeing the market, and then made my move.

Two properties.

Ten apartments between the two of them, and eight are already filled with tenants.

The least I can do is give one to Margo's dad.

He got a job in the city and has been commuting from Rose Hill. He joins Margo, Robert, and Lenora for dinner every Friday night. On Wednesdays, Margo goes to his Rose Hill apartment, occasionally accompanied by me.

The original plan was that Margo and I were going to move into the building after graduation. She got an acceptance letter to NYU a few weeks ago that I intercepted. But an even better one came today.

And I can't pass it up.

"Does Margo know?" He's at the window, staring out at the street.

"Not yet."

He runs his hand through his hair. It's gotten longer since his time in prison. When I look at him, I feel guilt.

Guilt that I harbored all this unnecessary anger, that I wasted years of my life festering in it. But if I hadn't, I might've moved on from them. From Margo.

"You should forgive yourself, son." Keith stops in front of me. "If you need forgiveness from me, you've got it. But... I never held anything against you."

I suck in a deep breath. I was less nervous negotiating a price for this place than I am talking to him. "I am guilty for believing their lies. If only I had—"

"No." His hand lands on my shoulder. "You were ten. Innocent in all of this."

"Margo got into her dream school." I pull out the acceptance letter. "Robert and Lenora intercepted it so I could surprise her. But it's going to take us away from here."

His eyes fill with tears. "My baby girl got into college?"

"Full ride scholarship and everything," I say, handing him the letter.

He turns away and slips it from the envelope, reading it silently. His shoulders move as he takes a deep breath, and he turns back around with a smile. "You grew up."

"I did my best under the circumstances."

Keith pats my shoulder. "Thank you. Seriously. Not many people would go to the lengths you have, first securing me a job, and then buying an apartment and not charging rent?"

"Buying the whole damn building," I correct. "And I was kind of hoping you'd be my building supervisor, seeing as how we won't be around..."

He laughs. "It's the least I can do."

"Do you ever wonder if you're making the wrong decision?"

He narrows his eyes. "I hope you're not referring to my daughter."

"No, no. Just..." I gesture around. "Maybe I should try to separate myself from him."

"It's okay to miss your dad, Caleb." He looks away. "But it's okay to recognize his faults and want to do better."

That's true.

We're both bad at heart-to-hearts, apparently. But besides Josh, he's the only one who's ever been close to a positive male role model.

"He was a good man. He helped me out, too, after my mother cut me off. We hadn't spoken in a few years, but he was glad to offer his home to Amber, Margo, and me." He exhales. "I forgave him for sleeping with my wife. He told me a few weeks before he died. It wasn't you or Margo who ruined the ruse—he died when your mother decided it was time."

My breath comes out shakily. "Margo had said as much. That you knew, and she didn't tell."

He nods. "I wasn't aware of the extent of her memory block, or what you knew or didn't know. It's only good to uproot the past if you're prepared to deal with the trauma."

"Margo wouldn't have been ready if she didn't talk to you." I grab the keys I had left on the counter for him. "I have one last thing I want to ask you."

MARGO

I shift each and every way, analyzing myself in the mirror.

My hair is longer. My skin clear and glowing. My makeup is flawless.

And yet, something feels... off.

"The dress," Riley says from the doorway.

I jump. Caught staring at myself like a fool.

"Huh?"

Riley chuckles. "The dress doesn't match the vibe. Which is fine—I brought you one." She holds up a plastic bag covering a black dress.

"I never thought I'd be going to prom," I admit. "And you're sure you don't want to go?"

"As much as I'd love to watch you slow dance with Caleb, I think I'm going to pass. I'd rather just help you get ready, then go home and watch *The Breakfast Club*."

I roll my eyes. "Eli's still...?"

Well, I wouldn't know exactly what he's still doing, since she's refused, for *months* to talk about it. She suffers in silence.

"Try this on," she orders, shoving the bag into my hands. "This is going to be so much better than the masquerade ball for you."

I raise my eyebrows. "Is it?"

"Yeah, because Caleb is in love with you and you're in love with him, and things have been... Good. Like, painful to witness good."

She has a point—about the painful to witness part anyway. Dad was released from prison shortly after David, Lydia, Tobias, and Claire were arrested. Mom was sent to a rehabilitation center, where she remains to this day, and Claire is in a juvenile detention center until she turns eighteen. Tobias surprised us by turning on everyone viciously, supplying evidence he had stored over the years.

Turns out, the ex-public defender knew just what to keep in order to incriminate... just about everyone.

It was impressive.

I stayed with Robert and Lenora. It was a decision the four of us made tearfully in the living room. All of us were a crying mess by the time the conversation was over. But the way they accepted Dad into the fold like he was part of their family, too? It broke my heart and healed it at the same time.

And Dad...

I let out a sigh, closing myself in the bathroom.

He knew me as a child. Ten years old, seeing only the good in the world. Now he has a seventeen-year-old daughter.

I've been through the foster system and survived.

Came out ahead, if you ask me.

Caleb is a stage five clinger—and I mean that in the best way possible. Once we returned to school, everyone magically backed off. He'd cast a magic spell. That... and hockey season was in full swing.

Fall semester was nothing compared to the spring. With the possibility of the state championship on the line, it seems like everyone is waiting breathlessly for the result of each game.

All Hail King Caleb. I snorted at the first person who said it, but it was a thing.

"Margo," Riley calls, knocking on the door. "Do you need help?"

I jump. Whoops.

"One second." I change into the dress, pulling the straps into place and struggling to zip it on my own. It fits like a glove—small miracles, since Riley is a size smaller than me.

When I open the door, her mouth drops open. "Damn."

It's a halter top with a deep V neckline, similar to the one Riley wore to the last dance we attended. This one is beaded, glittering. From my hips up, it's skintight. The silky fabric goes to the floor, but it's the slit that ends halfway up my thigh that's the real showstopper. Paired with skinny, strappy heels?

I kind of feel like a warrior princess. But also—

"I feel like I'm going to throw up. How many people are down there?"

"Just..." She rolls her eyes. "Don't think about it. It's just Caleb and Hanna, Iris, your foster parents and dad..."

I swallow. "Is that all?"

Iris has suddenly found herself in our circle. Along with the shocking revelation that Hanna and Caleb were half-siblings, and Hanna was pretty obviously attached to me, everyone involved decided that she shouldn't be kept away from us. Caleb and I have been including her on our weekend dates.

What started as Iris waiting in the car, staring stoically ahead, soon became her getting out of the car and chatting with Robert and Lenora on the porch. That transitioned into staying for a drink or dinner. And it wasn't too surprising when Iris dropped off Hanna to go out with Lenora and Robert.

"Lipstick," Riley suggests. She shows me a few different options from her purse. She has a mental debate, then hands me one. "Here."

I know better than to try to argue, so I take it from her hand and swipe it on. I'll give my best friend this: she knows how to pick her lipsticks.

"Thank you," I say quietly.

"Thank *you* for giving me this distraction." She smiles. "Besides, I'll go to prom next year once all of you are gone."

"What are you going to do without me?"

She throws her arms around my bare shoulders. "Don't get me started. Graduation day, I'm going to be a wreck with a capital W."

I hug her back. "It's not too late to come."

"It's definitely too late." She steps away. "Ready?"

"Yes."

She leaves before me, and it's oddly reminiscent of the masquerade ball. Except then...

Then, I wasn't half the woman I am now.

I take a moment to look at myself in the mirror.

Strength comes from being pushed to your limits and surviving. Dad told me that the day he got out of prison and straight into my arms.

And, my girl, you've survived.

I fix the edge of my lipstick and flip my hair over my shoulder, then go to the stairs. Down I go, reliving the déjà vu.

Caleb is waiting at the bottom just as I knew he would be. His gaze sweeps up and down my body, and his eyes darken. I take a moment to relish it before my cheeks heat up. Goosebumps scatter down my arms.

He offers his hand, and I take it. The soft squeeze tells me I'm not alone.

I look around, but... we *are* alone.

"Where'd they go?" I whisper.

"They're giving us privacy." He taps under my chin, unable to withhold his grin.

In the past few months, both of us have started smiling more. The smiles come freely, with wild abandon. It's the result of levity after months—*years*—of guilt and shame and anger.

Claire may have said I was just going from one cage to another, but that isn't true.

In the end, the truth has opened our doors.

We just need to fly away.

"You remember the apartment?" he asks me.

I frown. "The one in Brooklyn."

He was renovating. It wasn't just an apartment he *got*, it was an entire apartment building he *bought*. And then refinished. I helped him pick out colors and finishes, but every time I asked if it was ours, he said no.

"Yes," he says. "Well, I rented out all the apartments."

I suck in a breath.

"It was always our plan to move there, right?"

I squint at him. "Clearly not, since you just filled it. It was our plan that we'd both be going to college in the city.

Well—that was *your* plan. I'm just going to be a fast-food worker, or a receptionist at the company you own, or—"

"Easy," he murmurs. "You don't think you got in?"

"Literally *everyone* has heard about their schools except for me."

He removes something from his pocket.

An envelope.

I take it, unfolding it slowly.

"This is my mail." I look up at him. "You know it's illegal to open someone else's mail, right?"

He laughs. "Call Masters on me, then."

I roll my eyes. "And give him an excuse to throw you back in jail? I'll pass."

I return my attention to the envelope. My hands are shaking, but I pull open the paper and read it slowly.

I got in—but not to New York University.

My dream school.

The one I most certainly did not tell Caleb about.

"I... How?"

"'Dear Ms. Wolfe,'" Caleb recites, his eyes burning into mine. "'Congratulations! We're pleased to inform you that you have been accepted into Crown Point University.'"

I cover my mouth. Crown Point was a pipe dream.

"I'm going to college," I repeat. "Where are you going?"

Caleb snickers. "Same place, baby. You can't get rid of me that easy."

That's why he rented out the apartment building in Brooklyn. Because we're not going to New York... we're going to Crown Point.

"She's going to college!" my dad hollers, emerging from the dining room.

He's wearing a blue-and-white CPU t-shirt. Lenora, Robert, and Iris are close behind him, and they, too, are wearing the school's colors. Riley and Hanna appear with a hand-painted sign that says, *Congrats on being accepted to CPU!*

"Don't make me cry." I blink rapidly at the ceiling. My eyes burn. "Thank you all for the surprise, but I can't..."

"They gave you a full ride," Caleb says in my ear.

My mouth drops open. "What?"

He just shrugs, grinning.

I squint at him. He wouldn't have paid for it upfront, right? He's not *that* crazy...

He is.

I reach up on my tiptoes and kiss his cheek. "Thank you."

"One more thing," he says.

I cough. "You're kidding. This is just prom... What on earth are you doing?"

There's a black velvet box in his hand.

"Are you *proposing* to me?"

He looks around. "Why not? We're surrounded by everyone who loves us."

"Because—"

"You promised me forever," he says, kneeling. He takes my hand.

His thumb skates just below the bracelet on my wrist, eliciting a shiver.

"I just want to make it even more official."

"You..." I suck in a deep breath. "You're impossibly infuriating sometimes."

His brow furrows.

I continue, "And you just assume that I like surprises. Which, for the record, I don't. And you're bossy. And—"

"Are you just going to list my worst attributes while I'm trying to propose?"

"I'm just getting this off my chest, okay? It was my idea to marry you eight years ago. This isn't a new idea. And you've picked up some bad habits along the way—"

Riley snorts.

"But it doesn't mean I don't love you." I shrug and wiggle my fingers in his hand. "I don't want to know what *not* being in love with you feels like. So, okay. I'm ready."

He smirks. "You take things to an extreme, baby."

"Yes."

"Will you marry me? And love me until we're old and gray?"

I can't help it. In the eleventh hour, seconds left on the clock—we're doing sports analogies here, people—I glance at my dad.

Did I think he was ever going to walk me down the aisle, let alone be able to witness the man of my dreams propose? No.

He nods at me. A barely there movement.

He isn't surprised.

He knew.

And my heart... it just explodes with happiness. Because Caleb knew how much this would mean to me.

A lump forms in my throat.

"Yes," I answer. "It's not even a question—"

He rises almost too fast for me to track, lunging like a shark diving out of the water. He scoops me up and spins me around, holding me tightly to his chest. I hold on to his shoulders, laughing as we twirl.

"Not that I had any doubt," he says in my ear. "After all we've been through."

"You asked my dad?"

"I did. And Robert and Lenora, just to be safe."

I pull back so I can look him in the eye.

He's dead serious.

To hell with having an audience. I grab Caleb's face and kiss him. It's the only way to express how I feel.

I get to live my happily ever after with my best friend—my devious, loving, wicked man.

About the Author

S. Massery is a dark romance author who loves injecting a good dose of suspense into her stories. Originally from Massachusetts, she now lives in Southern California with her dog, Alice.

Before adventuring into the world of writing, she went to college in Boston and held a wide variety of jobs—including working on a dude ranch in Wyoming (a personal highlight). She has a love affair with coffee and chocolate. When S. Massery isn't writing, she can be found devouring books, playing outside with her dog, or trying to make people smile.

Join her newsletter to stay up to date on new releases: http://smassery.com/newsletter

Also by S. Massery

Hockey Gods

Brutal Obsession

Devious Obsession

Secret Obsession

Twisted Obsession

Fierce Obsession

Shadow Valley U (co-written with SJ Sylvis)

Sticks and Stones

Heart of Thorns

Sterling Falls

#0 THRILL

#1 THIEF

#2 FIGHTER

#3 REBEL

#4 QUEEN

Sterling Falls Rogues

#0 TERROR

DeSantis Mafia

#1 Ruthless Saint

#2 Savage Prince

#3 Stolen Crown

Broken Mercenaries

#1 Blood Sky

#2 Angel of Death

#3 Morning Star

More at http://smassery.com

Where to Find Sara

Thank you so much for coming along on these crazy boys' journeys with me.

If you like my stories, I'd highly encourage you to come join my Facebook group, S. Massery Squad. There's a lot of fun stuff happening in there, and they're who I go to for polls about future books (fun fact: some key details in this series is decided by their votes!), where I share teasers, etc!

My Patreon is also an awesome place to connect and get exclusive content! On release months, I do signed paperbacks. Plus, get ARCs, audiobooks, and artwork before the rest of the world. Find me here: http://patreon.com/smassery

And last but not least, here are some social media links for ya:

Facebook: Author S Massery

Where to Find Sara

Instagram: @authorsmassery
Tiktok: @smassery
Goodreads: S. Massery
Bookbub: S. Massery